JULIE ROWE

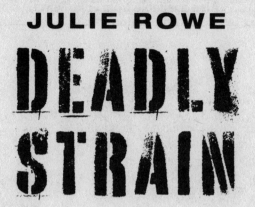

DEADLY STRAIN

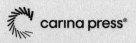

carina press®

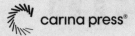

ISBN-13: 978-0-373-00321-1

Recycling programs
for this product may
not exist in your area.

Deadly Strain

Copyright © 2015 by Julie Rowe

All rights reserved. Except for use in any review, the reproduction or
utilization of this work in whole or in part in any form by any electronic,
mechanical or other means, now known or hereinafter invented, including
xerography, photocopying and recording, or in any information storage
or retrieval system, is forbidden without the written permission of the
publisher, Harlequin Enterprises Limited, 225 Duncan Mill Road,
Don Mills, Ontario M3B 3K9, Canada.

This is a work of fiction. Names, characters, places and incidents are
either the product of the author's imagination or are used fictitiously,
and any resemblance to actual persons, living or dead, business
establishments, events or locales is entirely coincidental.

This edition published by arrangement with Harlequin Books S.A.

® and TM are trademarks of the publisher. Trademarks indicated with
® are registered in the United States Patent and Trademark Office, the
Canadian Intellectual Property Office and in other countries.

www.CarinaPress.com

Printed in U.S.A.

To my husband, George, who never fails
in his support and love. I am a lucky, lucky woman.

Author Note

The inspiration for *Deadly Strain* and the other forthcoming books in the Biological Response Team series came out of research into some of the most deadly outbreaks in human history. The bubonic plague (Black Death), tuberculosis and cholera pandemics are just a few examples of pathogens that caused millions of deaths worldwide, some in reoccurring outbreaks lasting years. Many of these deadly organisms have been controlled through vaccination programs or with antibiotics. Many others can't be controlled so easily, and some are becoming resistant to the drugs we use to treat them.

In April of 2014, the World Health Organization published its first global report on antibiotic resistance (who.int/mediacentre/news/releases/2014/amr-report/en). In the report, the WHO reveals the full extent of antibiotic resistance across the world—it's everywhere. We're not headed for a post-antibiotic era, we're already there.

Information about how to use antibiotics safely and properly can be found at the Do Bugs Need Drugs website, dobugsneeddrugs.org.

DEADLY STRAIN

ONE

The battle line between good and evil runs through the heart of every man.

—Aleksandr Solzhenitsyn

"I'M SO DEAD." Dr. Grace Samuels stared at the chessboard. There was no hope. None. Not a single move left open to her.

Except for one.

She sighed, shook her head at the patience on her opponent's face. "I concede."

"Want to know where you went wrong?" he asked as he cleared the board. He set the pieces up again. Those big hands of his could bandage a wounded soldier, field strip a 9 mm and box her into checkmate with equal skill.

"I sat down in this chair," she answered with a straight face. The mess hall was busy with soldiers, American and Afghan alike, either beginning their day or ending their night.

"No," he said. "You played the board."

Grace thought about it for a second, but it still didn't make any sense. Then again, it was 0600 and she'd only been up for twenty minutes. "Huh?"

Special Forces Weapons Sergeant Jacob "Sharp" Foster looked at her earnestly. "You played the board," he repeated. "You should have been playing the man."

He winked and she had to fight not to roll her eyes. When she first met him she'd thought his flirting was for real, and had been worried she'd have to shut him down. She didn't want to, because he was hilarious, but the impropriety couldn't be ignored. Then, she discovered when he wasn't on the job, he had a wicked sense of humor, and everyone was a target.

"Then I suppose I'll have to study you." She leaned forward and made a show of giving him a thorough once-over.

He grinned and spread his hands wide. "By all means, study me."

Sharp was a big man, about six-two, and she'd guess he weighed about two hundred pounds. He flexed his biceps and waggled his eyebrows in response to her joke. Though he had brown hair, with a mustache and beard to match, he had the lightest blue eyes she'd ever seen—like looking into glacial ice.

Right now, those eyes were challenging her. She just wasn't sure if it was regarding the game or something she didn't want to talk about. At all.

Unfortunately, Sharp wasn't going to leave it alone. The chess game should have warned her. They usually played poker.

She watched him reset the chessboard while, for the first time in a week, letting her mind go back to the moment she realized she was in trouble. On her way to her quarters late at night. They'd arrived at Forward Operating Base Bostick the week before, and she'd been introduced to the base commander, Colonel Marshall. He'd barely spoken to her. So why was he waiting for her outside her quarters with clenched fists and a face so blank she knew he was in the grip of a powerful emotion?

The colonel wasn't known for any kind of emotion.

She stopped several feet away. "What are you doing here at this hour, sir?"

One corner of his upper lip lifted in a sneer and he snarled, "I wanted a private conversation."

His words triggered every internal red flag she had. "I don't understand."

Marshall's response was two words. One name. "Joseph Cranston."

A name she wished she could forget. "You...knew him?"

Scorn turned his words into weapons. "He was my son."

Oh God.

Grace took an involuntary step backward. Now that she knew, she could see the son in his father's face, the same eyes and jawline as the young man whose features she couldn't forget. As if conjured, his shade floated in front of her mind's eye, thrusting her into a memory she wanted desperately to erase. His face, covered with blood, whipped her heart into a gallop. Her breathing bellowed, lungs attempting to push air through her terror-closed throat. She fought the invisible hands pulling at her and her vision spiraled into a narrow tunnel.

Sharp had surfaced out of the dark, his presence breaking the memory's chokehold.

He'd crouched in front of her, calling her name, ordering her to respond before he did something stupid like give her mouth-to-mouth. She coughed out a response, couldn't remember what, and fought her way to her feet.

Sharp didn't try to hold her. He didn't touch her at all, but he shielded her body from prying eyes with his own. He refused to leave her, facing down Colonel Marshall, who showed no sympathy and less tolerance for her *fainting spell*. Two of Sharp's team members appeared and, after glaring at them all, Marshall left without saying anything else.

She managed to get inside her quarters before anyone could demand an explanation, shut the door and locked it. She'd only felt relief when no one knocked to ask for an explanation. It wasn't until the next day that she realized their lack of questions was as suspect as her behavior.

She hadn't expected to meet anyone connected to Joseph Cranston outside of the United States. Hadn't expected something that happened that long ago to thrust her into a memory like it was happening all over again.

Fool.

In the days since, Sharp had been mother-henning her like she was some fragile little chick, and she'd had about as much of that as she could take. She was a Samuels. Her father, also a military doctor, had just retired from the army, and her grandfather had run a MASH unit during the Korean War. He'd met her grandmother during WWII; she'd been one of the first Air Force service pilots. If there was one thing she wouldn't accept from anyone, it was pity.

"I've been studying you for a while." Sharp finished setting up the board and met her gaze. "You're a damn good doctor, a hellacious good shot on the range and you put up with our male stupidity with more patience than we deserve."

"I hear the *but* coming."

"What happened between you and Marshall?"

"None of your damn business."

When he continued to stare at her, she added, "Look,

I'm not going to saddle anyone else with my personal grievances or the fact that I don't get along with someone."

"Personal grievances?" Sharp asked. "Twice last week I thought you were going to damage a guy for jostling you in the chow line. What's going on with you?"

Shit, of course he would notice. She'd damn near freaked out each time, a scream hovering on her lips, her hands and feet moving to defend against an enemy who wasn't there.

The enemy wasn't there. No gunfire. No weapons pointed at her, yet she still found herself reacting as if it were happening all over again.

She hadn't been reacting that way until Marshall had confronted her. Meeting the father of a soldier who'd died an unnecessary death in front of her must have detonated an emotional trip wire in her head. One she needed to deal with.

Not an easy thing when on active duty and nowhere near a base with more than a glorified first-aid station.

It seemed like anywhere she went on the base, Sharp or one of the guys from the A-Team was there. Not doing anything, just there. They weren't fooling her.

Damn alpha males and their overprotective tendencies.

"Nothing I can't handle. I take care of myself." She narrowed her eyes. Her sidearm, a Beretta M9, might have to make an appearance. Then Sharp's words sunk all the way in. "Wait. Are you telling me I should play chess with the same mind-set as *poker*?" She buried his ass *every* time they played poker. He was terrible at keeping his attention on his cards and lousy at pretending he wasn't checking her out—not that he was serious about it. He knew the rules same as she, and she was glad, *ridiculously* glad, she had a friend she could count on, someone she could trust.

"Sort of. Chess demands more of you than poker, but the principles are the same."

Them's fightin' words. "The hell you say." She'd been playing poker with her dad since she was ten years old. He'd taught her how to bluff anyone.

"Doc," Sharp said, chuckling. "If I were lying, you'd be beating me, but you aren't."

"Ha." She leaned forward and tapped the board. "Make your move."

Sharp opened his mouth to respond, but he never got a chance to say anything before another Beret, the team's other weapons sergeant, Harvey Runnel, strode over to them. It wasn't the speed he was moving that drew her and Sharp's attention, it was the look on the soldier's face. Flattened lips, clenched jaw and a slightly flared nose. She couldn't see his eyes due to the tinted safety glasses he wore, but she could guess that the skin around them would be tight—a man who was on full alert.

Special Forces soldiers did not get amped up for no reason.

"Playtime's over," Runnel said. "Doc, grab your go-bag."

A mental blanket sank over her, numbing her to the horror to come. It was the first self-preservation tactic doctors learned. Compartmentalize all that terrible stuff or go crazy in a week. Sometimes she wondered when all those boxes in her mind would break open and rip her apart from the inside out.

There was an entire crate named Joseph Cranston.

"Warm or cold?" She asked even though she already

knew the answer. Runnel never looked this rattled. *Please say warm.*

Her warm go-bag was a trauma kit, a backpack with everything she'd need if she was dealing with bullet holes, shrapnel lacerations or broken bones. The typical things most people expected her to treat since she was a trauma surgeon. But that wasn't all she was.

She was also an infectious disease specialist.

Her cold go-bag contained the very latest in biological detection technology. One- or two-step tests that identified anything from anthrax to Ebola to a weaponized flu. She was a member of a select group of virologists, microbiologists and infectious disease specialists the US Army relied on to train not only their own troops, but the soldiers of other nations, in the detection of and protection against biological weapons. They were known officially as the Biological Rapid Response team, but most soldiers called them Icemen or Icequeens.

Lately the army had been assigning BRR team members to work with Army Special Forces teams—Green Berets. She'd been working with Sharp's team for almost a year. Her job was to assist in training Afghan forces in everything from combat and demolitions to the most survivable responses to biological, chemical or nuclear weapons.

"Cold," Runnel said. "No drill."

Shit.

Adrenaline spiked through her system as Grace got up and followed Runnel. He led the way back to whoever was calling the shots, Sharp right behind her as they ran at a trot. She might be the base's resident expert on biological weapons, but it was knowledge she wished fervently she didn't have to use.

They entered the staging area where she'd been doing some of the training. Several members of Sharp's team were using it to gear up. Runnel glanced at her and angled his head toward the base commander, a tall man in his forties who wore a permanent frown. He was looking at a map with several ranking officers, including the A-Team's commander, Geoffry Cutter.

Cutter glanced at her. "The major is here, sir."

Base Commander Colonel Marshall gave her a glare before returning his attention to the map in front of him.

He'd called her a *fucking quack* yesterday as he walked past her. If he kept demeaning her in front of the Afghan forces and their own soldiers, she'd lose the credibility she needed to successfully train them.

"Major," Marshall said without looking at her. "One of our patrols reported in about ten minutes ago with what *appears* to be a biological incident."

She waited, but he didn't add any more details. "What led them to believe that, sir?"

He met her gaze with an even colder expression. "An entire village dead. Some of the bodies show lesions and bleeding from the nose, mouth and eyes."

Holy Mother of God.

Bad. This was very bad.

"I concur with their assessment of the situation, sir. Your orders?"

"Get the fuck out there," he snarled at her. "Figure out what happened and fix it."

That part she knew already. *Asshat.* She'd hoped he'd give her some detailed orders, with a timeline and what kind of manpower she could expect. Not more sarcasm and snark. She came to attention and saluted. "Yes, sir."

He took two steps, then stopped and turned around.

He addressed Cutter and only Cutter, who had somehow inched his way over until he was right next to her, with Sharp on the other side. What a couple of papa bears. "Send half of your A-Team with the Icequeen. The other half will stay here in case I need a second team to go in."

Grace bit her tongue hard to keep from telling what she thought of him and his orders, and mentally promoted him to *asshole*.

"Yes, sir." Cutter saluted. "The location of the village is here." He glanced at Grace and pointed to a spot on the map. From a distance Cutter looked like the least threatening person in the room. He was the shortest, skinniest guy on the A-Team, but he more than made up for that in stubbornness and stamina.

Grace moved closer so she could get a better look. "How far is it from the Pakistan border?"

"About two klicks."

"Not very damn far." She ran her index finger over the spot on the map. "Mountain valley?"

"Yeah. It's a small village. Less than one hundred people."

"The patrol found no one alive?"

"No one."

Grace breathed in through her nose and out through her mouth. "Did they get their breathing gear on right away?"

"According to their report they did, but they're nervous. Whatever killed those people, killed them fast."

"Okay. I don't have to tell you guys how to prep. You're as well trained as I am. Consider this a live weapon."

"Will do," Cutter responded. He looked at Sharp

standing next to her. "I'm assigning Sharp to ride herd on you, Doc. Where you go, he goes."

"I'm not arguing, Commander. I've worked with Sharp plenty of times."

"Good. We leave in fifteen." Cutter nodded at her, gave Sharp a nod, then moved off to brief the rest of his team.

"I have to get my go-bag and the rest of my gear," she said to Sharp, her mind on the eight million things she needed to do before those fifteen minutes were up.

"I'll give you a hand."

"Thanks, but I don't need any help." She was going to have to deal with his protective crap sooner rather than later, but carefully. "I do need every friend I can get, though. Are you in for that?"

At his grin, she relaxed a little and refocused on the job at hand.

SHARP WATCHED GRACE rush away for about two seconds too long.

"Do I need to replace you with Runnel?" Cutter asked.

He jerked his head around to stare at his commander. He'd thought Cutter had been briefing the rest of the team. "No."

Cutter stood with his arms crossed over his chest and his feet apart. "Then pull your tongue back into your head. You're damn near panting after her."

"Not fucking likely. She's just the only person on this base who can beat me in poker. If something happens to her, I'll have nothing to do for the next month," he said. "Besides, something's not right. She's been off her game since Marshall decided to be an ass. She's our number-one asset. I'm worried." The way he'd found her the other day, damn near passed out, shaking and hyperventilating like she was about to fly apart... It had hit him—a sucker punch to the gut. She was reliving something awful.

Post-traumatic stress disorder.

How many guys did he know who lived with PTSD? Ten, twenty, fifty?

What was Marshall's connection? Something he'd done or said had set off a bomb in Grace's head.

Even weirder, Marshall hadn't liked it when Sharp wouldn't leave Grace alone with him.

What the hell had Grace been involved with that earned her the dislike of a career military man who normally didn't give a rat's ass about what a doctor like her might be doing or not doing?

"Still, watch yourself. Word around the base is, he's got a hate on for the doc and you got in the way."

"What do you know, Cutter?"

"Nothing specific. Marshall hasn't talked, but his attitude toward the doc is clear. He hates her guts."

Cutter was right, Marshall's face had been twisted by disgust and hostility as he stared at her the night he got between her and the colonel. What had happened to cause it? Whatever it was, Sharp wasn't going to let anyone hurt her. She worked just as hard and long at training their allied troops as the A-Team did. And she was *good*.

"Sharp." Cutter's voice had a wary edge and he took a step closer. "Be careful, man. I like the doc, too. Hell, the whole team likes her, but you and I both know falling for someone while on deployment is a mistake."

"Preaching to the choir here, boss. I might enjoy the

view on occasion, but there's a line I have no interest in crossing."

They'd both watched as a former team member fell hard for a woman he'd met while overseas. The relationship disintegrated within weeks after he'd been reassigned. It had damn near broke him, and he'd left the military altogether.

"I respect her," Sharp told his commander. "She's smart and she's worked her ass off this last year. I also think Marshall has some kind of vendetta against her. The look on his face the other night..." Sharp shook his head. "He'd have killed her if he could have. She belongs to *us*."

Cutter was silent for a couple of moments, his gaze steady on Sharp's face. Finally, he angled his head toward the knot of soldiers and gear. "Come on, no one is going to bother her now. Marshall needs her. Get your shit together."

Cutter had one thing right. He needed to keep his focus on the mission. Sharp followed the other man, but there wasn't much for any of them to do, since they were always ready to move out on a moment's notice. Every man on the team had developed the habit during training and had only refined it since. One of their instructors used to say that an unprepared soldier was a dead soldier.

Sharp joined the rest of his team, double-checked his weapons, pulled on his battered gear and bio-suit and got out of the way. *Focus.*

Cutter was talking with Bart, one of their communications guys, when Colonel Marshall walked in a few minutes later with another half-dozen soldiers behind him and headed straight for the Special Forces group.

"Cutter, storm coming at twelve o'clock," Sharp informed him quietly.

By the time Marshall came to a stop, the entire A-Team was standing at attention.

"Sir," Cutter said with a salute. "The go-team is ready, sir."

"Where's that damn doctor?"

"She'll be here in six minutes, sir."

Marshall grunted. "You're taking these men with you on this mission. Two additional medics, Yanik and Anderson, and four of my infantry for security. Your mission objective is to assist Major Samuels."

For the first time since their arrival two weeks ago, Marshall was actually helping a situation rather than shitting all over it.

"And make sure that bitch doesn't screw up," Marshall added. "I want the men on that patrol back in one piece. Understand?"

"Yes, sir."

The team saluted and Marshall stalked off like he was Patton or something.

"So much for that guy not being a tremendous bag of dicks," the team's second in command, John Leonard, said in an undertone.

TWO

GRACE ENTERED HER quarters at a run, slamming the door against the wall.

Down, girl.

She came to a stop, closed her eyes and breathed in and out slowly three times. Having an aneurism now would not be good, but her racing pulse didn't seem to be listening.

Too damn bad. Time to work.

Grace pulled on her bio-suit and her equipment packs.

Altogether, she carried fifty pounds of additional equipment.

She wasn't going to whine. Sharp and the rest of his team each carried at least one hundred pounds of weapons, ammunition and survival gear.

Grace headed toward the area of the base where air support landed and found Sharp coming toward her.

He looked her over, taking in her holstered sidearm, pack and bio-suit. He appeared to take note of everything in once glance, his nod satisfied as he turned to walk with her to the base's landing pad.

Really? He was checking her gear like she didn't know what to bring? The time was coming when she was going to have to knock some sense into big ol' papa bear Sharp.

Commander Cutter was helping to load the helicopter

and giving last-minute orders to the other team members accompanying them.

When she approached the bird, he pulled her aside and yelled in her ear, "When it comes to the source of what killed those villagers, you're in charge. If the situation changes and it becomes necessary to bug out of there, you do whatever Sharp and Leonard tell you. Got that?" Cutter pulled back to look her straight in the eyes. "Sharp's got one job on this mission and that's to keep you alive so you can figure out this shit. Don't make it difficult for him."

"Sharp is teaching me to play chess," she told Cutter. "I can't let anyone kill him until *after* I've beaten him at least once."

Cutter looked at her like she'd lost her mind, shook his head and pointed at the helicopter.

She took it as an order to get on board.

The bird was cramped with gear and men, but Sharp had a jump seat for her smack-dab in the middle of the aircraft. She stowed her backpack under her feet and buckled up. Leonard flashed a hand signal to the pilot and they lifted off.

The helicopter shook like an alcoholic drying out for the first time. The vibration always did something funky to her stomach. There wasn't anything she could do until they landed except hang on to the bottom of the jump seat and talk her guts into some kind of truce.

Sharp nudged her arm a few times and she glanced at him. He gave her the universal thumbs-up and down hand waggle to ask how she was feeling.

She would have liked to flip him a bird, but she'd have to let go of the seat, so she stuck her tongue out at him.

He shook his head at her, but left her alone to suffer

in relative silence. Or as silent as it got on a giant, vibrating, flying washing machine. The landscape outside the helicopter flashed by in muted browns, beiges and creams. A rolling, rocky, ravenous country that had devoured invaders for centuries.

An entire village this time.

How many more would die?

She didn't bother trying to count the minutes; it wouldn't do her any good, and it might even make her feel worse, so she let herself fall into an uncomfortable doze. It was a trick she'd learned to do during residency when she often had to work thirty-six-hour shifts. It didn't matter where she rested her head: a desk, a gurney, even sitting up with her head jammed in a corner. She could sleep anywhere, for about twenty minutes.

The next thing she knew, Sharp was shaking her arm.

Grace opened her eyes and looked around. They were descending into a dry valley, mountains all around.

As the helicopter landed she could see low buildings—some wood, some stone—and a few soldiers waiting for them.

They weren't wearing full bio-suits, just full-faced breathing masks.

The team disembarked, Grace in the middle of the pack, the safest spot.

The helicopter took off as soon as the last man was away.

As soon as it was far enough away for them to talk with the first soldiers on scene, she said, "I'm Dr. Samuels, the on-site bug expert, and this is my team." She gestured at Sharp and the men ranged on either side. "We received a very short summary of what happened." If you could call Colonel Marshall's angry two-line description any kind of explanation. "Can you run us through it again?"

"Ma'am," one of the soldiers said with a salute. Must be the patrol's leader. The mask partially obscured his face and muffled his voice. "We arrived at zero-four-thirty. It was still dark, so we weren't concerned when we didn't see anyone at first."

"At first?" Her breathing ground to a halt. "When did you realize there was a problem?"

"About fifteen minutes after we arrived."

Fifteen minutes was a long time to be in the same environment as a lethal agent without any protection. Marshall had made it sound like they'd gotten their breathing gear on right away.

"We secured the perimeter and all was quiet, so we went to the home of one of the villagers who's a friend. He's given us good intel, food and water in the past. He was dead, along with his brother, sister-in-law and their kids." The soldier stopped to clear his throat.

It must have been bad.

It was probably going to get worse.

"I'm going to tell you an old doctor's trick," she said to him. "When you look at the dead, remember these aren't people anymore. What made them human is gone now. We have a duty to figure out what happened here so no one else dies. Focus on that." She paused, then added, "Mourn for them later, as you should."

"Yes, ma'am." He nodded and continued in a more professional tone, "We got out of there as soon as we saw what had happened. We checked the next home and realized they were dead too. We put on our masks and called for help."

"Where did you put your masks on? Here or farther away?" she asked.

"Over there, ma'am." He pointed at a spot about fifty yards east of their position near the village well.

Not far enough.

"I'd like you and your men to give a more detailed report to..." She glanced at Leonard.

"Sergeant Bart, communications," he said with a chin gesture in the right direction.

She picked where Leonard left off. "While I begin my assessment."

The soldier saluted and walked toward Bart.

"I need all the homes checked for possible survivors," Grace said to Leonard. "Who do you—?"

"Rasker," Leonard barked. "Do a perimeter check. Williams, Lee, start checking the rest of the village. Make sure the patrol didn't miss anyone." He looked at her as they headed off. "Anything else, Doc?"

"No, you've got everything covered."

With a nod to Sharp, who hovered behind her, she approached the first house. Grace pulled out a small digital video recorder, sucked in a deep breath and prepared herself to see whatever awful thing was waiting for them.

She walked inside. Sharp followed.

The house was small. A hearth dominated the middle of the room, probably so it could heat the space evenly. The bodies were huddled together against the far wall under blankets as if they'd just gone to sleep.

Sharp shone his flashlight on their faces. Blood trails ran down from their noses, eyes, mouths and ears. Everyone had bloody lesions on their exposed skin. The victims' eyes were all open and varying expressions of agony had been frozen on their faces.

Whatever caused their deaths involved pain and suffering.

This kind of kill rate narrowed the field of possible agents to a viral hemorrhagic fever caused by something like the Marburg or Ebola viruses, another virus that attacked the liver or even anthrax. The problem was, none of them killed in just a few hours. An influenza virus like SARS or MERS could kill quickly, but the timeline was still too short and the symptoms were off.

What the hell was this?

She shunted shock, horror and fear into a locked box deep in her head. "Are these all the occupants of this house?" she asked Sharp. "If someone died before the others, would they have moved the body somewhere else?"

"Maybe." He turned around and said to someone, "Check the rest of the house and outside for more bodies or recent graves."

She took a closer look at the victims. Three adults and three children.

The lesions on the faces of the children looked no different from the ones on the adults. That might mean the disease progressed the same way, regardless of age.

She reexamined the position of the children, between the adults, wrapped tightly head to toe in blankets. The adults were clearly positioned to protect the children and keep them warm, indicating that they likely got sick at the same time as the adults.

Grace went back to the hearth and lifted the lid on a small pot sitting on top. It was filled with something that looked like water. She poured some out into a bowl sitting in a stack on the floor close by. Tea?

No other recent source of food was immediately evident.

Was this the source of the agent that killed them?

From the condition of the bodies—no burns, evidence of seizures or skin discoloration—she could cross off chemical weapons.

Was the agent airborne or did the victims have to have direct contact with infected fluids or tissue?

So many questions and, so far, no answers.

"I want to look in the other homes."

"Is it me or does everyone look the same?" Sharp asked.

He had a good eye for details. "It's not just you."

They left the first house and entered another and another. The same horror greeted them in each home: entire families, young and old, men and women, all of them dead. All of them with bleeding eyes, noses, mouths and ears. All of them with bloody lesions.

It appeared that everyone in the village got sick at the same time. The chances of that happening by accident were nonexistent.

Water, food, air or more than one?

Grace and Sharp went through a half-dozen homes before she decided she'd seen enough. She needed to collect samples and determine what it was that killed all these people.

She and Sharp joined Leonard and Bart at their hastily erected communication post, where Bart manned the satellite phone and computer. She gave Leonard a brief report.

"Man, so many little kids," Leonard said, shaking his head.

"I'm going to start collecting samples," she said to him in a tone so cold she expected frost to coat the air between them. She knew it made her sound unfeeling, but what they didn't know was she paid dearly for her professionalism in emotional pain after the crisis was over. "Anything else in the patrol's report that might be pertinent?"

Leonard swallowed hard, but answered readily enough, "The last real-time contact anyone outside the village had with anyone inside the village was a little over sixteen hours ago. Contact with another patrol through here. No indication of a problem."

Grace checked her watch. It was now zero-seven-thirty. "Bart, contact the base and have that patrol placed in isolation. I want them checked to be sure they aren't carrying our deadly agent."

"Yes, ma'am."

She turned to Sharp. "So, something happened in less than seventeen hours to kill every person in this village."

"Sixty-eight people," Sharp added. "So far."

"Do we have an idea of how many permanent residents there are in this village?"

"I'm afraid not. The only census taken in Afghanistan was back in the seventies. Nothing since. The population can be very mobile if there's a natural or man-made disaster. They just move to another part of the country."

"So, we have no idea if any survivors packed up and left in the middle of the night?"

He shrugged. "Extended family, traders or even someone just traveling through the area could have stopped here."

"Well, the news can't get any worse." If someone had left the village and taken the illness with them, the infection could spread.

"Doc," someone shouted, stress making the word sound higher-pitched than it should.

Here came the worse news. She should've kept her mouth shut.

Grace squinted at the soldier coming toward her at a run. It was Rasker.

"Did you find any survivors?"

"No, ma'am, we found more bodies."

Rasker hadn't been coming from the village, but toward it. "Someone leaving or returning?" she asked him when he got close enough.

He shook his head. "Not people."

Not people? She'd thought she couldn't get any more afraid of whatever this was.

She was wrong.

Any disease affecting animals as well as people, especially bacteria or viruses, ran a much higher risk of becoming a pandemic. A worldwide killer.

"Show me."

THREE

RASKER LED HER past the houses and into a partially fenced pasture. Over a small rise was a carcass. A cow, bloated to a grotesque size. A quick examination revealed none of the lesions evident on the human bodies.

"There are thirty of them," Rasker said.

"Thirty?" She looked out over the field. Dead cows, their distended legs sticking out at unnatural angles, seemed to be everywhere.

An ice-cold rock settled in the pit of her stomach. "I don't suppose you know when the cows started dying?"

"We'll have to check to see if it was reported by the last patrol through here," Sharp said, his voice so calm she knew he was anything but.

"You do that." Her whole body shook. If the same disease had killed the cows and the people here, it would be her worse nightmare come to life. "You do that."

HE STARED AT Grace's face for a moment. She looked like she was about to pass out. "What's special about cows?"

"Any disease capable of jumping from one species of animal to another is dangerous. Rabies, malaria and bird flu are good examples. If the animal is a common one, the bug is easy to come into contact with and easily transmitted to people. Cows, aside from mad cow disease, are not common vectors, but they're everywhere.

They also represent a significant cost to buy and own, so people will hesitate to destroy them."

"Yeah, I remember the mad cow scare. Maybe people won't be so slow this time."

A grimace came and went on her face, telling him she wasn't just worried, she was terrified. He'd only seen that look on her face once before, the night he found Colonel Marshall talking to her outside of her quarters.

"Mad cow is a prion disease you can only get if you eat infected brain and nervous tissue," she told him. "It can take weeks for infected persons to show symptoms. This disease appears much more contagious. It kills in hours. There's no comparison. This agent has the potential to become an outbreak."

She stopped, thinking so hard he could almost hear the gears in her head. "Okay, here's what I need to happen as quickly as possible. First, I need samples taken from as many people in the village as possible. I also want samples taken from at least six of the cows. I'm going to run a cross section of the samples through the Sandwich to see if it can tell us what we're dealing with. We also need to determine how the agent was introduced into this environment. How were the victims exposed to it? Decontamination can only occur after we've gotten all the answers." As she spoke, her composure firmed up until she appeared as calm and composed as usual.

Hot damn, they had a plan. "Gotcha, Doc," Sharp said. "Let's get moving."

He herded her back to their meeting point, and flashed a hand signal. Eight or nine soldiers jogged over.

The four guys from the A-Team formed up in front of them with an unconscious precision that spoke of years in the service. The other soldiers followed suit.

"How many teams?" he asked her.

"Four besides you and me. One to collect samples from the humans and one to collect from the cows. I need a team to collect water samples and the last team to collect samples from any of the food that's been eaten. You and I will collect additional samples for the lab to investigate further."

"Good plan."

He and Leonard got the teams organized while Grace got the equipment ready. By the time he was done and the men were prepared to head out, she was ready to hand out sample kits to them.

The whole thing took about five minutes. Effective and efficient. Just the way he liked it.

Sharp shadowed Grace back to the first house as she took blood samples from every member of the family. Then they removed the clothing from one adult male and photographed his body, front and back. The lesions were visible head to toe, but were concentrated in the sweat regions under the arms, and around the neck and genitals.

He watched her hands and her face, especially when they examined the kids, but she was as calm and composed as ever.

She photographed the other members of the family, careful to maintain proper confidentiality and documentation with each photo. The army had developed procedures for just this sort of situation, with strict rules on how men, women and children could be treated after death.

She swabbed lesions on each of the other members of the family, as well.

Sharp was surprised at how consistent the lesions were.

Once Grace finished, she prepped the samples for testing in the Sandwich and started the process. The results were ready five minutes later.

She read it. Then read it again. Her gaze fastened on the ticker-tape paper the machine had spit out with a horror he could almost feel. Slowly, she raised it to lock with his.

She looked as shocked as someone who'd just been shot in the chest.

Fuck.

"Doc?" Sharp fit a thousand questions into one word.

"Anthrax," she told him. "And for it to have acted this fast, it had to be weaponized. If it also killed the cows..." Her voice trailed off.

"We have a treatment for anthrax," he said. "Cipro-floxacin. We're vaccinated for it, too."

"Our military members are vaccinated, but the civilian population isn't and I don't know if the Afghan defense forces are vaccinated."

He didn't have to do any math in his head to know this was bad. This was a mostly agrarian society. People traveled to trade and buy goods all the time. "How long would it take to get the vaccine over here?"

GRACE SWALLOWED DOWN a mouthful of bitter fear. "A day, maybe two, but we don't have a lot of vaccine available to us here and there's not much Cipro, either. If this spreads, it could get away from us fast."

"Marshall needs a report."

"A *very* preliminary one. There's still a lot of work to be done before I'll be comfortable giving him even a formal preliminary report."

She walked toward Leonard and Bart and the sat

phone, but before they could reach them, Rasker sprinted toward them.

More bad news?

Sharp immediately brought his weapon up and began searching the surrounding hills for signs of the enemy.

"What's wrong?" she asked Rasker.

He came to a skidding stop in front of her and said, "One of the members of the discovery patrol is sick."

One word. That was all it took, one word to flood her system with adrenaline. "Define *sick*."

"Sweating, fever and coughing up blood."

Grace's chest seized as everything inside her came to a sudden stop. *Holy shit.* "Are lesions visible?"

"No." His tone said, *not yet.*

"Where is he?"

Rasker led her and Sharp, and they picked up Leonard as they passed the communication post, past a couple of houses and to a man in a face mask sitting on a rock. He was coughing, and when she got close she could see a fine spray of blood on the inside of his face plate. He looked up as she came to a stop and crouched in front of him.

It was the American patrol leader. The first one to find the dead. He'd gone inside two houses before putting on his breathing gear.

"Is your anthrax vaccine up-to-date?" she asked him.

He nodded and coughed again. More blood dotted the clear plastic.

"Is that what I've got, Doc?" he asked. "Anthrax?"

"Possibly. I'm not one hundred percent sure yet." She put a hand on his arm. "But I'm going to find out."

She turned to Leonard. "I want a tent set up at least one hundred yards away from the village and those cows, and *all* the members of the discovery patrol brought together so we can watch them for signs of disease." She thought hard. What was their top priority? If this was a man-made biological weapon, were these soldiers or victims?

Her job right now wasn't to play hospital; it was to detect disease, determine which one it was, provide answers to her chain of command and assist with decontamination. After all that was done, then she could hold the hands of the recovering. Or the dying.

The Sandwich was telling her the disease was bacterial, anthrax, but the physical presentation of symptoms was off. This disease progressed faster than any strain of anthrax she had ever heard of. It killed so damn quickly, she couldn't be certain the results were accurate.

"I need to talk to my commander," she told Sharp. "Stay here," she ordered the sick man, "until the medical tent is set up."

After the soldier nodded, she turned on her heel and strode toward Bart.

"Colonel Marshall?" Sharp asked, disbelief coloring his words.

She snorted. Like she'd ever ask Marshall for advice. "No, *my* commander. Colonel Maximillian."

Sharp was silent for about three seconds, then he asked, "Is he good?"

She didn't even have to think. "Yes."

"Better than you?"

She nodded. "Yes." She considered her next words very carefully. "Battling biological weapons is his life's work. There's no one I would rather have working with me on a case than Max." She glanced at Sharp. "He's the guy everyone calls *the* Iceman."

"Everyone calls you *the* Icequeen," Sharp told her.

"No," Grace said. "That would be Max's ex-wife. Coldest bitch I've ever met in my life."

They reached Bart, who was talking to someone on the sat phone. He glanced at her, then at Sharp, raised an eyebrow and saluted.

Sharp shook his head.

Bart barked a "yes, sir" into the phone, then ended the call.

"Marshall?" Sharp asked.

"Yeah, he wants a report so he can decontaminate the village, pronto. He gave us another thirty minutes to finish up before he sends in a cleanup crew."

"He can't do that," Grace protested. "Not until I've determined the agent."

"He seems to think he can."

"What's he planning to do?" she asked, not bothering to hide her derision. "Bomb the place?"

"Something like that."

Grace mentally demoted Marshall to useless fuck. "Until I locate the source of the agent, we can't decontaminate anything." She looked at Sharp and Bart for support.

They looked back at her. Expressionless.

Men.

"Give me the phone."

She must have sounded as irritated as she felt because Bart handed it over, then raised his hands as if washing them of the entire situation.

Grace punched in her commanding officer's direct phone number.

He answered on the first ring. "Max."

"Dr. Samuels here, sir. I'm at the site of the release of

a probable anthrax attack. I believe *weaponized* anthrax was released here, sir, but I haven't figured out how it was introduced into this environment. Plus, it's killing people in hours, Max, *hours*. Not days. And if the death rate is as high as I think it is, this could be a worst-case-scenario weapon."

"Slow down, Grace," Max ordered. "What's got you in a panic? Our procedures can deal with this."

"I need someone to talk Forward Operating Base Commander Marshall out of *cleaning* the site in approximately thirty minutes. I've also just discovered we have a possible secondary infection."

"Secondary?"

"I won't know until I take samples from one of the soldiers who found the bodies and have them analyzed. He may have been infected by the same spores as the dead villagers."

"How many dead?"

"Sixty-eight."

"How many alive?"

"None." An impenetrable silence followed the word.

Finally, Max asked in an incredulous tone, "None?"

Grace swallowed to wet a throat gone dry. "Yes, sir. Like I said, it took less than seventeen hours for the infection to run its course. There's also a possibility the strain killed thirty cows at the same time it was killing people."

He swore. "I've never heard of a naturally occurring anthrax doing that within the time frame. Someone designed a nightmare."

"That's my feeling, as well, sir. Orders?"

"I'll get in touch with Colonel Marshall and tell him to stand down on his cleanup plans. We can't afford to do that until after we know *exactly* what we're dealing with, and we discover if this secondary infection is even the same contagion. This anthrax is too virulent, too deadly to skimp on confirming the identity of the pathogen and how it's being transmitted. If we're dealing with anthrax spores, they're airborne. If their creator releases them in a densely populated area, we'd be looking at a major disaster. It might only be another six to twelve hours to wait, but those are valuable hours to us. Have you got samples collected for lab verification?"

"Almost done. I just need to check on the discovery patrol members and get samples from them."

"Good work. Do that, then get in a helicopter and get them to me as fast as you can. I'll talk to Marshall and have him stand down his cleaning crew."

"Yes, sir."

"Anyone not involved in bringing the samples needs to stay in that village. No one else is allowed in or out."

"I'll order the quarantine."

She ended the call and turned to the waiting men. "I've got orders from Colonel Maximillian to examine the discovery patrol and collect samples from them. Once that's done, I need to get the samples to Max as fast as possible. This area is not to be decontaminated until we're sure we know what we've got here. He's as worried as I am about how fast this infection progresses and the possibility it's crossed the species barrier. This is a unique pathogen that is already a devastating weapon. If we don't do this right, we could make things infinitely worse."

It took a couple of seconds for anyone to respond. "Marshall won't like it," Sharp finally said.

"He doesn't have to. Colonel Maximillian is in charge

of this situation now." She turned to Leonard. "I'm going to check in on the patrol. Can you and Bart contact the base and let them know they have to wait until Colonel Maximillian gives the word before any decontamination can begin?"

"What do you want us to say if Marshall insists on talking to you?" Leonard asked.

He probably would. "I don't have time for long explanations, but if he wants a short report from me directly, he can have one after I've finished with the discovery patrol." She walked away.

The medical tent was up, but that was all it was: a tent with three sides down, the fourth open to the air. Grace grabbed one of the larger first-aid kits and took stock of what she had. The kit had the supplies to treat everything from broken bones to heart attacks, but not enough supplies to treat multiple patients with the same illness or injury.

She might have to get creative.

She laid a thermal blanket on the ground and went to find the patrol leader.

He waited only a few feet away and started walking as soon as she made eye contact with him, but he stumbled after only a few steps, coughing hard.

She went to him, holding on to his arm and taking some of his weight so he didn't fall over. It took several seconds for him to calm his breathing and straighten, but when he did, she had to hold back a horrified gasp.

His face plate was completely obscured by blood. The mask wasn't helping him at all and the filter was probably saturated. "Can you walk?" she asked him.

He nodded and walked with obvious difficulty into

the tent. He lay down on the blanket and she slipped the face mask off him. "This isn't helping you."

He didn't complain, just closed his eyes and lay quivering on the ground.

"Are you experiencing any pain?"

"My joints." As he spoke, she heard popping sounds from deep in his chest, like an old-fashioned coffee percolator.

She picked up his hands and noted slight swelling in them. "Your knees, too?"

He nodded. "Hard to breathe."

"I'm sorry this is difficult for you, just try to breathe normally." She couldn't use a stethoscope without taking her suit off, so she leaned in close to listen to him breathe.

Definitely fluid in his lungs.

He managed two good breaths before he started to cough again. Blood sprayed out from between his lips with every exhalation he made.

Sharp crouched down on the other side of the soldier and used some Wet Wipes to clean off the sick man's face.

"I need to take your clothing off from your waist up," she said to her patient.

He didn't complain, just kept coughing and nodded.

Sharp helped her remove the soldier's upper body armor, uniform shirt and undershirt. She took a flashlight and peered at his armpits. Small lesions were visible under both arms.

Grace grabbed swabs and sampled the discharge from the lesions, then she drew a couple of vials of blood from the soldier.

"Am I going to die?" he asked her, his eyes dull and frightened.

No doctor ever had a good answer for that question. "I need to know more about what's making you sick. It might be the same thing as what killed these villagers, it might not." She patted his arm. "I'll be right back." She looked at Sharp. "Stay with him, please."

Sharp was shaking his head before she could finish talking. "I can't do that, Doc. You know my orders."

"I'll stay with him," another soldier said. One of Marshall's medics.

"Thank you."

She gathered up her samples and went back to the Sandwich.

She didn't want to accidently contaminate any of the samples with cast-off expectorant, so she used a spray bottle of bleach from among the supplies included with the analyzer to clean off all the blood the patrol leader had coughed onto her suit.

She input one, put half of the samples in her container to go with her to the lab and put the remainder inside the Sandwich's cooled storage compartment.

The machine spit out the result and Grace made herself read it.

Anthrax.

Fuck.

"Anthrax," Sharp breathed. He stood right behind her and had obviously read the result over her shoulder. "That sucks donkey's balls."

FOUR

Grace groaned. "Shut up." She searched the area and found Leonard still standing with Bart by the communications station. As she walked toward him, he began waving at her to come quickly.

"Marshall is on the phone," Leonard said. "He's insisting on speaking to you."

She sucked in a deep breath and took the sat phone from Bart.

"Yes, sir."

"What the fuck is going on?" Marshall's tone could have sliced her into very thin slivers.

"Sir," she began, injecting calm and confidence into her tone. "One member of the discovery patrol has tested positive for anthrax. If it's the same strain as the one that killed the villagers, we could be looking at a devastating weapon."

"What did you do to endanger my men?" His bellow could easily be heard by all three men around her.

Marshall was angry and looking for someone to blame. If she tried to defend herself, he'd stop listening. She needed him to listen. Needed him to understand and agree with the next steps in the process to correctly identify and destroy the pathogen.

"I believe the pathogen was still active in the environment when the discovery patrol arrived. I believe it might still be active. I need time to properly identify this strain and discover how it was introduced into the environment."

"Now," Marshall said in a doomsday tone, "is not the time to hesitate."

Grace flinched. "I'm not hesitating, I'm taking appropriate precautions."

"Your precautions didn't save my patrol, did they?"

"Sir, their team leader went into two homes containing bodies with evidence of disease before putting on his breathing gear."

"You were the one who trained my men on how to respond to possible biological weapons," Marshall spit out. "I'm not going to take the word of an inept bitch who obviously doesn't know what she's doing. If this bug is as dangerous as you say, then cleaning the site will stop any further infection."

"This appears to be a man-made strain, sir. If we don't properly identify the strain and how it was created now, we might not have a chance to do it later. A few extra hours at this point could mean the difference in living and dying for more soldiers in the future."

"My men are not guinea pigs for you to test your theories on. You will follow established protocols, identify the agent and evacuate the area for decontamination. Now."

"I've identified the agent, sir, but—"

"Are you arguing with me, Major?" Marshall's purr wound its way up her spine, leaving a trail of cold sweat in its wake.

She shook off the implied threat. "With all due respect, Colonel, the situation calls for extraordinary measures."

"Not your call to make." He sounded like he enjoyed saying it.

"You're correct, sir, which is why I contacted Colonel Maximillian. As the head of the Biological Rapid Response team, the decision is his."

When Marshall didn't respond, she continued with, "Colonel Maximillian has ordered the area quarantined and protected until we can be sure we've identified the specific strain of the pathogen and method of delivery."

Still no response from Marshall.

"Sir, are you there?" she asked as diffidently as she could.

He disconnected the call.

She handed the sat phone to Bart and prayed Marshall wouldn't do anything stupid.

"What did Marshall say there at the end?" Leonard asked.

"He didn't say anything, he hung up on me."

Leonard winced, but said, "You've made your report and we have a plan of action. Time to execute it. I'm going to stay here and enforce the quarantine. You two head out with the samples."

"You got it," Sharp said.

"Don't let anyone blow anything up while I'm gone," Grace told Leonard as he walked away.

"Yes, ma'am." He gave her a crisp salute.

"Don't salute me. I'm not in command of this situation."

"Yes, you are," Sharp told her.

She shook her head. "No. The anthrax is in charge here and none of us can afford to forget it. There's *no* room for ego or hurt feelings." She sucked in a deep breath. "How should we split up the team? Some need to stay here and monitor the situation."

"You, me, Rasker, Williams and three of Marshall's men." He watched her face for a second. "Don't let Marshall's stupidity rattle you."

"The problem is, he has a point. Too many things have gone wrong here."

"No plan survives first engagement. Things always change. There's no way you could have predicted this."

She couldn't maintain eye contact and let her gaze skitter away. "Strategy, tactics and figuring out who the enemy is are not my strong suit."

"That's not what I've seen from you before now and definitely not what I've heard."

That caught her attention. "Heard?"

"You were awarded the Bronze Star a couple of years ago." He said it almost gently and she scowled at him.

She shouldn't be surprised he knew about that. Hell, the whole A-Team probably knew about it. There was just one problem. She wasn't proud of what happened two years ago. "I was doing my job and it went horribly wrong." She spun around and took a couple of steps toward the Sandwich. "Other people deserved that medal more than I did."

"That's what all the heroes say." It was a low whisper.

She jerked to a stop and stared at him, but he was already talking to Bart. "Get us a ride. Something close and fast."

"One magic carpet ride coming up," he said. "ETA, ten minutes."

"That *was* fast," Grace said to Bart. "What did you do, make the request when I wasn't looking?"

"Leonard had the aircraft waiting on standby in case we needed a quick pickup."

"You guys think of everything."

Sharp nodded at her. "Have you got everything you need?"

She glanced at the Sandwich. "Everything I need is right there."

"Get it ready for transport, boss."

As she moved to do it, Sharp called for Rasker, Williams and three of their security detail to join them.

Grace got the samples squared away in multiple zipped plastic Baggies, then put them all in a biohazard travel container and threw the strap over her head.

She took the bleach and sprayed down the suits of everyone leaving so they wouldn't contaminate the interior of the bird.

The thud of the helicopter's rotors beat against her skin before she saw it. Sharp and the men who were coming with her gathered around her in a protective huddle.

It came in to land, kicking up dust and dirt, and they raced to get in. Sharp leaned over the pilot's shoulder for a minute and she could tell from the rising tension in his body that the conversation wasn't all happy, happy, joy, joy.

Finally, Sharp patted the pilot on the shoulder and sat down in the jump seat next to her. The helicopter took off.

"What were you and the pilot talking about?" she yelled at Sharp.

"Our destination," he yelled back. "He had orders to return to the forward base, but I told him Marshall wasn't in charge of this party anymore."

"Marshall had given him *other* orders?" Wanting to get the job done quickly was one thing. Interfering with an investigation of this magnitude was another. She had hoped to avoid another confrontation with Marshall, but it looked like one was going to happen anyway.

"Yeah, but don't worry. One doctor, two Green Berets and one situation-specific colonel beat one regular army colonel in this poker hand."

She scowled at Sharp. "We're not playing poker."

"Sure, we are," he said. "We're playing to win." He patted her knee. "Close your eyes and pretend you're sleeping, Doc. We're okay."

Oh, she very much doubted that.

The flight got bumpy. Enough to bounce her out of her seat had she not been strapped down.

"I hate flying," she yelled at the world as she hung on to her harness and prayed for deliverance. The constant engine vibration and turbulence bumps had her stomach on strike and trying to crawl up her throat. "I *really* hate helicopters."

"Want a barf bag, Doc?" the soldier sitting on the other side of her asked as he tried to hide a grin. Tried and failed. Vomiting *inside* her suit would be very uncomfortable.

Asshole. "No, I was planning on taking my suit helmet off and puking on your lap."

The soldier stopped grinning and leaned away from her. "Seriously?"

"If we don't get out of this turbulence, I'm very serious."

"Sorry." A plastic bag was thrust in front of her face. "Just in case," he said.

She rolled her eyes and took it. It would take hours of bone-jarring air travel before they arrived at the naval base in Bahrain where Max waited to confirm the Sandwich's test results, and they'd have to stop for fuel before the Iranian border.

"How did you get tapped for this duty if you get airsick?" the soldier asked.

She gave him a sidelong look. Did he think trauma doctors or infectious disease specialists grew on trees? "It's only flying that makes me sick. A lot of the time I don't have to fly to where I'm needed."

All told, there were seven people on the helicopter besides the pilot and copilot. Everyone else was there to keep her, and her samples, safe. Three of them could kill a person with their little finger.

She leaned back against the harness of her jump seat, closed her eyes and began a relaxation technique to put herself to sleep.

She'd need all the sleep she could get now, because she had the suspicion not a lot of it was going to be available later.

GRACE WOKE WITH a start, dizzy and disoriented. They were still in the air, but they weren't flying, they were falling. The helicopter was twisting and turning like an insane amusement park ride, losing altitude fast. Sharp was out of his jump seat yelling at the pilot and the soldier beside her trying to get out of his harness.

Where the hell did he think he was going to go?

She watched as he finally hit the release on his harness. There was a flash and a deafening *bang*.

The world went dark.

WHY COULDN'T SHE breathe?

Grace inhaled, but the air choked her like it had hands around her throat.

Coughing, she clawed at those invisible fingers, opened her eyes and realized there were no bumps or vibration. They were on the ground. Smoke formed a black wall around her, shutting her away from the rest of the world. Smoke, inside her suit helmet. She forced her mind to think.

The aircraft was down. That meant injuries and death.

Her suit was compromised. That meant possible exposure to infection and death.

For a moment her stomach took over, rolling like they were still in the air, but she wrestled it into a lockdown and forced herself to think through the shock of what had happened. *Injuries, infection and death.*

Her limbs and lungs all seemed to be working. Time to get at it. She released her harness and pitched out of the seat and onto her hands and knees.

Next to her left hand was the face of the soldier who'd been sitting next to her. He was staring up at her, his mouth slack, eyes fixed and pupils dilated. Blood was splattered all over his bio-suit, inside and out, and a piece of the aircraft stuck out of his temple.

She stared at him unblinking for a couple of seconds, her stomach twisting tighter than it ever had while she was the air.

She'd just been talking to him and now he was dead.

She tried to push her jumbled emotions aside, but there were too many. Old traumas and the new twisted together into an uncontrollable boiling mass of confusion and pain.

Her body had only one way to get rid of it.

The world narrowed and grayed, and she wrenched her bio-suit helmet off as she vomited all over the soldier's chest. She scrambled sideways to get away from the body, her stomach still heaving.

A sound penetrated her mental haze. Screaming.

It was hard to see where the noise was coming from. Between the smoke and the jumbled debris all around, it was hard to even believe the wreck had once been a helicopter.

She crawled around a large piece of metal paneling that probably had once been part of the rear bulkhead. Her hands landed on a suit-covered boot and she felt her way up the body to search for evidence of injury.

Another of Marshall's men. He'd been decapitated.

Horror worked its way up to choke her, freezing her in place like the day the IED went off and she'd been faced with an extremist with a weapon. Then, the only thing that saved her had been the quick actions of another soldier.

No. She wrenched her mind out of the past.

Focus. Where was Sharp?

She searched the area, but there was no sign of him. He could be hurt or dead. No, not him. *She hadn't beaten him at chess yet.*

She'd find him, then she'd worry about everything else.

She discovered a second body, dead, then got to the source of the screaming. It was one of men on her security detail. One of his arms was trapped under mangled pieces of the wreckage, pinning him to the ground.

There was a lot of blood.

Too much blood.

She began to pat him down, searching for the injury and the source of all the blood.

His left foot was missing. Completely gone.

"I need some help here," she yelled as she jerked at a piece of harness. It came loose and she quickly used it to put a tourniquet at the end of the stump to stop the bleeding. The screaming stopped as the soldier passed out. She turned, hoping to see assistance in the form of Williams or Rasker or Sharp. No one.

Where was Sharp?

She'd have to get an IV going and push fluids into the injured soldier if there was any hope of saving him. Did they even have those kinds of medical supplies on this bird?

No one was there.

The smoke had dissipated a little, allowing her to see better, but all she saw was a dead aircraft filled with broken bodies.

Despair grabbed hold and shook her like a hunting dog with a rat. She wanted to throw up some more, then crawl into a hole and never come out, but the soldier needed her.

He was going to die if she didn't get moving.

The biohazard container hanging around her neck bumped into her arm. It appeared intact. Thank God.

She stripped off her suit—it wasn't any use now—then crab-crawled below the smoke and over debris and bodies toward where the emergency supplies were supposed to be stowed. Stored in a series of bulkhead cabinets in padded containers and locked to the fuselage by heavy-duty straps, some of it should be okay. As long as there were IV sets and saline, she could cobble something together to keep the soldier alive.

She dug out one case, but it was full of bandages and splints. She'd gotten her hands on another one when she heard the voices and the laughter. From the sound of their baritones, men. From the language, Dari or Persian, locals rather than a rescue team. From their laughter, extremists or insurgents.

The soldier started screaming again.

There was a burst of gunfire and the screaming stopped.

She didn't have to see it to know what happened. They'd killed the soldier. Murdered him. A wounded man, pinned to the ground, who had no hope of defending himself.

Anger rushed through her system like a firestorm, heating her blood and completely clearing her head for the first time since the crash.

The men laughed some more and she could hear the crash of debris being thrown aside. Gunfire erupted for a second time and her hands curled into fists.

They'd killed her patient, then moved on to shoot someone else.

They thought it was funny.

She was going to show them funny.

She was going to ram funny right down their throats.

She put the crate down with suddenly steady hands and searched for something she could use to school those giggling idiots. Next to the medical supplies was a small rack of backup weapons, three Beretta M9s. She pulled one out, grabbed a fifteen-bullet magazine and slowly, carefully loaded the weapon.

Gunfire echoed around her. They'd moved away, probably to the other side of the aircraft.

She crept out of the hidey-hole she'd been in and listened carefully to the voices, judging direction and distance. There was still enough smoke to make visual contact somewhat hit-or-miss, so she kept low and moved slowly toward them.

Movement had her ducking down. Two men in typical Afghan clothing, chattering away at each other in what she was sure now was Dari, walked quickly away from the wreckage. She couldn't see where they were going, but they started to run, so it must have been something important.

She peeked over a piece of bulkhead and stopped breathing when she saw what they were after.

A soldier in a bio-suit lay at the end of a trail of debris as if he'd been spit out of the helicopter like a mouthful of something that tasted awful.

The two Afghans were only steps away from him, their weapons raised.

Grace lunged out of the aircraft and sprinted toward them. She yelled, "Hey!" dropped to one knee and fired two shots in rapid succession when they turned to see who'd called out.

They both fell. She leaped to her feet, running toward them, her gun up and ready to fire again if those first shots hadn't done their job.

But they had. Both Afghans were dead.

She turned and looked at the American.

He blinked up at her like he'd just awoken from an unwelcome sleep. "Doc?"

"Sharp?" Grace nearly wept in relief. *He was alive.* "Can you stand? Are you injured? Your suit is torn." She looked around, watching for more bad guys. "Did those men shoot you? There might be more of them."

"I'm mobile and don't need medical attention at the

moment. How about I handle the shooting and you handle the first aid." He held out his hand.

"Yeah." She handed him the pistol and he palmed it with the ease of long familiarity. "I need to check for more wounded."

He accepted her hand up and they walked toward the helicopter.

She noted his limp, but it would have to wait until their immediate problems were addressed.

"What did I miss?" he asked.

"We crashed."

"I got that."

She told him what she remembered of the crash and what happened after.

He glanced back at the two Afghani bodies lying on the ground. "How many bullets did it take to lay them out?"

"One each."

"Damn, Doc, that's fine work."

She stared at him blankly. Too tired, too heart-sore to respond.

"Are you injured?" he asked.

"No." She looked down at herself. Splatters of blood covered her uniform, but none of it seemed to belong to her.

"Anyone else alive?"

"I don't know. I haven't had time to look."

"Okay, let's look now. I'm also going to arm myself to the teeth and see if I can radio for help." He took two steps away, then stopped and turned back to her. "You took your suit off?"

"It was torn in several places. Just like yours."

"Good point." He pulled it off.

They entered the wreck and Grace began checking for more wounded. She found Williams first, but he was dead, one side of his skull crushed. He'd always been so quiet, but the second she ever needed anything he'd be there helping out or pitching in any way he could. Grief surged to the surface of her mind, but she shoved it back down and put a lock on it. Next, she found another soldier from her security detail, a bullet hole in his head. Finally, after some digging through debris, she found Rasker. He was breathing, but unconscious. Her palms moved up his body, checking for injuries, and found broken bones and at least one skull fracture.

"Doc."

She glanced up. Sharp crouched in front of her cradling an M4 in one arm with the pistol she'd fired in his other hand, butt toward her. "I want you to keep this."

She took it and holstered it. "The pilot?"

Sharp's expression was so carefully bland she knew the news was bad before he said it. "Dead along with the copilot. The radio is junk too."

FIVE

GRACE'S STOMACH DOVE into her combat boots. "How long until we can expect a rescue?"

"Don't know," Sharp said, his gaze roaming the area around the aircraft. "It depends on whether the pilot was able to radio our situation out before we crashed or not. If he did, then we should see help soon. If he didn't, we'll be on our own for a while." He glanced down, a grimace creasing his face. "How's Rasker?"

"He needs immediate surgery. He's got a skull fracture and probably a hematoma."

"His brain is swelling?"

"Yeah. If it swells too much, it could kill him."

"Can you do anything to help him now?"

"The only thing that's going to help him is if I drill a hole through his skull and drain away some of the fluid collecting in the bruise."

"Fuck."

"I don't have the equipment or the drugs. Plus, so far, it's just you and me. And one of us needs to watch out for more bad guys with guns. We need another pair of hands."

"I'll keep a lookout and stay with him while you see if we can find anyone else who might be in better shape and able to help."

Sharp turned to move away, but she stopped him with

a hand on his arm. "Wait. Your leg. It's bleeding pretty steady. Let me bandage that up for you."

He looked like he was going to refuse, but then he nodded. "Make it quick."

She grabbed a bandage out of the pile of medical supplies she'd found earlier and quickly wrapped his thigh. "I'll need to take a closer look later." He nodded while scanning the area outside the aircraft.

She left Rasker with Sharp and continued searching, praying she'd find someone else who was healthy enough to help her. But she only found bodies, none of them alive.

Time to talk to Sharp.

She headed back to where she'd left him watching over Rasker, but Sharp wasn't there.

Gunfire erupted and she ducked down over her patient, then looked to see where it had come from. Sharp was laid out on the ground a few feet from the aircraft, firing his rifle at three Afghan men. They returned fire, bullets ploughing into the ground all around him, but Sharp didn't move or stop firing until all three were dead.

He left them where they lay, got up into a crouch and approached her. "Any luck?"

She snorted. "No. Everyone else is...dead." That last word got stuck in her throat and she had to struggle to breathe around it.

She glanced at Sharp. He was staring at her hands. They were covered in blood and shaking.

His gaze met hers and he asked, "How much water do we have?"

"I don't know, hadn't even thought about it." She should have. Had the crash scrambled her brains?

"Can you take stock of what's useable? Water, food, first aid. Gather what you can and get it ready in case we have to leave in a hurry to find shelter."

"I'm not leaving Rasker. Not unless there's..." The words stuck in her throat, but she shoved them out anyway. "No hope."

"Doc, I don't want to leave him either, but we've got to have a plan B ready. Okay?"

He was talking to her like she was a two-year-old. "I'm not going to freak out."

He smiled at her; it wasn't on his face long, but it was enough to tell her he didn't believe a word.

"I hate it when you do that."

"Do what?"

"Give me the *I'll take care of the poor defenseless female* look. I did save your life a few minutes ago, remember?"

"That you did. My apologies."

"Don't worry, I'll let you know if I need you to slap me out of my hysterics."

That made him laugh and he shook his head. "I'm never bored around you, Doc. You say the craziest things."

She let out a sigh. "For some reason crazy doesn't seem like a bad thing right now."

"Ready to get back to work?"

"Yeah." She glanced around. Smoke from the wreckage rose into the air. It was probably visible for miles. "How much trouble are we in?"

"This is going to draw unwanted attention, but if we leave, our rescue won't be able to find us."

She looked out over the desert, searching for movement or the flash of sunlight reflected off a weapon in the distance. "How long can we stay?"

"As long as we can. How's Rasker?"

She went back to check on his vitals. Sharp followed, his gaze alternating between watching her and the landscape.

"Not good. His breathing is shallow. If we can't get him some advanced medical assistance very soon..." She didn't finish. She didn't need to.

"Understood." His voice vibrated with restrained violence. "I'm going to walk the perimeter. Gather supplies as you can."

Men often dealt with grief by getting mad at it. It was probably the healthiest response for the situation, but she was going to have to watch him close. Make sure he didn't do something stupid. Or brave. Or both.

Grace checked her patient again—no change—then began collecting water, food and assembling a comprehensive first-aid kit that wouldn't slow them down if they needed to run. She found and grabbed three additional magazines for her gun, then added them to the pile.

"How's it going, Doc?"

"Bare necessities are ready, but time is running out for Rasker."

"We've got movement," he said, sliding behind a large piece of metal. "Take cover."

Grace moved to try to cover the injured man with anything that might protect him from gunfire.

She was dragging a wrecked jump seat over when Sharp yelled at her, "Get down, Doc."

A bullet pinged off something metal above her head. She dove for the ground, and discovered the Beretta in her hand. She stared at it like it was a live grenade for about half a second before turning and firing it out at the desert and the men coming toward them.

"Sharp?"

"I've got incoming on my side, too!"

"I've only got one extra magazine on me!"

"Look in your back pocket."

She slapped a hand on her back pockets and discovered one additional magazine. "How the hell did you put that in there without me knowing?"

"I did it when you were having your hysterics."

The cad. "So you figured that was a good time to cop a feel?"

"I'm a guy. It's always a good time for that."

They'd survived a helicopter crash that killed most of their team, armed extremists were trying to kill them and he was thinking about getting his hands in her pants? "Asshole," she yelled.

"What? I can't hear you over the hail of bullets trying to kill us."

"You're lucky there are worse assholes for me to shoot at."

"Promises, promises, Doc."

"Just don't get shot. If anyone gets to shoot you today, it should be me."

"Yes, ma'am."

She focused on the men approaching her side of the wreck. She hadn't hit anyone yet and she was down to five bullets. Taking time to reload was dangerous. Dare she change her tactics? Would hesitating now, letting them rush forward to give her bigger targets, make the situation worse or better? She'd hesitated before while under fire and had regretted it ever since. She chose to wait, her stomach twisting, hands shaking and breathing coming in pants. She waited, allowing them to get closer. Closer. *Closer.*

She took aim and fired.

One. Two. Three. Dead.

Relief shot champagne into her blood, which went straight to her head. *This time she'd made the right choice.* "You still shooting at yours?" she asked Sharp.

The only answer was a burst of gunfire. "Not anymore." He came through the wreckage and glanced out at the bodies on her side. "You're a good shot, Doc."

She'd killed three more people. Five altogether. The fizzy feeling went flat. "Yay me."

"When you say it in a monotone like that, it doesn't sound so happy."

She stared at her hands, which were vibrating at a rate that would have done an earthquake proud. She'd been fine, *fine* until Marshall had reopened the emotional wounds Cranston's death caused. *Son of a bitch.* She wasn't like this. Wasn't someone who couldn't handle her shit. Until today happened. "Sharp, I think I need that slap now. Um, just as soon as I throw up." She stumbled a few steps away and let her stomach complete its protest. She stood there bent at the waist, her hands braced on her knees until the nausea and dizziness passed.

She turned to check Rasker's pulse. Weak and slow. He didn't have long.

She glanced outside. The sun beat down on the desert with unrelenting heat, but it was getting closer to the horizon. Nighttime wasn't far off, and darkness would bring out even more predators. Rasker wouldn't make it without surgery. If he didn't get that surgery soon, he wouldn't make it at all.

Time, the weather and the men trying to kill them were all the enemy. She and Sharp had precious little to fight them off with.

"Have you been thinking about our escape plan?" she asked him.

He didn't stop his inspection of the horizon. Moving from side to side of the aircraft, watching for more unfriendlies. "Yes."

"I've got everything you asked me to gather. I just need to find a couple of packs to carry it in."

"Check the same spot as those medical supplies. There might be some at the very back."

She did and found three that were relatively undamaged. She quickly packed two of them and placed them where they could grab them on the run if they had to.

"Have you got enough ammunition?" she asked.

"I grabbed everything I could get my hands on."

She glanced out at the desert. Desolate and empty of life. No help or safe place in sight. "Is it going to be enough?"

"Probably not."

She grunted. Sharp had something huge going for him. He didn't lie.

Grace checked Rasker's pulse again and found it had slowed even more. He wasn't going to make it and there wasn't a damn thing she could do to change it. Tears cooled her face, but she let them fall. No one besides Sharp would see them.

People said she was cold behind her back, thinking she didn't care, that she really was as unfeeling as she often appeared, but they were wrong. She cared too much, and sometimes her emotions got away from her no matter how hard she tried to lock them down.

Keeping the fingers of her right hand on his carotid pulse point, she smoothed her left index finger down his nose. "It's okay to go, Rasker," she whispered to him. "It's okay."

The pulse under her fingertips slowed and disappeared.

She stood, looking down at the dead body of her brother-in-arms, then glanced at Sharp. "I'm done," she said, and was shocked at how bleak her tone sounded. "I'm so done."

He looked at her. "I wish we could *be* done, but for us the shit's just getting started."

She glanced at him. His face was drawn in sad, angry lines, his mouth pressed tight and the muscles in his jaw clenching and unclenching. "I need you to keep up. Can you do that?"

She swallowed a bitter mouthful of regret. "Okay."

Sharp came over and picked up one of the packs. "We'll head northeast for a bit, get lost in those hills." He paused for a moment, then met her gaze with a frankness that told her she might not like what he was about to say. "I won't let anything happen to you, Doc."

Who did he think he was, a superhero? "Don't make promises you can't keep, Sharp."

He put his hand under her chin and took a small step closer. "I don't make those kinds of promises."

Despite the temperature, she shivered and stepped into him so she could soak up his body heat and strength. She was going to need it. "I'm one lucky gal to have a friend who's as badass as you."

He didn't answer, just stared down into her eyes as if trying to convey a lifetime of messages in just a few seconds.

The moment passed, he stepped back and moved out.

She grabbed the other pack, shouldered it and followed him away from the wreckage.

How would a rescue team find them now?

How long could they last on their own?

SIX

THE HEAT SUCKED every bit of moisture out of the air. Grace's tongue felt two times too big for her mouth, and at the pace Sharp set, all she wanted to do was hang it out and pant.

He had them moving toward the nearest hills at a ground-eating trot, his head roving from side to side, watching for possible threats. After a few minutes, the terrain changed from barren stony hills to low scrub brush and washout ravines, the only sound the skitter of small creatures running for cover.

Was there room for her under one of their rocks?

Sharp came to a stop, his head poised to listen, one hand extended behind him with his palm out in a stop gesture.

She stopped.

He waved that hand toward the ground.

She crouched, the butt of the Beretta rough against her palms. Her stomach tightened until breathing was painful. It had become second nature for her to hold the weapon at ready, safety off during training, but at this moment it felt wrong. She was a doctor, a surgeon. Her muscles should remember what to do with a scalpel, not a gun.

Nausea threatened, but she beat it down with ruthless anger. No time to panic, freak out or let her inner pansy ass out to throw up on the situation. That bitch had already had enough airtime today.

There was only room for the soldier to be in control.

She closed her eyes for five seconds. Took in three deep breaths and deliberately relaxed her shoulders. They would get through this. They had to. She wasn't ready to die, and Sharp didn't look like he was interested in it much either.

They waited for a long time. Shadows grew and lengthened like pulled taffy, turning the desert into a moonscape of craters and valleys an eternity from home. The pack on her back gained weight with every passing second, and the sample container dug invisible claws into her side.

Finally, long after the muscles in her thighs and calves began to burn, his fingers lifted in a come-closer sign.

She walked slowly, quietly until she was right behind him, then reached out with her left hand and placed it on his shoulder so he'd know she was there.

His reaction was a subtle relaxation in the muscles under her hand. "Stay on my ass," he whispered, the sound more of a sigh than a vocalization.

She attempted to reply as quietly. "Understood."

He moved forward, weapon ready, the butt of his rifle anchored in the hollow of his shoulder.

She followed, keeping as close as possible without tripping over him.

They traveled for what seemed like hours, following the ravines until Sharp paused extra-long looking at a collection of prickly brush perched about ten feet up from the bottom of the ravine.

He signaled her to remain where she was, then rushed

up to the vegetation. A second later she couldn't see him at all.

Grace waited, growing unease twisting in her chest until she could barely breathe. Finally, Sharp appeared out of the darkness as if he were made of the same shadows cast by the half-moon in the sky.

He waved at her to follow and she found herself climbing the rocks, sliding behind some low brush and into the dark.

A cave.

The opening wasn't large. She had to bend over almost in half, but it opened up a bit more a few feet inside.

A snap echoed softly, then an orange glow-in-the-dark stick lit up and illuminated the cave. It wasn't high enough for Sharp to stand up in it, but she almost could. There were animal tracks on the dirt floor of the cave, but none were large or looked recent. The cave ended after about ten feet, making it just large enough for the two of them to be comfortable.

She snorted at the thought. Comfortable was not a word she'd be using to describe her situation for the foreseeable future. Her father had always told her a comfortable soldier was a lazy soldier, but he couldn't have meant this.

"Is this place safe?" she asked, afraid to speak too loud in case the cave created an echo.

"As safe as we're going to get," Sharp said. "I'm going to go out, scout around and see if I can erase any tracks we might have left on our way up here."

"What do you want me to do?"

"Wait here. No noise, no moving around."

"Got it." A second later he was gone, a silent ghost among the shadows.

She knelt down, unslung the container of samples, placing it in a small nook near the mouth of the case, then took her pack off. Inside were three water bottles. She took one and drank slow and careful from it, stopping before her thirst was quenched. They were going to have to ration it and she might as well start now.

The temperature outside the cave was dropping fast, but inside, it was still warm. She sat down, using her pack as a back brace, and watched the entrance for Sharp's return.

At first she kept a careful watch, every sound bringing her to attention and leaning forward to check for someone sneaking close. After a while she began to recognize insect noise and birdcalls. All good things to hear. It was when they got quiet that she would have to worry about another human being in the area. After a while, her muscles began to relax, her mind drifted and flashes of memory struck like snakes after prey.

The smiling face of the soldier next to her on the plane was shoved aside by his death mask.

Her anger at the senseless killing of her teammates by the Afghan men. The freeze of seeing their bodies lying still and bloody on the ground after she shot them.

Hope at finding Rasker alive.

Anguish at giving him permission to die.

Conflicting emotions, images and utter confusion at having no escape, no outlet for the cacophony, threatened to suck her into a tornado of despair with the power to drown her in her own guilt and self-doubt.

She should have died too. She should have been able to protect and help those men, yet every one of them now lay dead in the helicopter's carcass, their blood coating the smoking broken bones of the aircraft and the greedy sand beneath it.

She was the reason those men had gotten into that doomed machine.

Their deaths were on her hands.

A sound broke through the mental haze and she realized something, someone, was closing in to the entrance to the cave. Her hands moved before she could decide what to do, the Beretta poised and ready.

A voice floated through the night with a stealth she could only dream of someday accomplishing. "Doc?"

"Sharp." She let out the breath she hadn't known she was holding and her arms fell to her sides. She had no strength left, no armor for her feelings and no skills left to cope with the meltdown she could feel beginning inside the core of her soul.

He slipped inside the cave, but stayed at the entrance, anchoring branches he must have taken from other brush and bushes, creating a screen to hide them.

"Where did you get all that?" she asked quietly.

"Here and there." He moved back from his handiwork and took a look at it. "That should do for camouflage."

He seemed concerned. "Are we going to need it?"

"Yeah." His response was a sigh she felt more than heard. "I went back to take a look at the crash site."

When he didn't continue, she asked, "And?"

"It was being watched."

"By who?"

"Several whos. From several locations."

It took her a moment to digest his answer, but when she did, nausea threatened again. "We can't go back, can we?"

"Not if we want to stay alive."

"Will they look for us?"

"Probably."

"How will our guys even know we survived if we're not at the helicopter? Couldn't we find a closer place to wait? So we'll hear them coming?"

"In my opinion, closer isn't safe. There are extremists all over these hills and they're now waiting for a rescue helicopter, too, so they can try to shoot it down. If we jump up and wave our arms in the air, they're going to shoot us first."

"Point to you. How will our people know we survived?"

Sharp's reply took a moment or two. "There aren't enough bodies."

"What do you mean? At the crash site? There are plenty of bodies. More than there should be." She was responsible for some of those bodies.

"Not American soldiers. They'll look and they'll count. The bastards who shot us down are most likely looking for whoever killed their men. They know we're out here, hunkered down somewhere, waiting for help. They'll be watching for a chance to kill us before we can be safely extracted."

"What are we going to do, then?"

"Our guys can't leave the wreckage to be picked over. There are a lot of usable supplies and gear on board. Plus, they're going to want to recover the bodies. We'll have to wait until a full retrieval team gets here. Then we can make a run for it."

"How long until that happens?"

He shrugged. "Maybe six to twelve hours. If we stay hidden and quiet, we have a good chance of making it."

He scuttled farther into the cave. "In the meantime, why don't we figure out where you're wounded?"

"What are you talking about? I wasn't hurt."

"Doc, you're bleeding from somewhere. I found a blood trail one of us left, and since you bandaged me up already, it sure isn't me."

Sure, she had a few sore spots, her left arm ached, as did her left calf, but she was sure they were just bumps and bruises. "I'm fine."

"I know that, but it isn't relevant to this conversation."

Wait, *what did he say?* "Are you trying to *flirt* with me?"

"I don't know. Is it working?" He gave her a once-over that was *so* not appropriate.

"It's pissing me off." She wanted to smack him, yell at him, beat her fists against his chest.

He shrugged. "I'll take pissed off over nothing at all."

"Stop talking. You're not making any sense." She glared at him, daring him to say something more.

He smiled grimly at her. "Doc, get your butt over here."

She stared at him. He wasn't kidding.

Pffft. She wasn't bleeding and she'd prove it. Grace pushed to her feet, crouching a little so she didn't hit her head on the ceiling of the cave, and looked down.

There was a wet spot on the dirt where she'd been sitting. She palpated it with two fingers and brought the bit of sand closer to her face so she could smell it. The bitterness of iron coated the back of her throat.

Blood. *Shit.*

Sharp wasn't going to let her live this down.

"Doc?"

"Yeah, yeah, I'm coming." She moved farther in.

"Let's check my left side. It hurts more than anywhere else."

"Where exactly?"

"Bicep and calf."

He reached for her leg, then wrapped his hand around the muscle. She was surprised by the sting of pain that went with it. "Ow."

"Looks like something here. Where else?"

She sat down and he did the same exam to her arm.

"Blood here too."

She was an idiot. "I can't believe I got hurt and didn't know it."

"Adrenaline is a marvelous thing," Sharp said as he urged her to take off her body armor. "I've seen guys keep running, fighting or firing after getting hit with a fatal strike. Your brain can keep going for a surprisingly long time before it realizes you're dead."

Her mouth twisted into a grimace. "If you're trying to cheer me up, it's not working."

"Just keeping it real, Doc." Sharp turned away to open his pack and pull out one of the first-aid kits. "Let's start with your leg." He gave her left leg a moment's consideration, then lifted a hand toward her fly.

She stepped back before she could stop herself and he froze.

He dropped his hand, wiggled his eyebrows at her and said, "Take off your pants."

SEVEN

GRACE BIT HER LIPS. No. She wasn't going to laugh. It wasn't funny. He wasn't funny. "Are you trying to make me want to kill you?"

"No. Not really." He seemed to think about it for another second or two. "Okay, maybe a little."

She hovered between wanting to laugh and wanting to cry. Her best buddy was trying his hardest to help her, but she wasn't entirely sure his flirting was all fun and games. There was a serious glint in his eye she'd never seen before.

"You're nuts, you know that?" she asked as she began removing the gun holster strapped to her right leg, then moving on to the belt with forty-two different things hanging off it. "You've been cracking jokes since the crash, and none of this is *funny*." Oh God, her face was wet. "Why aren't you angry?"

"I'm angry, but not at you." The smile on his face lost its razor edge. "Never at you."

Tears clouded her vision and her chest stuttered with silent sobs she refused to let out. One escaped and strong hands and hard arms grabbed her up and she found herself drawn onto Sharp's lap, her head buried in the hollow of his shoulder. She shook both of them with the force of her restrained cries.

Her father would be mortified if he knew she was crying on someone's shoulder. She'd heard his stories of operating in sandstorms during the Iraq War. He'd survived horrible situations with his sense of humor and dignity intact. Why couldn't she?

She was so focused on keeping quiet, controlling the crest of grief flooding through her, she lost track of time. Eventually, she came back to herself only to realize her situation was no less emotionally explosive and dangerous now as when she started crying.

She faced Sharp, straddling his lap with her knees on either side of his hips, plastered to him like a lover who took what she wanted. Between her legs she could feel his response. No amount of clothing could hide the long, hot length telling her he was big all over.

He wanted her.

It was the crazy situation, not because he *actually* wanted her.

So why did feeling his erection between her legs, proving they were both still alive, give her so much pleasure?

She wanted him.

Was it wrong to want, to feel something other than horror and fear? If she moved against him, would he offer the comfort of his body?

Of course he would. He was a good man, the kind of man who'd do everything he could to help her get through this until they were safe.

She couldn't do it. Couldn't use him like that.

Grief and guilt formed a tsunami of nausea that rolled up from deep in her gut, and she tried to jerk herself out of his tight embrace. How sick did she have to be to want a man only an hour after being in a crash that killed several men, after *she'd* killed men?

Sharp held her tighter. She fought, pounding his back

and using the strength of her thighs to push away from him. He held her tighter still and whispered words of reassurance that made no sense in her ear. He should be angry at *her*, she hadn't been able to save Rasker's life. *His friend's life.*

She shoved, punched and pushed until her muscles trembled with exhaustion. Panting, she stilled, waiting for an opportunity for him to relax his vigilance, and finally understood what he was whispering to her.

"It's okay, Grace. You're good, honey. You're good. I'm going to keep you safe, I promise." Over and over he repeated the words.

"Sharp?" she managed to say, her heartbeat a thunder of drums in her ears.

"The bad guys don't know where we are. You're safe."

"Sharp?" she said again. "I'm okay, sort of, now."

He sighed and held her even tighter for a moment. "God, I thought you were never coming back."

"Neither did I." She trembled and returned his embrace, her hands flexing against his body armor, needing to feel him, solid and real. "What's wrong with me?"

"We've all got ghosts haunting us," he said, his voice rumbling out of his chest. "You need to let go of a few of yours, that's all."

She tilted her face up to tell him to stop placating her, she needed the truth, but never got the chance to say a word.

He kissed her.

His mouth was hard and hot on hers, his tongue stroking past her lips, his taste waking something cold and alone inside her.

So good.

Oh God, no kiss had *ever* felt this good before.

A voice in the back of her head whispered that this was bad. This would change things between them.

A whip of pleasure silenced the voice, blinded her to everything else, and she kissed him back, groaning, needing this connection to the real world. To him. Her hips rocked against the erection confined to his pants and she lapped up the growl that came out of him as a result.

"Grace." He jerked her closer, pressing her pelvis against him with one hand on her lower back as he rocked upward.

She wanted that.

She needed him. Now. Her hands clawed at his body armor, trying to rip it off. When that didn't work she shimmied backward far enough to work her hand between them to find the long length of his cock, then squeezed.

He wrenched his head away, breathing hard. "*Fuck.*"

Grace nipped and sucked at his neck, but his hands pushed her away so he could catch her gaze with his.

"Grace, honey, slow down," he crooned to her.

She blinked, desire a fog clouding her mind. "What?"

"Tell me you're with me, sweetheart." His words were spoken with the same gentleness a man might use to coax a wary animal or small child.

The fog lifted and reality, with all its cold, harsh truths, intruded.

They'd survived a helicopter crash, killed extremists who would have killed them, and there was no guarantee they would survive the next twenty-four hours, let alone get rescued.

Oh, and her best friend turned out to kiss like something out of her most intimate fantasies.

She still had his cock in her hands.

She stroked him through his clothing. "I don't want to slow down or stop." She did it again and got a groan out of him. "Are *you* with *me*?"

"Oh, holy fuck, *yes*," he hissed between gritted teeth.

She nibbled on his neck again and was rewarded with hands cupping her ass, his fingers curving under her bottom and stroking her through her pants.

Her breathing had become as ragged as her pulse. What he was doing with his fingers had to be illegal.

"What," he growled into her ear, "will get you off?"

At that moment, he stroked over her, his fingers finding her clit through her clothes, his thumb rimming the sensitive tissues of her body. It didn't matter that there were several layers of clothing between them. It felt like they were skin to skin.

She shuddered and whispered in his ear, "Penetration."

He reacted like she'd shocked him with an electrode. He jerked her up and took her mouth in a kiss so carnal she was surprised they hadn't self-combusted. His tongue fucked her mouth while his hands shifted her back until he could open her pants and get his hand down the front of them. His fingers found her clit and began to circle it.

Then he put the other one down the back of her pants. One long finger entered her and began fucking her hard and fast.

She ground and rocked against him until she thought she was going to lose her mind. The orgasm that resulted blew every circuit she had.

He was still kissing her when she finally came down

from the high enough to recognize it was his turn to lose it.

She sucked his tongue into her mouth, opened his pants and took him in hand. Not a small job. He filled her palm, a handful and then some, his length a delicious tease.

He growled into her mouth, took over the kiss, and his hands were everywhere. Touching her, grasping her, making her wish they were naked in a bed with a locked door between them and the rest of the world.

When he came, his whole body shook, his head falling back as he gave himself over to it. She stroked him until the shaking stopped.

His head came down and he looked at her like she was someone he'd never seen before. "Penetration, huh?"

His question cleared the haze clouding her mind.

"Oh my God," she breathed. She was plastered to him, his taste in her mouth, his lips so close to hers she could feel every breath he exhaled on her face. Her hand full of his cock. "We just..."

Had sex. In a cave. With God only knows how many bad guys trying to kill them.

She didn't even want to think about the best-friends label she'd stuck on his forehead, now irrevocably ripped off.

He must think her a fool. She let go of his erection, now at only half-mast, and tried to jerk herself out of his arms. "I'm sorry... I shouldn't have—"

"Whoa," he interrupted, kissing her temple and gathering her close despite the stiffness of her body. "Nothing to be sorry about. I started it."

"Then I attacked you." She rested her head against his

shoulder and relaxed a little. How was she ever going to look him in the face again?

"I have to admit, I wasn't expecting it," he said. "I figured kissing you might distract you a little from the shit we'd been through, but you know, if I have to defend myself against a beautiful woman and give her an amazing orgasm..." He sighed theatrically. "It's hard being me."

She snorted into his shirt. Shock. That must be what she was feeling. There could be no other explanation for the burst of humor grabbing hold of her frazzled nerve endings and calming them. Not only calmed, but made their situation a tiny bit humorous.

She lifted her head and looked him right in the eye. "You are the strangest guy I have ever met."

He raised a brow. "That's a good thing, 'cause a minute ago you were trying really hard to fly apart."

"Yeah. I guess I was." Now what was she going to do? How was she going to look at his face without remembering the expression he wore when his own orgasm overtook him? She shivered, the pleasure in watching him a glow warming her from the inside out.

"Hey," he whispered into her ear. "Can you move back a little so I can get at my pocket?"

Her hand was sticky, and she scooted backward, intending to get off him entirely. He stopped her.

"Whoa, hold still."

She froze. Had she done something wrong?

He opened a pocket and pulled out a package of Wet Wipes. After quickly cleaning himself, he offered her one, as well. He took it from her when she was done and put the used wipes into a small sealable plastic baggy from the same pocket.

"What else have you got in there?" she asked, momentarily distracted.

"Shampoo, hand sanitizer and a little Vaseline."

She blinked. "Vaseline?"

"Yeah, you never know when you're going to need to lubricate...something."

She swallowed hard, staring at his chest. "How bad did we just screw up?"

He didn't answer right away, and after a few seconds, she finally looked up to meet his gaze.

He considered her for a long moment. "You know I care about you, right?"

She nodded.

"And you care about me?"

She nodded again.

"Then where's the mistake? 'Cause I don't see one. We needed each other."

"That's it?" She couldn't quite believe it was as simple as he made it sound.

"Does it have to be complicated? Would you have rather screamed murder at the top of your lungs?"

"I suppose not, it's just...intimacy isn't casual for me." If it was casual for him, she didn't know how she'd ever look him in the face again.

"Hey." He leaned down to catch her gaze again. "It's not for me either." He kissed her forehead.

He made it sound like sex was a coping mechanism. "Has this ever happened to you before?"

He grunted. "Nope. Never survived a helicopter crash, killed a bunch of bad guys and had to calm down a woman having a panic attack before."

She nodded. "Okay, you can let go of me now."

He didn't just drop his arms, he gradually released

her, comfort-rubbing her back before she found herself in front of him on her butt in the sandy dirt of the cave.

The need to crawl right back into his arms was overwhelming.

She stared at him, her whole body trembling, trying to figure out what to say or do next. She had no idea. He'd surprised her, done nothing she'd expected.

She'd done nothing she'd expected. She didn't know this other Grace, a woman who took her pleasure, and gave it, without hesitation.

He watched her, his shoulders relaxed, his hands limp as they dangled off his knees, but his eyes were far from tranquil. She'd seen that look on his face, the one where the wrinkles around his eyes flexed and the furrow between his brows appeared. It was the one he wore when he was waiting for an attack, or preparing to make one. Battle ready.

Her breathing became deeper, labored, and she had to focus on it before she could calm herself down. "Stop looking at me like I'm a bomb about to go off."

He gave her a crooked smile. "Are you kidding? You already went off. I'm just waiting to see if there are any aftershocks."

"I'm not going to go screaming out into the night," she said, then paused. "I don't think."

His gaze examined her with unrelenting focus. "Is something else bothering you?"

She didn't know if he was asking her about the crash, her reaction to their lovemaking or something else entirely. It didn't matter. She was done talking. "No."

He didn't react except to ask, "Who am I?"

"You're Sharp—Jacob Foster."

When he didn't respond, she added, "Special Forces Weapons Sergeant Jacob 'Sharp' Foster."

He shook his head. "I want to know who I am to *you*."

The sneaky bastard. Did he think he was some kind of weekend psychologist?

She leaned forward, narrowed her eyes and bared her teeth. "Right now, you're an irritant, like all men who think asking the same question a different way is going to get you what you want. But when you're not being an ass, you're usually my best friend."

"Yes, exactly, we're best friends. Something hasn't been right with you since we arrived at Bostick. What the hell is going on between you and Marshall? Did he try to hurt you?"

Sneaky, *sneaky* bastard. She opened her mouth to yell at him, to let the anger boiling beneath her skin out into the space between them to batter him with the truths he thought he could easily ferret out.

He spoke before she could utter a sound. "Don't throw me a bullshit flag. There's a history there, right? You weren't alone with him long enough to start a new argument."

"You're right, it's not new, and there isn't anything anyone can do about it, so, please just drop it."

He watched her face as she struggled to decide whether she should say anything. "Look, I get it. Shit happens. In my case, my dad beat the hell out of me on a regular basis when I was a kid." Sharp snorted. "He said it was character building. He wanted me to be tough." Sharp's face reflected pain, fear, anger and despair. "Breaking a kid's arm in three places doesn't make them tough."

He'd been *abused*? Oh God, no. Horror's frozen fingers wrapped around her throat. "Did you fight back?" It came out as a quivering whisper. She'd fought. When the enemy attacked, she'd killed.

Sharp's chuckle was unexpected, and it loosened the cold grip cutting off her air. "Not in the traditional sense."

"Traditional?"

"I didn't hit back. After he broke my arm, there was a social worker who figured out what happened, but she couldn't prove it and I wasn't talking. Instead of badgering me, she saw to it that the community center where I went every day after school offered martial arts training." He paused. "I forged my dad's signature on the permission form."

"*What?*"

A grin came and went so fast on his face she wasn't sure she'd seen it. "She made sure I could hit back, if I wanted to."

"But you said you didn't."

"I didn't. What I did was block every punch my father tried to throw at me. I never hit back. I didn't shove or kick. I just blocked. Blocked and blocked until my arms were bruised and my father realized he'd succeeded."

After that litany of pain she couldn't reconcile the last word with the rest. "Succeeded?"

"I'd become what he wanted...tough."

What a sad, awful way to grow up. Yet, here he was, healthy, strong and resilient. "What happened then?"

"On my eighteenth birthday I signed up for the army. I haven't talked to him since."

"Has he tried to communicate with you?"

"He did at first. He doesn't anymore."

"Well, that just sucks." She released a breath and

made a decision. Rationally, she knew he was safe and no threat to her, even if the primitive part of her brain had been programmed by circumstances to protect herself emotionally by whatever means necessary. The only way to reprogram herself was to leave her comfort zone.

Ever since the IED explosion, she'd stayed away from making emotional connections with people. She'd loosened up enough to befriend Sharp and the other men on the A-Team, but it had happened only because they'd ended up training together for nearly a year. Anyone else, she'd kept at arm's length.

Change of plan. She was going to put herself in his hands. Again.

"Okay. Right." She swallowed hard, met his gaze and held it. "Here's who you are to me: my friend, my partner and the one man I trust. I can't promise I won't freak out again, because I just did, but I know you'd never hurt me."

"Yeah?"

"Yeah."

There was a long silence.

"So," he said drawing out the word. "Are you ready to talk?"

She tried, she even opened her mouth, but admitting she'd made mistakes that resulted in the death of a fellow soldier, no matter the circumstances, was more than she could do. "Could we compromise? Could we talk about it after I've had a chance to..." She glanced around at the cave, at the two of them bloodied, dirty and tired. "Wrap my head around everything?"

He considered her for a long moment. "Yeah, I think I can agree to that."

Relief was a balm on her frayed nerve endings.

"Next question. Are you going to take off your pants?"

She blinked. "You...are the weirdest guy. It's a good thing you're my friend or I'd have to—"

"Kill me?" he finished for her.

"I can't joke about that right now." The young soldier's dead face flashed across her vision. Followed closely by the sight of the bodies of the five men she'd shot today. Other memories surfaced. Memories she wished she could forget. "I'm not sure if I'll ever be able to joke about it."

"Fair enough. You look like you've got your groove back, so I'll lay off the jokes, but I reserve the right to go back to being funny if you lose it again."

She blinked away sudden tears. "I did lose it, didn't I?"

He shrugged, as if it was all good. "It's been a pretty shitty day."

That's when she noticed he had tear tracks running down his face. "Did you lose it too?"

He snorted. "You'd know if I'd lost it. I prefer something a little more...physical."

SHE SUCKED IN a breath, but responded with a shaky smile. "Right, the martial arts stuff. What do you do to blow off steam, break a bunch of boards?"

She looked so confused, uncertain and shocked, Sharp had to force himself not to take her in his arms and hold her until the sorrow left her face. He wanted to touch her again, to put his hands on her and watch the pleasure make her light up like a fucking Christmas tree again.

"Punching bag is more my style. Sometimes I spar with another one of the guys. Rasker..." The rage he normally kept locked down threatened to explode. He had to forcibly stuff it down into the mental prison he'd constructed back when he was a kid. Everything that went in there never came out.

"Rasker and I liked to keep our skills sharp."

A soft, feminine hand slid over one of his to squeeze and stroke. "I'm sorry. I wish I could have saved him."

"Not your fault. The assholes who shot our aircraft down are to blame."

She stroked his hand once more before pulling hers away. "Sounds like we're both going to need therapy when we get out of this mess."

"That's my girl." She wasn't his. He had to keep telling himself that, because the second he didn't, he was claiming her in his head.

Kissing her.

Taking her on the dirt.

Get a hold of yourself, asshole. She was a career officer, and a damn good one. This was not a woman he could romance and see when he was on leave. The rules of fraternization were clear. She was a major and he was a long way down the chain from that. If they were found out, they'd both lose big. He had to stop creating X-rated fantasies of her in his head. What happened today was a onetime thing born out of the stress and danger they were in. That was all. He was a professional, damn it. She was a fellow soldier and a good friend. Nothing more, nothing less.

She sighed, shook her head, got up on her knees and opened her pants. She had to wiggle a little to get the waist down over her butt, then she sat down in the dirt and pulled her left leg out.

Her panties were pink.

The panties his hands had just been inside were *fucking pink*.

Holy Mother of God, he was going to go to hell. He couldn't take his eyes off the scrap of fabric between her legs, and he could almost feel the wet heat of her against his fingers again. Then she let out a pain-filled groan and his gaze jerked loose to land on her bloodied calf. It was still oozing blood.

"Damn it," Grace hissed between clenched teeth. "I think I just tore the scab off."

He should shoot himself in the foot for lusting after a wounded woman. "What made the wound? A piece of shrapnel or a bullet?" Sharp scooted over until he could get a good look at it. He reached into a pocket on his right thigh and pulled out a small LED flashlight covered by red translucent tape. He turned it on and shone it at her leg.

"Shrapnel probably. During the crash," she answered.

He palpated the skin around the wound, trying to discover if anything was in it that shouldn't be there. "I don't feel anything."

"Close it with a few Steri-Strips and bandage it up," she ordered, sounding much more like her normal businesslike self. "I can get it properly cleaned out when we get to a base."

He had a few of those small, but useful bandages in another pocket, but he didn't want to use them up until he had to. "We got extras of those?"

She reached into the backpack behind her and pulled out a compact first-aid kit. It had everything he needed inside.

He cleaned up her leg first, using a few iodine swabs. He waited for that to dry, then closed the jagged-edged wound with four Steri-Strips, covered it all up with a nonstick dressing pad then wound a self-adhering bandage around her calf until he was certain it wouldn't come undone.

She watched him silently throughout the whole operation, but as he finished she said, "Nice job. Ever thought of going into medicine?"

"Not really, though adding medic to my skill list wouldn't be a bad idea. Uncle Sam likes us special soldiers to have as many skills as possible."

She snorted at that, got to her feet, tried to stand on one so she could put her pants back on but wobbled badly.

He surged up and caught her, wrapping both arms around her waist and back before she landed in the dirt. "I've got you, you're okay," he whispered.

Her whole body shook once, then she pressed her face into his neck, took a deep breath and seemed to completely relax. "Oh."

Since she wasn't screaming or trying to get away, he was going to go on holding her, earning himself another decade or five in hell. A few seconds passed before he asked carefully, "You okay?"

"Yeah, you just smell good."

"Finally, a use for my dirty, stinky laundry."

"Oh no," she said, her elbow in his ribs telling him to let go. "You're not turning me into your laundress."

"Laundress?" he asked, loosening his hold on her until he was sure she wasn't going to fall over. "Who uses the word *laundress*?"

"Fine. Housekeeper, maid, girl Friday, whatever you want to call a woman who cleans up after you. I'm not it."

Sharp sighed with all the theatrical *oomph* he could muster and said, "Mom?"

Grace pushed him over with a shove from both hands.

He rolled with it until he was a couple feet away. Thank God he'd managed to keep her off the ledge this time with nothing more than his sweaty self. He glanced up and froze at the sight of Grace taking her shirt off. She shrugged out of the left sleeve and lifted her arm up to eye level. "This one isn't as bad as the one on my leg."

Sharp hardly heard her, he was too busy staring at the finest set of breasts he'd ever seen. She wasn't wearing any fancy lingerie, just the opposite. Her bra was beige, plain and appeared to be more solid than some canvas tents. No, what had his attention were breasts bigger than he'd imagined, and he'd imagined hers a lot. And her waist was smaller than he'd expected. Her body armor made her look more padded around the midsection than she really was.

She was *hot*.

And very, very quiet.

He lifted his gaze to meet hers. Oops, she was giving him the stink eye. "I'm sorry, I couldn't help it. They're—" he glanced down again real quick "—amazing, and wow, you're totally gorgeous, you know that, right?" So much for professional, jackass.

She rolled her eyes. "I can't believe you turned into a college junior just by looking at my boobs. I'm wearing more fabric than most bikinis."

He squeezed his eyes shut. "Don't put that image in my head. Have you no compassion? No pity?"

"Fine. Here. They're covered up."

He cracked open one eye. She'd brought her shirt across her chest to cover herself.

"Now, can we get on with dealing with my arm?"

Damn. That fabulous view was all gone. He should have kept his mouth shut.

Patching up her arm took less time than her leg. Then she turned around and put her shirt back on.

Spoilsport.

"Your turn," she said. "Take off your pants. I want to take a look at your thigh."

On one hand, he was happy to take off his pants and get that wound dealt with. The problem was, now he knew just how much she loved being touched, how her internal muscles had gripped his finger, and he could imagine what it would feel like when they gripped his cock. He was primed and ready to go all over again.

Waiting was only going to make her pissed at him again. Might as well get the yelling over with. He began to disarm all the extra gear strapped to that leg, then went to work on his belt. Just before he pulled down his fly, he cleared his throat and said, "Don't take this *too* personally, okay?"

Grace frowned. "Take what personally?"

He pulled his pants down enough to pull his leg out, and managed to keep the bulge in his underwear somewhat hidden. He wasn't sure if he wanted her to notice or not. A smart man would go for not, but he'd been all kinds of stupid today. "Never mind."

Grace shook her head and leaned forward to prod his thigh.

Having her head so close to him made things even bigger than they already were. Fuck, she was killing him.

"Looks like a through-and-through. I'll clean it now, but it may need to be cleaned again."

"No problem, Doc. I expected that." If she didn't hurry up, he was going to poke a hole in his shorts.

She didn't use Steri-Strips on him; rather, she used iodine to clean the wounds, packed the holes, front and back, then covered them with pads and began bandaging them both to his leg with another self-adhesive bandage. They were rapidly running out of those.

She couldn't quite get the roll of bandage around his leg. He was still holding his pants over his crotch. She nudged his hand.

"Uh, Doc, maybe I could do this part?"

"You need two hands and a clear view of where the bandage is going. Not happening. Move."

He hesitated. This was going to suck.

He removed his hand, taking the material he'd been hiding behind with it.

She moved to continue with the bandage, but stopped suddenly as she noticed his aching boner.

Her mouth dropped open. "Holy shit, Sharp. Do you always rearm this fast, or has it been a while?"

EIGHT

It wasn't the amazement in her voice or how her jaw dropped open that made him laugh. It was the question.

His whole body shook with the effort it took to keep the guffaws from exiting his big mouth.

She didn't frown, she glared at him with her whole face. Brows low, upper lip retracted, teeth clenched and nose screwed up like she was trying hard not to smell something reeking worse than a week-old corpse.

"Really?" she asked.

"I just don't know if I should feel embarrassed or proud," he managed to get out without making too much noise. "You should see the look on your face."

She scowled at him for another moment, then went back to bandaging his leg, muttering, "Men."

He shrugged. "It's a natural physical response."

Her hands finished bandaging up his leg. "Who are you trying to convince? Me or National Geographic?"

National Geographic? For a moment, he wanted to laugh at her comment, but there was something... He studied her. She was joking like she always did, but there was an underlying thread in her tone containing no humor at all. He was tempted to let her do it, to go along with the penis joke, play it safe. But her shoulders were tense and she wasn't looking him in the eyes.

"You." He let his answer stand on its own for a moment, then added, "Right now, you're the only person who matters. We *will* survive. We *will* get back to base. I won't accept anything less."

Her expression turned solemn as she looked at him, like she wanted to believe him, but wasn't sure she could.

He needed her to understand that when it came to what was between them, she was in charge. "We're a team, Grace. I'm your weapon and you're mine."

She bent her head to finish with his leg. "I've never wanted to be a weapon." She paused for a moment. "I'm a third-generation military doctor who shoots at the marksman level, but I hate firing a gun. I killed five people today. I know it was in self-defense and there wasn't any other choice, but it still hurts me that I did it."

"You're allowed to be a human being," he told her, taking her hands in his. "Even stubborn assholes like me have to work through the shit we see and do. That's why the team is so important. We support each other, and you." He pointed at her. "You've earned your spot on our team."

"Our team?"

"Yeah, ours. As far as all the guys are concerned, you're *our* doctor."

"So, what we did earlier, that was you taking *care* of me?"

He watched her face, trying to determine how she really felt about it. Was there an ember of anger there? He couldn't tell. Had to be sure. "That was a man showing a woman how gorgeous she is." He hesitated, waited for her to respond, but she seemed deep in thought.

Shit. Her whole family was in the army, one way or another. "When we get back to base, I'll talk to Cutter, get reassigned."

Her startled gaze reconnected with his. "What?"

"You're too important to the training mission. I'm replaceable, you're not."

"What the hell kind of bullshit is that?" Now she sounded angry.

"I crossed a line..."

"I sprinted across it." She poked him in the shoulder. "You tried to slow me down, but I distinctly recall dragging you along with me for the ride."

He snorted. "I started it."

"I finished it," she told him, glancing at his groin. "You're not telling Cutter anything." She stopped, frowned and asked, "Unless you want to be reassigned?"

"No." He smiled. "Not a chance. Of course, we have to get out of this mess first."

She shook her head. "I know how creative you are, Sharp. I'll bet you ten bucks you've got a plan already."

"You think so?"

"Yeah. I've played chess with you too many times not to know you're a man who plans two moves ahead."

"Predicting what my opponent is going to do on a chessboard is a hell of a lot easier than in combat, or even poker."

"Touché." She put the first-aid kit into the backpack, then faced him and glanced at his leg. "Pants?"

The woman wasn't going to give an inch. "So, are we good or not?"

"We're good," she said after a moment or two. "It's just..." She sighed and swallowed hard. "Earlier, when I freaked out...I *really* freaked out. I had no control over myself and that's not me, but I can't seem to stop it from happening. I hate it. How can I do my job if I'm..." She shook her head and pressed her lips together. "I'm damaged."

What had fucked her up so bad? "Hey, no harm, no foul. Feel free to freak out whenever you need to. You've earned a free one or two. Hell, I've seen you knock a marine off his feet who was too amped up on adrenaline to realize his flesh wound was bleeding buckets. That guy was twice the size of you, but you didn't back down when he got all mouthy. You told him if he didn't cooperate, you were going to fix it so his wife never had to use birth control again." Sharp wished he could choke whoever put that look on her face. "We're all damaged, and, fair warning, Doc, I have a protective streak a mile wide. I reserve the right to stick with you no matter how hard you flip your shit."

She nodded, but he could tell from her jerky movements she was already regretting telling him as much as she had. He had to get her refocused on their situation, demonstrate that he could keep his mouth shut and be the man she could count on.

"Okay." He gave her a sharp nod. "Here are our priorities. Stay alive and out of sight." He ticked off finger after finger. "Watch for a rescue and/or retrieval team. Get the samples to your lab. Save the world."

She looked at him like he was a few bullets short of a magazine. "Save the world, huh?"

He winked. "That's what puts the *special* in Special Forces."

"Ham." She rolled her eyes. "So, how do we achieve our priorities?" She gestured at the cave around them. "We seem to be alive and out of sight. What about the rest? If we don't get these samples to the lab within the next twenty-four hours..." She paused, tensed, then continued, "The anthrax attack in the village was probably a test. To see how the strain would perform in a relatively controlled environment."

"It performed too well."

"It could kill hundreds, even thousands in *hours*. We have no time to waste, but we're stuck here." The last word was spoken in a frustrated tone bordering on anger and sorrow at the same time.

PEOPLE WERE GOING to die. A lot of people, and there wasn't a damn thing Grace could do about it. If the person who'd created the anthrax strain in her samples were within her grasp, she'd cheerfully choke them to death.

Sharp looked at her like she was some kind of pity case. Maybe she was, but she was also a doctor and a soldier, and she'd be damned if she'd allow some backroom herbalist who believed he could create and control a plague let his monster loose on anyone he pleased.

This anthrax would consume everyone it came in contact with.

Everyone.

It could make the latest Ebola outbreak in northern Africa look like a minor blip on the world's heart monitor.

Sharp leaned forward and put his hands on her shoulders.

She stilled, her gaze on his, her emotions balanced on the edge of a knife made slick by blood of their dead lying in the husk of the helicopter they left behind.

"We reach our goals by putting one foot in front of the other," he said with a voice as solid as steel. "Staying calm and remembering who we are."

She wanted to grab hold of him and never let go, but

was he all talk and no substance? Would he dissolve into a mist at the first sign of trouble? "Who are we?"

"I'm Special Forces Weapons Sergeant Jacob Foster, and you're Dr. Grace Samuels, trauma surgeon and infectious disease specialist." He leaned forward until his forehead touched hers. "We're the best, the very best at what we do. We're going to figure out our shit and we're going to complete our mission. Right?"

She swallowed. "Right."

One of his eyebrows rose. "Convince me, Doc, 'cause I'm not feeling it."

She narrowed her eyes, bared her teeth and spit the word at him. "*Right.*"

He leaned back. "Much better. For a second I thought I was going to have to slap you out of your hysterics again."

"Ha. Stay out of my back pockets, soldier." She sucked in a deep breath, pulled the backpack beside her over and began digging in it. The words were superficial, but safe, and they soothed something frayed and hurting deep inside her chest. She didn't want to lose her friend, and he'd figured out how to give her what she needed again. "Guess we should take stock of what we have."

He grabbed the other backpack and opened it up, laying out its contents. Three bottles of water, medical supplies, granola bars, two MREs, two magazines for a Beretta, rope, knife, matches, emergency blanket, plastic sheeting, standard survival tin and a compass.

Her backpack's contents were very similar, but with two unopened bottles of water, one opened and two bandages less than Sharp's.

"If we stay in this cave," he said. "We've got enough water for a couple of days."

"We can't stay that long for a lot of reasons."

He nodded slowly. "We're going to grab a few hours of sleep then try to get to the most likely place they'd extract us from."

"Where?"

He pulled a map out of one of his pockets, and using the flashlight with the red tape, showed her a point on it circled in red. "I think we're within a couple of klicks of this spot. There used to be a village there, but most of it was blown up back when the Russians invaded. Our intel says it's deserted."

"Can we get there before dawn?"

"If we push, yeah."

"What's our plan B?"

"Run like hell."

"Well," she drawled. "As long as we know where we're going."

He folded up the map and put it back in his pocket. "You know me, always looking ahead." He pulled an emergency blanket out of his backpack and spread it on the sandy bottom of the cave. "Bedtime." He lay down, leaving what looked like room for three other people.

She lowered herself carefully onto the middle of the blanket, her back to him. "You don't snore, do you?"

"Not allowed." He scooted a little closer. "Too noisy." His arm went over her and he inched closer until he spooned in behind her completely.

He was big, warm and his arm curved over her waist in a way that made her feel protected. "Another one of those things that puts the *special* in Special Forces?"

"Now you're catching on." His lips whispered the words against the sensitive skin behind her ear. "Sleep. I'll wake you when it's time to go."

Her eyelids sagged, as if his giving her permission was the one thing she needed to succumb to the exhaustion attempting to pull her under. There was one thing she wanted to do first, though. Something important.

Grace put her hand over Sharp's where it curled around her waist, tangled her fingers with his and squeezed. The last thing she remembered before sleep rolled over her was his hand squeezing back.

"GRACE."

She came awake all at once, but not in a panic. Lately, she woke ready to go down fighting. Her nightmares, filled with explosions and gunfire, following her into wakefulness. Not this time. Her sleep had been deep and dreamless.

"Grace."

"I'm here," she whispered.

Sharp withdrew his arm from her waist in a slow slide that made her want to catch his hand and hold it. As if they were two lovers, waking to do normal things on a normal day. What was normal anyway? A home in a place where you didn't fear bullets coming through the door of your vehicle or explosions bringing down the roof?

Would she ever have that? Would her nightmares ever retreat to a point where loud noises didn't make her want to hide under a rock?

She sat up. The cave was as dark as when she'd lain down. "What time is it?"

"About zero two hundred." He sat up next to her, took a drink out of the water bottle she'd opened and handed it to her.

The water was warm and she sipped it slowly.

"We slept about four hours," he told her. "How do you feel? Wounds bothering you?"

"Not really. Yours?"

"Nope. You tie a mean bandage, Doc." He sounded so cheerful it was irritating.

"Yeah, I'm sure that's what you really wanted while I was down there." Shit. Why had she brought that up? She was the one leading the charge on pretending it didn't happen.

His body shook in a silent chuckle. "I plead the Fifth."

She waited for him to push, to make a suggestive joke, but none came. Instead, he offered her a granola bar and busied himself with folding the blanket they'd slept on.

Was she ever going to understand this complicated man? It would take a lifetime, but they only had weeks left in their Afghan training mission. After that, she'd be heading to the base in Bahrain. *If* they survived and got back to Bostick.

It took them only a minute or so to eat, pack up and crouch at the entrance of the cave to see if it was safe to leave.

"We're going to move like we did before," he told her. "Follow me, stay close and keep watch around and behind us. I'll worry about what's in front."

"Got it."

"If you need my attention for anything, put your hand on my back." He glanced out again. "It's clear out there and the moon is about half-full, so we've got enough light to see. If it's too dark for you, though, you can hang on to my belt."

She nodded.

Sharp slipped out with all the noise of a wraith, and she followed. How did a man his size move so quietly?

They made their way steadily west through dry gullies, over deserted plateaus and around coulees of prickly brush. They encountered no people or animals beyond the sort that scurried away from their faint moon shadows.

It seemed like they walked for days when the horizon turned a deep azure, signaling dawn's arrival. Sharp drew her close to speak his dead-whisper in her ear. "We're still a quarter mile away and there may be people between us and the pickup site."

"What do you want to do?"

"Hide."

A shout echoed, then another.

Her body dumped enough adrenaline into her system to mobilize a fossil, but she didn't know which direction to go.

Sharp put a hand on the back of her neck and pushed her down just as she shifted her weight. Balance gone, she tried to catch herself with her hands. One landed on the edge of a rock while the other tangled with a bush. She fell through it and kept on falling into a narrow trench the plants had hidden.

Grace landed on her side with enough force to knock the wind out of her.

While she caught her breath, Sharp hissed, "Stay there." The crunch of running feet on rock told her he'd gone.

Yelling, voices raised, speaking Dari. Several gunshots punctured the air. More than one person ran past her hiding spot.

Had they found him?

Her thoughts raced as she listened to the commotion slowly die down. It didn't sound like they were celebrating, but they didn't sound angry either.

What happened?

She was about to leave when two men, chattering away in Dari, walked past. They carried water canteens, ammunition and rifles. Men on a mission. With that much water, a long one.

She waited a few minutes, while the area grew quiet and the sun rose in the sky. Finally, she crept silently out of her dark hole and listened. Voices were audible to the west.

Not very far away, but between her and them was a ridge of rock. She moved cautiously closer. What she'd thought was a ridge was what remained of a man-made wall.

She looked around it.

Four men were visible. Three in traditional Afghan dress, one in an American military uniform. Sharp.

He was seated, his hands tied behind his back, his head bowed over knees drawn up to his chest. His feet were tied together. She could see his chest moving with every breath. Breathing heavy. Too heavy.

Damn it. He was hurt.

The Afghans were talking and cooking around a small fire inside a rock oven. They smiled at each other, their gestures large and excited.

They'd bagged an American soldier. They probably thought they'd really accomplished something. All three were armed with the same Soviet-made rifles as the two who'd left had worn, and loops of ammo were draped across their chests.

Wonderful. She was outnumbered and outgunned three to one, and she only had one thing on her side. Surprise.

NINE

Surprise wasn't enough, but if she added a distraction, it might cause the confusion she needed to get Sharp out of there.

She knew what Sharp would say. *The mission was more important than him. She should get out while she could.*

Too bad for him he wasn't in a position to stop her from doing something stupid.

Distraction, distraction. What did she have that would work?

She had a couple of smoke flares. Setting one or two of them off would certainly be distracting. She didn't dare wait. How long could he last, bleeding who knows how much, with no medical treatment? Were they giving him water or food?

She was careful and quiet as she made her way back to her hiding place. She found a small gully a short distance away and threw the flare into it as hard as she could.

She ducked into her hidey hole.

Shouting followed after only twenty or thirty seconds.

Several people rushed past her haven, yelling and shouting, toward the place she'd thrown the flare. Two gunshots followed, but they weren't close. Sounded like they'd come from the direction where Sharp was held prisoner. An aggressive *oorah* was cut off by gunfire.

Grace's breathing staggered to a halt.

Had they just shot Sharp?

Had her distraction gotten him killed?

Oh God, *oh God.* She'd thought she was so clever and sneaky. Provide the perfect distraction so she could tip-toe in and rescue Sharp with no one the wiser. Only min-utes ago she'd been patting herself on the back for her ingenious plan. She should have left well enough alone. Sharp had probably had a plan of escape.

Now he wouldn't be going anywhere, because he was *dead.*

Self-loathing, regret and indecision held her hostage. Now what? Her situation had only gotten worse. She was trapped in her refuge, alone with only a day's worth of water and a case of anthrax samples strapped to her back.

She caressed the butt of her Beretta, dark thoughts making her hands shake as tears flowed down her face.

How could she have been so stupid?

Another burst of yelling caught her attention. At first, she wasn't sure why, until she began hearing words shouted in English, in a voice sounding remarkably like Sharp's.

He was alive?

"I don't know," he yelled. It was definitely Sharp. "Whoever did is a long way from here."

There was a grunt of pain, then nothing audible for several minutes.

Someone had probably hit him.

What were they doing now? Were they hitting him, *torturing* him?

Another pain-filled sound echoed and she found it difficult to suck a proper breath in. She had to stop it, save him. She couldn't bear the thought of him hurt, and she knew, *knew* he'd never say anything to risk her safety.

Well, she wasn't willing to give his life to save her own. He was her friend, her *best* friend... Oh, who was she kidding? He was more than that, even though she didn't have a label for what they were to each other. She cared about him and couldn't leave him in the hands of men who were going to kill him.

She worked at calming her breathing. Sharp was alive and well enough to holler. The thing was, did setting off the flare help or hinder her chances of getting to him and getting them both out of here?

Just as she was about to leave her shelter, several men walked past, one talking, the others only adding a word or two here and there.

She waited for a long time before easing out of her hole and making her way back to the wall.

She peeked.

Sharp wasn't sitting up anymore. He was lying in a fetal position, motionless except for breathing.

At least he was still alive.

Two men were tending the fire and talking softly to each other. No one else was visible.

Perhaps the rest were out hunting the person who set off the flare. She hoped they were searching farther away, because if the rest of those men were close, her goose and Sharp's were both cooked.

She palmed her gun, took in a deep breath and resigned herself to killing at least two more people, then popped out from behind the wall and shot the first man in the chest and head.

The second man raised his weapon, but he was standing close to Sharp, who kicked out at the man's knees, proving the Green Beret was only playing possum, knocking the Afghan down. He didn't get up.

Grace ran over, gun in front and ready to fire, to check the man, but sightless eyes stared back at her.

"He must have hit his head on a rock," she said to Sharp as she went to work on the knots in the rope binding his hands behind his back. "Where are you injured?"

"Gunshot to my right leg, some contusions and a possible concussion." His voice was low and tight.

Grace looked him in the eyes. Both pupils seemed the same size. "Headache?"

"Yeah, and I was a little nauseated after one of them punched me around for a while. You set off a flare?" Sharp asked as he grabbed a knife from the dead man next to him and cut the rope tying his feet together.

Grace looked around, waiting for another man in Afghan garb to appear. "It was the only distraction I could think of."

He growled at her as he shouldered one of the Soviet rifles. "About that. Why the hell didn't you make a run for it after I was captured?" He took three limping strides, then plucked his backpack out of a pile of stuff tossed to the side. Then he grabbed her by the arm and towed her with him as he jogged away from the bodies, heading in the opposite direction from the one the Afghans took earlier.

"I was thinking you might appreciate a rescue. You know, from certain death?"

"Death is everywhere, including the Christmas present attached to your back. You want to try for a better answer?"

Anger gave her the strength to yank her arm out of

his grasp. "There's a difference between you dying at eighty-six of a stroke, and dying because I didn't do anything while some asshole put a bullet through your head." She poked him with one finger. "Besides, you're a thousand times better at the survival-in-the-field stuff than I am. I need you."

"It's damn difficult to plan an attack or a response to one if I can't predict what you're going to do. It's my job to protect you, not the other way around. Stop thinking with your heart and start using your head."

"Well, excuse me for giving a shit, Sergeant," she said through clenched teeth. "But don't we have somewhere to go?"

He paused. "Fuck me." He looked around, they'd stopped some time during their argument. He grabbed her hand and pulled her along with him, muttering, "Damn doctors always wanting to save everyone but themselves. How can I keep you safe when you throw yourself into harm's way every other hour?"

"I thought we were a team. You know, the kind where we help and protect each other?"

"This team," he said, pointing at himself and her, "has very defined roles. It's my job to keep you alive and get you back to base. It's your job to do nothing to jeopardize your own safety." He started walking again, but kept hold of her hand so he could tug her along.

What did he think she was going to do? Have a hissy fit and run off like some spoiled brat?

"What a load of bullshit," she said to his back.

He didn't respond except to squeeze her hand, then drop it.

Scream at him or silence. It was a difficult decision, but she chose silence rather than give away their position.

Sharp set a tough pace, one she struggled to keep up with. His helmet was gone, so were his body armor and the rifle he loved like a pet, and he was even dirtier than before. For a man who had the kinds of injuries he did, and then was beaten and shot on top of it all, showed how strong, how fierce a warrior he was.

She found herself watching the rocky ground as she jogged behind Sharp, trying to be sure she didn't put a foot down wrong and twist her ankle.

There was blood on the ground.

"Sharp, your leg. We need to stop and bandage it up."

"We don't have time."

"You're leaving a trail."

He swore and veered to one side toward a large boulder. He was already tearing his pants open so she could see the wound.

Matching entry and exit wounds on the meaty part of his thigh were easy to find.

"These have bled a lot. You need stitches and probably a transfusion."

"It'll hold," he said. It sounded like his teeth were so tightly clenched he was chewing on the words.

"Really? How wonderful, you're a doctor now? Able to diagnose injury at a glance and run long distances in an arid country with no water and no protective gear? How about I just give you a superhero name?"

He gave her a *what the fuck* look. "What's got your panties in a bunch? We're alive, aren't we? You've got your samples, right?"

"Oh yes." She let her frustration drip off the words. "All the necessities of life, right there."

"We don't have time for anything else."

"I know, and I hate it." She was so angry all she could

do was shake, because if she let herself do anything else, she'd probably make a fool of herself. "God, I'm going to need so much therapy when I get home."

She pulled off her backpack and grabbed two nonstick gauze pads, one for each wound, then secured them to his leg as tight as she could with a pressure bandage. Hopefully it would keep everything in place despite Sharp's acrobatics.

He didn't say anything to her after she finished, just grabbed her hand and urged her to her feet. He went back to that ground-eating jog. They went east for a while, then south, then northwest. After that he didn't waver on speed or direction.

She wasn't sure how long they'd been running when the echoing sound of gunshots reached them. Sharp didn't look back, but she did.

How far had they run?

Was it far enough?

Finally, sometime later, Sharp slowed and seemed to be looking for something.

"Sharp?"

"We need another cave." His voice sounded raspy, dry. Tired.

"How long will that take?" He was probably dehydrated and in pain. Damn it, what was it with tough men never allowing anyone to know they need help? Suffering in silence was stupid, especially when one word, *one word*, to her would get him the water he needed.

"Not long. Our team studied topographical maps of this area. It's full of caves."

His voice, with slight hesitation at the end of the sentence, made her ask, "But?"

"But...we have to be careful not to pick an occupied one. People use caves in this area for homes sometimes."

"Great," she breathed.

He moved on, continuing to examine both the ground close to them and look for signs of caves.

He picked up his pace again and they detoured into a small gully, and despite the fact that the whole place looked like solid ground all around, led her into a cave. This one was much bigger than the first one they'd stayed in. Unlike the last time, Sharp sat down with a thump.

Grace crouched next to him. He should have been sweating. Instead his skin looked dry and wrinkled, his eyes sunken. She put her fingers to his neck to check his heart rate.

"Headache?"

"Yeah," he whispered.

"Let me see your tongue."

An unholy grin wiped the pain and fatigue from his face. "Just see?"

She wasn't going to slap him. She wasn't. She wanted to, but she wasn't. "Let. Me. See. Your. Tongue."

He stuck it out. It looked dry and leathery.

"You're seriously dehydrated. Your heart rate is high and you're not sweating." She pulled open her backpack, pulled out one of the full water bottles and handed it to him. "Drink all of this."

"No, we might need..."

Her head came up and she gave him her specially crafted *don't fuck with me* look. "If you don't rehydrate, your kidneys will shut down. Stop being a goddamn martyr and drink."

He swore under his breath, but he took the water and began drinking.

"Let me see your leg," she ordered.

"Bossy."

His thigh wounds had bled through, leaving his pants leg and sock bloody.

"Shit," he said after swallowing another mouthful of water.

She knew what he was thinking. "Did we leave a trail?"

"Did you notice any blood on the ground?"

"No."

"That will have to do, because you're right. I'm..."

"You need recovery time," she said, finishing his sentence.

"Yeah."

"Let me check the rest of you."

"For what?"

"I know they beat you, I could hear it." She swallowed hard. "It was all I could do to stay hidden."

Sharp surprised her by snatching her hands and shook her. "Damn right you stayed hid. You're more important to this mission. You're the expert. You have the samples."

"I will not leave someone I—a friend—to die of broken bones and internal injuries," she snarled. "Why do you think I set off that flare? To give me a chance to get to you. To get you out."

"It was a stupid rookie mistake."

"So, I should've left you to be tortured and murdered?"

"Yes," he hissed.

Her mouth fell open and she gaped at him for a couple of long seconds. "You...you *suck*."

He snickered, let go of her hands and sat back again. "Don't say that in front of the team. I'll get a reputation."

"This is not *funny*." She was so angry with him, she might hit him after all.

"Sure, it is. It's a damn comedy of errors. Nothing on this mission has gone right. Not from the get-go."

She opened and closed her mouth a couple of times as his words penetrated her own mental fog of exhaustion and stress. "You sound suspicious," she said, pointing at him and then the floor of the cave.

He got the hint and lay down. "I'm beyond that. I think this has been planned for a long time. Someone has studied our responses to other...emergencies and very carefully crafted a way to strike at the Afghan authorities and their American allies in multiple ways during the same event."

"Emergencies," Grace huffed. "You make it sound like you're firemen or something."

"Different training, similar mind-set. We all put our lives on the line to save others."

Oh yes, the noble sacrifices men make. "What about the people who love you? Do you think about what your *sacrifice* does to them?"

"I don't give a shit if my dad likes it or not. My mom succeeded in working herself to death when I was sixteen." He speared her with a glance. "She was a nurse."

Grace wasn't going anywhere near that, not even with a bio-suit on. "And your girlfriend? How does she feel about it?"

He shook his head. "Don't have one. I've watched too many guys get Dear Johned. That shit can fuck you up." He cleared his throat. "Not that I think you'd do that."

Me? He was out of his mind. "Do *not* go there."

"Where?"

"Crazyland."

"I don't know, crazy can be a good place sometimes. A necessary place." He looked around them at the cave they were in. "Better than this place."

TEN

SHARP WATCHED GRACE'S face as she thought about what he said and didn't say.

He opened his mouth, but he never got the chance to say anything.

She kissed him.

He froze, letting those soft lips slide against his own.

After a couple of seconds, he let his lips follow hers, allowed her to take the lead. When she nibbled on his bottom lip, he groaned. She took total advantage of his lapse by sending her tongue on a teasing foray into his mouth. He had to fight with himself to keep his hands off her, to let her set the pace.

She pulled back with a frown. "What the hell am I doing?"

Sharp played dumb. "Kissing?"

"Exactly. First we're kissing, then we're fighting, then we're kissing again. We shouldn't be kissing at all."

"Just for the record, it doesn't bother me in the slightest."

She snorted. "You are a menace."

"To what?"

"My peace of mind."

"If I had a nickel for every time a woman said that to me..."

"You'd have five cents."

"Probably. What do you say, Doc, want to get some rest?"

She answered with a chuckle that told him she was okay.

Despite the pain from his injuries, the lack of sleep and the precariousness of their situation, he'd never felt better. He settled into the uneven ground beneath him with a twitch of his shoulders and damn near purred, "Anytime you want to make out, I'm your guy."

GRACE WOKE TO Sharp shaking her with one hand and holding the other over her mouth. Fear spiked through her, leaving her shaking. It took a few seconds for her vision to adjust to the darkness and for her to realize what was happening.

The sound of feet scuffing against the rocky ground outside their cave had her nodding at Sharp to let her go and reaching for her Beretta.

Sharp put his hand on her wrist and pushed hers down. When she glanced at him, he sat up, pulled a knife and motioned for her to back away from the entrance.

What was he going to do, kill whoever was outside in hand-to-hand combat?

Idiot, of course that's what he's going to do.

By the time she thought of questioning his plan, he was already gone, out into the gathering darkness with no sound at all.

Would the man he was about to kill hear him coming, or die not knowing he was being hunted?

Grace waited, straining to hear any sound that might tell her what was going on outside. A short, faint moan was all she heard, gone almost immediately. No sounds of movement reached her. No sounds at all other than faint insect noises.

A dark wraith slipped into the cave and came to rest in front of her. It surprised the hell out of her and she sucked in a breath.

Two fingers covered her lips and she relaxed as she recognized Sharp's touch. He leaned in and put his mouth to her ear. "Only one man," he said in that soundless whisper she wished she could reproduce. "I put him down and hid the body in another cave. There are others searching for us, though. We need to move."

"Where?" she asked. "You're injured. How far are we likely to get?"

"I heard helicopter blades out there. I think those flares you used may have been seen by our guys and they're now looking for us. We need to find another spot to set off another flare. Someplace defendable."

"You know of a place?"

"Yeah, about a half mile from here."

"How's your leg?"

"It'll hold. How are you?"

She had so many cuts, bruises and aches she wondered if any part of her was injury free. "I'll make it. There's no other choice."

He grabbed her hand and squeezed. "We have to go now."

She nodded and he led her out of the cave.

She'd been wrong about how late it was. The sun was just setting, but it was overcast and the clouds were low and dark.

A few feet away from the cave, there was a wet patch on the sandy soil, with a trail of blood leading a few feet toward the surrounding rocks.

More blood. Lots and lots of blood.

As long as it wasn't Sharp's blood.

Grace forced herself to follow Sharp, who moved quickly and silently. How he could do it in his current condition, she had no idea.

He'd probably smirk and say, *That's what put the special in Special Forces.*

Twice, they had to hide from Afghan men. Sharp whispered that it was better if they didn't kill anyone else, since that person could be missed or the body discovered, alerting all the searchers.

That was just fine with her.

They were approaching a plateau when a helicopter seemed to emerge out of the cooling air. The markings on the bird proclaimed its allegiance and function. It was American. A Combat Rescue team.

Relief spurred her feet and she ran with Sharp toward the craft.

Unfortunately they weren't the only ones.

From three o'clock came movement on the ground, along with gunfire.

Sharp put his stolen rifle to his shoulder and returned fire. So did soldiers on the bird. As they came closer to the helicopter, now hovering a few feet above the ground, the Afghans rushed the aircraft.

Grace pulled her Beretta and fired until her clip was empty.

Sharp stumbled and fell to one knee, but was up, firing and running at the same time almost immediately, with one difference.

He was limping worse than before.

"Are you injured?" she yelled at him.

He didn't answer.

She scanned his body, trying to see what had happened and narrowed her gaze on his right leg. It looked wet. Again. Bloody. Again. "Have you been shot?"

"Not now, Grace. You can screech at me later. If we survive."

"*Screech?*" Ha. She was going to take a strip off of him, she really was. She was also very tired of being shot at.

More shots were fired behind them. Sharp shoved her down behind a pile of rocks, spun and returned fire. They were only ten or fifteen feet from the helicopter.

"Get over here, you moron," she yelled. "You don't have any body armor on!" Okay, maybe she was screeching a little.

But the gunfire directed at the helicopter stopped. Sharp grabbed her by the scruff of her uniform and dragged her with him as he continued on.

"Sharp, how bad is your leg?"

"It's still attached," he barked at her. "Get in the bird."

A soldier manning the doorway, returned fire over Grace's head as Sharp threw her inside and covered her body on the floor of the helicopter.

She tried to get up, but he yelled in her ear, "Stay down." With his entire weight on her, she didn't have any choice.

More bullets pinged overhead as they lifted off. This time two soldiers fired back before slamming the door shut. She couldn't see much, but she could tell the men on board were yelling at each other, trading hand signals and preparing for God knows what.

Sharp finally got off her and helped her up. She immediately looked at his leg. Damn it, he had blood all over himself. She got in his face and yelled, "Sit down. I want to see your leg."

He hesitated, like he was going to argue, but sat down in one of the jump seats instead. She put her hands on his leg and began searching for the wound.

Someone put a headset over her ears.

"Ma'am," a man said over the headset. "I need to check your injuries."

She looked over her shoulder at the soldier behind her. He wore a paramedic patch on his shoulder and his helmet.

"I'm a trauma surgeon. Major Samuels," she told him calmly. "My injuries are minor and can wait. Sergeant Foster has sustained multiple wounds to his leg. He's first priority."

"Yes, ma'am," he replied. He dipped his head and came up with a pair of scissors.

She loved working with the Combat Rescue guys. They were prepared for everything.

Grace cut Sharp's pants where the blood seemed heaviest and found the bullet wound she'd bandaged hours before sluggishly bleeding. She checked the back of his thigh to see if there was anything new there, but aside from more bleeding, it was okay. She reached up and squeezed Sharp's hand.

"Through and through happened a few hours ago," she said to the paramedic. "Doesn't seem to have involved the femoral artery, but he might need a transfusion. Let's pack it for now. He can be sewn up at the base."

She and the medic went to work, put an IV line in and had him bandaged up in a few minutes.

"Am I gonna live?" Sharp asked, now wearing his own headset.

"Yep. You might have some muscle damage, but nothing that should put you on the sidelines for long."

A grimace etched lines onto his forehead and around his mouth. "Sidelines? I don't want to go there at all, Doc."

She got herself strapped into the jump seat facing her patient. "You don't get a choice, Sharp."

His grimace dug in deeper. "We might all have fewer choices when we get back to the base."

That sounded ominous. "What does that mean?"

"I mean, these guys—" Sharp glanced around at the soldiers surrounding them "—say Marshall is not a happy camper. He's pissed. At you."

"Because I went over his head about his cleaning plans?" She pressed her lips together. "Too damn bad. It's not a situation he's in control of. He doesn't have enough info to make the right decisions."

"He doesn't agree."

"He doesn't need to. This is over his head and his pay grade."

"He can still make trouble. Slow things down."

"Why would he do that? He'd be risking lives of soldiers and civilians both."

"I didn't say I agreed with him, I said what I think he's going to do. Right or wrong, the guy was king shit of his island until you voted him out without a paddle or a canoe."

And here she thought the man couldn't get any lower or behave any worse. "Well, that's just fucking perfect."

ELEVEN

A GRIN CAME and went on Sharp's face. "Wow, so you do know how to swear."

She looked at the other soldiers on the helicopter. Most of them still wore grins, but a couple didn't. They frowned and avoided her gaze. Great. Marshall was probably going to hear a complete report of everything they'd said here within minutes of their arrival at the base. She'd need to talk to Max ASAP to make sure Marshall didn't get in the way of what needed to be done, rather than what one power-hungry asshole wanted done.

He was going to come at her with everything he had, which was a lot. His initial patrol infected, the helicopter crash and her having gone over his head before she left.

Yep, he was going to attempt to tear her limb from limb.

She let one of the combat rescue medics check her over and re-dress the injuries on her left arm and leg. Sharp was lying quietly on his gurney on the floor of the aircraft, staring at the bulkhead above him or at her face. She listened as he asked the medic monitoring him how much longer until they arrived at the base.

Fifteen minutes.

Grace let her head fall back. Fifteen minutes of relative peace before having to face Marshall and the rest of Sharp's team. Rasker and Williams had died in the crash, and so had the rest of the men with them. All of them soldiers. All of them her responsibility.

No matter how rational an explanation there was for their deaths, she was the reason they'd been in that helicopter, the reason they died.

Maybe she deserved to get yelled at, because she'd accomplished nothing. She still had the original samples, yes, but they were over twenty hours old now, and they'd had the shit shaken out of them.

She was going to have to go back to the village and get fresh ones.

Marshall wasn't going to like that.

Something nudged her foot. She glanced down at Sharp, who tapped his headset. She checked hers and realized she'd shut it off.

"What?" she asked after she turned it back on.

"How long will it take for you to fix me up?"

Geez, he sounded like it was as easy as fixing a car. A few stitches here, a unit of blood there and he'd be as good as new.

"You need at least one unit of blood, probably two. Your bullet wounds, large and small, need to be cleaned out and sewn up. You'll need a complete set of X-rays to make sure you don't have any broken bones, and you need at least eight hours of uninterrupted sleep. You tell me, how long will it take?"

"Too fucking long."

She shrugged. "That sounds about right."

His narrow gaze told her he suspected something. "What are you going to do when we land?"

"I need to go back and get fresh samples."

"You're not going back to that village alone." He said it like he was the major and she was the sergeant.

"Of course I won't. I'm sure Marshall will assign several soldiers to accompany me."

Sharp lifted his lips in a silent snarl, showing her just how much he didn't like that idea. She didn't like it much either, but her list of choices in regard to how she completed her mission was getting shorter and shorter. She gave him a long, direct look that said *protest all you want, buddy, it's going to happen.*

"Make contact with Cutter as soon as we're on the ground," Sharp said. "He'll support you in whatever you have to do."

"Are you sure about that? Rasker and Williams are dead." Grace fought tears. Again.

"Not your fault."

She shook her head. She was the reason they'd gone.

"Hey." Sharp rapped his knuckles against her leg. "*Not your fault.*"

"Then whose fault is it?"

"The son of a bitch who's playing around with a bacteria that could easily kill a whole lot of people." He wrapped his hand around her ankle. "Don't lose focus. Stay on task. Complete the mission."

"I wish it was that easy."

"It isn't easy."

She sighed. "Let me guess, it's what puts the *special* in Special Forces?"

The medic on the other side of Sharp's gurney stifled a laugh.

"Now, now," Sharp said with a grin in his voice. "No giving away trade secrets."

"Ha, as if. What I know about how you guys get to be what you are would fit in a shot glass."

The pilot broke in to their conversation. "Two minutes to touchdown. Medical standing by."

Everyone onboard shifted in anticipation of landing.

"Remember what I said," Sharp ordered, his hand on her ankle again. "Make contact with Commander Cutter."

"I won't forget. I want to tell him personally how sorry I am for the loss of Rasker and Williams."

"Tell him I want beans for breakfast, okay?"

"Beans?"

"Don't knock 'em. They're good for when you've got a long haul ahead of you or when you need to heal."

At that moment the helicopter landed and two medics were unstrapping Sharp's gurney and rushing him out as fast as they could.

Grace released her jump harness and followed them into the base hospital. She quickly related the history of Sharp's injuries to the on-duty doctor, who insisted on taking care of Sharp himself, while she got checked out by another physician.

She ended up needing a few stitches on her left leg and arm. The doctor had finished sewing her up and was talking to her about giving her antibiotics despite the fact that no visual infection seemed present, when Colonel Marshall strode into the curtained cubicle treatment room she was in.

Colonel Marshall was an old-school officer. Big on discipline, short on excuses and zero on failure. She anticipated anger, frustration and dislike.

He looked like he wanted to kill someone—her. She held herself very, very still.

"Is she medically fit?" he asked the attending doctor without looking away from her.

"Yes, sir," the doctor replied. He'd also frozen into immobility, his back against the wall.

"Dismissed."

The doctor glanced at Grace, then left without saying anything else.

Coward.

Marshall waited a couple of seconds, then snarled, "My patrol is dead. Every last man."

"I'm sorry, sir."

"I don't want your goddamn apology," he spat at her. "I want a fucking explanation for why you chose to leave the majority of your team, and my men, to die."

"They're *all* dead?" No one had mentioned anything to her. No one had even brought up the village and what was happening there.

"My entire original patrol is dead, thanks to you. The rest of the A-Team that went with you are fine, for now, but they won't stay that way for long. Insurgents have taken up positions around the village and are trying to pick them off."

"Did you send in some support?"

"Don't tell me how to do my job," he yelled, not an inch from her face. She jerked back as his spittle landed on her eyes, nose and mouth. "I sent support, but guess what, their helicopter came under heavy fire short of the village and barely made it back here intact."

He walked around her, shoving her away from the exam table she was standing in front of, until he could circle her. "I was told you left in a bird with three of my men and two from the A-Team. Where are they?"

Was this some kind of trick question? "We were shot down, sir."

He walked around her one full circuit before saying, "And you survived with a couple of scratches. How convenient."

Ooh, that was the wrong word to use. "Convenient would have been arriving at my destination with my samples and my escort intact," she said in as even a tone as she could manage. "Convenient would have been identifying the pathogen that killed everyone in that village *and* your men, and determining the correct procedure to contain and eradicate the pathogen."

"What a load of sanctimonious bullshit," he sneered at her.

"It wasn't bullshit to regain consciousness after the crash to realize that most of the people with me were dead. Insurgents reached our crash site in minutes. *Minutes*, Colonel, and when they got there they proceeded to shoot everyone they found, alive or dead, in the head."

"Explain to me how you and your boyfriend got away with so few injuries."

She narrowed her gaze. "I'd found someone alive, one of your men. I was trying to find the emergency medical supplies when two Afghan insurgents arrived and began shooting everyone. I was hidden behind a piece of bulkhead, and though I hadn't found the medical supplies, I'd found the backup weapons' locker. I loaded a Beretta and shot them both."

"You shot them?"

"Yes."

"And your boyfriend?"

"Who are you referring to? I don't have a boyfriend."

"That sniper pal of yours, the one who never leaves you alone."

"He'd been thrown clear of the aircraft. The two insurgents had spotted him and were moving in to kill him. I shot them first."

"Well, isn't that a nice, neat little story." His sneer twisted even further. "I don't buy any of it."

"Excuse me?"

"You're lying."

His accusation made no sense whatsoever. "Why would I lie?"

"To cover up your earlier mistakes at the village that allowed my men to die of whatever bug killed them."

"I made no mistakes."

"I've got eight bodies that say otherwise." He stepped back and signaled to two armed soldiers standing a few feet away. "Lock her up."

They approached her, one with handcuffs out. "What? Why?"

"I'm charging you with dereliction of duty, abandoning your post and reckless disregard for human life," Marshall said as his goons cuffed her and then started to march her out of the medical building.

"None of that is true!"

No one paid her any attention. Not even Marshall spared her another glance once his men had her under control.

She twisted her body and head around as far as she could in order to yell, "Wait! We have to go back to the village and get new samples. The ones I took are probably contaminated."

No response.

A few members of the medical staff flicked glances at her and she could tell they were worried, but with Marshall in no mood to listen to anyone, no one said anything.

"Colonel, please," she begged. "Send another team."

Her two jailers marched her faster.

The last thing she heard was Marshall ordering Sharp locked up with her under the same charges.

Holy shit. Marshall had just made a horrible situation a thousand times worse.

There was nothing she could do to stop him.

SHARP LAY ON the gurney, playing possum for all he was worth. The last thing he wanted anyone to know was that he was conscious. Grace had talked to the doc who was still sewing him up. This was the third wound he'd put stitches in and there might still be a fourth. They'd also stuck an IV in his arm and were giving him a unit of blood. He felt better already.

He'd pretended to pass out during his first stitching up, mumbling something about being afraid of needles.

His gurney was on the other side of the cloth wall from where Grace got checked out and stitched up, so he'd heard every word Marshall said to her.

The guy was a paranoid buck-passer, but the charges he'd leveled against Grace were no joke. Things were FUBAR and Marshall had decided to make her the scapegoat. Along with Sharp's A-Team.

Not a smart move.

Sharp continued his lights-out routine as the doctor finished up, then played dead when Marshall came and breathed right on his face.

Someone needed a mint.

"Why isn't he awake?" Marshall demanded. "I was told he was talking to the bitch on the bird."

"Maybe he was, but from all the bruising and swelling

he's had his bell rung at least twice. He lost consciousness while I was sewing him up."

Marshall stepped away and grunted. "Move him to the brig."

"I'm afraid I can't allow that, Colonel," the doctor said. "Sergeant Foster needs to remain immobile until after I've done a scan of his head. If he's got the concussion I think he has, I might even need to perform emergency surgery."

No one said anything for a moment, then Marshall grunted again. "He's under arrest for the same charges as Samuels. When he wakes up, contact me."

"Yes, sir," the doctor said.

Heavy footsteps walked away, followed by a couple of others.

Other people started talking, mostly medical-speak.

One of those voices belonged to his doctor, who ordered the cleanup of the exam room he was in and the one where Grace had been. After a few minutes, things seemed to calm right down.

A soft sound told him someone was standing close by.

The doctor whispered in his ear, "You can stop faking now."

TWELVE

SHARP OPENED HIS eyes to meet the gaze of the doctor who'd sewn him up. "Concussion, huh?" he asked quietly.

"A CT scan might take a few hours." The doctor glanced around, then continued, "Marshall fully intends to prosecute Dr. Samuels for insubordination and all those other charges. I've tried to tell him she was correct in her assessment of the situation at the village, but when she went over his head, he took it personally. Then his men in the original patrol died and that cemented his opinion she's at fault."

"She thinks it's some sort of super-anthrax," Sharp told the doctor. "Fast-acting, and she thinks it might be in the air and water supply, but she isn't sure."

The doctor paled. "That's not good."

"No shit. Has Marshall done anything right since we left?"

"No. Some of your A-Team are still there. Cutter wanted to take the rest of the team out there, but Marshall ordered them to stand down."

"Have you heard what the status is at the village?"

"Not in the last couple of hours."

"Shit." Sharp glanced at the bag of blood hanging over his head. It looked empty. "I may not make that CT scan."

"You're in no condition to go anywhere," the doctor said as Sharp sat up.

He reached for the IV line, intending to yank it out. "Doesn't matter, I've got a job to do."

The doctor moved surprisingly fast. "I'll do it. I don't want you spilling all the blood we just poured into you." He took out the IV line and put a bandage over the hole in the back of Sharp's hand. The doctor ducked down and pulled something out of a box stored underneath the exam table and handed Sharp a bottle of electrolyte water. "Drink all of this before you leave the base, and eat something substantial or you're going to fall over in a few hours."

"Thanks, Dad," Sharp said with a grin. He cracked open the bottle and drank several swallows. "So where's the rest of my team?"

"After your aircraft disappeared, they moved their gear to a shack next to the helicopter landing area. I think in anticipation of going to that village, but Marshall told them to stay put, and confiscated their SINGCAR radios when they tried to contact Colonel Maximillian."

"They're under arrest?" Sidelining an A-Team wasn't what Sharp would call a smart move. They had their own orders to follow, and their own chain of command to keep in contact with.

"No, I would say they're grounded to the base. No one is stopping them from going to the mess, chapel or medical. They just can't leave or call out."

Sharp finished the bottle of water and stood. No dizziness, good. "Marshall is digging himself a deep hole."

The doctor nodded. "Do yourself a favor and don't jump in it with him."

"I'll try, Doc, but I've always been a curious fellow."

Sharp glanced down at himself. The medical people had cut his clothes to get at his wounds. "Got anything I could wear over this?"

The doctor handed him a lab coat, which Sharp put on and buttoned up. "Good luck," he said to Sharp. "I'd rather not have to sew you up again."

"Me too. Thanks." They shook hands, then Sharp left the medical center and headed toward the landing field like he had an errand to run for someone important.

No one looked twice at him.

Bonus.

He entered the shack and found his team, their gear stowed near the door, ready to go, talking quietly as a group. "You lazy bums on a coffee break or something?"

Most people would have jumped to their feet, called out greetings and patted him on the back. These guys were too smart to do that. They all got to their feet with shit-eating grins on their faces, but not one voice rose in volume.

"About time you got here," Cutter said, waving Sharp over. "Where the hell have you been?"

"I was on an all-expenses paid trip to the beach, but the food sucked, so I came home to this fabulous address." His shoulders slumped. "I'm sorry, boss. We got shot down. Rasker and Williams didn't make it."

"What about the doc?" Cutter asked.

Sharp frowned. "You don't know?"

"We're out of the loop. Marshall won't tell us jack-shit. His ass is going to be grass when the brass finds what a clusterfuck he's whipped up here."

"She survived the crash, too. We hauled ass to get back here as fast as we could, but it was close a couple of times. Marshall arrested her on a bunch of charges and has her in some brig somewhere on the base. She tried to tell him she has to get her samples to her lab, but Marshall isn't having any of it. This shit is serious. If we don't get it figured out soon, like twenty-four hours soon, a lot of people are going to die."

"What do you mean?" Cutter asked.

"I mean, someone created the bug that killed everyone at the village. It kills fast and hard and everyone who's been exposed to it has died. It's one hell of a weapon."

"Fuck me," Runnel said.

"No thanks, you're not my type," Sharp said and the moment of humor served to center everyone's attention. "We have to bust Grace out of jail and get her wherever she needs to go."

"Grace, huh?" Cutter said, crossing his arms over his chest.

"Hey, you bleed all over someone, you end up on a first-name basis."

Cutter's eyebrows rose. "Really?"

"Really. I'd have her at my back any day."

"You and her, huh, Sharp?" Runnel asked with a suggestive smile.

"Nah, facing death and dismemberment isn't the time to make a move." The fact that he had was beside the point. Grace was too good for all of them, including himself. "So, you guys want to bust her out, or what?"

Runnel grinned. "I vote yes. Can you imagine the look on Marshall's face?"

Everyone else nodded their agreement, and Cutter turned to Sharp. "We're go. Why don't you put on some real clothes? We'll find you a weapon and some essentials."

"Sounds good to me, boss." He put actions to the words and was re-equipped and ready to go in a few minutes.

Runnel handed him a rifle case.

"What's this?" Sharp asked. His rifle was in pieces on the desert floor and Runnel's was strapped to his back.

"It's my backup rifle."

"Wow, and all I brought was a backup Beretta."

"Well, she's not as shiny as the A-1 you were shooting, but she's a good weapon. Accurate."

"Thanks." Sharp shook his teammate's hand. "I'll take good care of it."

"Make sure you do. No dropping it out of an aircraft."

"Ah, come on. It's only happened once."

"Cut the chatter, you two," Cutter said. "Clark and Smoke, you two find us a helicopter we can steal. The rest of us will spirit the good doctor out of lockup. Ping me when you've found a bird."

"Yes, sir," Clark said while Smoke nodded.

Cutter led the way, followed by Hernandez, March, Runnel and Sharp. Sharp kept his head down, so his face wasn't front and center. He was just one of the guys, no one special.

Marshall had set up some kind of brig in a prefab metal rectangle building. It was hot, the air smelled stale and the walls and floors were a uniform grey color. Immediately to the right of the entrance was a hallway with several doors on either side.

An armed guard sat on a chair at either end of the hallway. None of the doors were open.

The guard at the door got to his feet real quick when Cutter walked in. "This building is off-limits."

"You got that lady doctor stashed in here?" Cutter asked him.

"Prisoners are not allowed contact with anyone."

Cutter snorted. "I'm not her lawyer. My guys and I are going to get thrown into the mess she left up north. I need to ask her two questions so we don't get shot to shit when we land. That's it."

"The colonel said—"

Cutter cut him off. "I know what the colonel said. He was referring to her calling some bug expert who thinks the world revolves around him, not us getting intel from her. I've got to know how to protect my guys."

The guard hesitated another second, glanced at the rest of their group, his gaze jumping from their obvious readiness, then back to Cutter's face. He checked his watch. "Marshall should be back in ten minutes."

"We've got to leave in five. That's why we're here now and not later with Marshall."

The guard turned and nodded at the other one, then stepped aside. "Okay. She's not talking to anyone, though."

"I think she'll talk to us." Cutter smiled a shark's smile at him. "Which door?"

"Second on the left."

Cutter and Sharp went to the door while Runnel and Hernandez stayed behind with the first guard. March continued down the hall a little toward the second guard and leaned against the wall like he was bored.

Cutter opened the door, let Sharp in, then closed the door.

Grace had been lying on a narrow cot. She sat up and blinked owlishly at them. "What are you two doing here?"

She was fine. Just fine. Lying there like she was on vacation. No hysteria. No panic. Something raw and bloody inside Sharp healed over. "Breaking you out," he answered her.

Her jaw dropped open. "Are you nuts? Marshall will have both of you in handcuffs in the next room."

"Don't think so," Cutter said. "There's seven of us."

"Besides," Sharp added. "We're planning on stealing a helicopter too."

"God." She flopped back on her cot, sighed then said to the ceiling, "I see someone left the bag of idiots open again."

Cutter choked back a laugh.

"Is that any way to talk about your liberators?" Sharp asked.

Grace rolled her eyes. "It is when they're about to do something supremely stupid."

"There's two kinds of stupid," Sharp explained. "There's dead stupid and live stupid. We're the latter."

She squinted at him. "I have no idea what you just said."

"Never mind, Doc," Sharp said. "Let's go."

"But—"

"No buts. We've got a world to save."

Cutter opened the door while Sharp grabbed the doctor. It soothed that hurt place deep inside him to touch her warm, soft skin again, to know she was okay.

"Here," he said, handing her a military ball cap. "Put this on."

They stepped out in the hall to find the two guards tied up and on the floor, the rest of their team waiting for them by the door. No one said anything. They just walked out of the building and marched, with her in the

middle of their five-sided formation, toward the landing field.

"Doc," Cutter said quietly. "Do you need those other
samples?"

"It would be better to get new ones," she replied. "The
old ones are still dangerous, though. They need to be
disposed of properly."

"We'll worry about that when we're not breaking
enough orders to cause an earthquake. Do you have all
the equipment you need at the village?"

"As long as no one has blown up the Sandwich or
shot it all up, probably. But I have no protective gear.
Do you guys?"

"No. Marshall did something with our bio-suits."

The landing field came into view.

"So, we're not stopping to grab anything?" she asked,
her tone betraying her nervousness.

"No time," Cutter told her. He'd stepped up the pace,
leading them in a ground-eating march that still wasn't
out of place on the base.

"What about a cell phone? My SINGCAR radio was
destroyed in the crash."

"Nope. The Grinch took our phones and radios yesterday."

"Why am I not surprised," Grace said, no trace of a
question in her statement.

Their group approached the helicopter where Smoke
and Clark were talking with one of the pilots in front of
an open panel near the rear rotor.

"Guys, I just got a heads-up on that mission we
worked up last night," Cutter said to Smoke and Clark.
He turned to the pilot. "Marshall wants to talk to you

personally before he okays the mission. He doesn't want another bird going down."

"No problem," the pilot said, closing up the panel. "I'm fueled and ready to go. You guys make yourselves at home." He headed out at a trot.

Cutter turned and said to the team, "Let's go."

Sharp urged Grace inside the bird. "Grab a seat."

"I need a weapon, and—" she glanced down at herself "—everything else."

"We'll figure it out." He strapped in next to her. He wanted to reassure her that everything would be fine, but he couldn't. He couldn't even promise they'd land at the village without trouble.

The rest of the team piled into the bird, Smoke and Clark up front in the pilot and copilot seats.

The engine started and the rotors began to spin.

A couple of soldiers glanced at them curiously. Sharp grinned and waved. The soldiers returned to whatever they were doing.

Across the aisle, Cutter put a headset on. He spoke into the mike, his lips moving to form the words in a precise manner that told Sharp he was addressing a senior officer.

No, sir.

No, sir.

A long pause, then very distinctly Cutter's lips formed the words: *I can't do that, sir.*

Shit had hit the fan.

Cutter reached around and smacked Smoke on the shoulder and gave the *get us out of here now* hand signal.

The helicopter began to rise off the ground.

Movement on the tarmac caught Sharp's attention. Soldiers were racing toward them with weapons raised.

No one was firing yet, but that was probably going to change.

Cutter took his hands off his weapon and raised them in the air. Sharp and the other guys followed suit. So did Grace.

That seemed to give everyone pointing guns at them pause.

Their helicopter continued to rise, more rapidly every second.

Marshall appeared out of the growing crowd of soldiers watching them leave. He made a chopping gesture toward their helicopter, yelling something.

For a moment, no one seemed to respond.

The next second, bullets pinged all around them.

THIRTEEN

GRACE DUCKED, HAVING already heard more bullets coming at her than she ever wanted to hear. Fear, disbelief and horror made her normal nausea while flying seem like the calm before the storm.

Their own people were shooting at them.

Next to her, Sharp threw himself over her, covering her body with his. The damn hero. She tried to shove him, to get him to move, but he just pressed down harder.

More bullets echoed around them, then it all stopped suddenly.

Someone jostled Sharp, which shook her, then he let her up. She saw why immediately.

Cutter had been shot.

The left side of his chest and shoulder were bloody, his head dangling down like a marionette with its strings cut.

"Doc!" Next to Cutter, Hernandez twisted in his jump seat and put pressure on his commander's chest. He turned and yelled at her again. "Doc!"

She was already moving, hitting the release on her harness and falling forward onto her hands and knees.

There was a lot of blood soaking the front of his uniform and body armor. Too much blood and he appeared completely unresponsive.

Sharp grabbed her by the arm and hauled her to her feet. She thought he was trying to stop her from helping, and she tried to rip her arm out of his grip, yelling, "I have to help him."

He urged her toward Cutter, yelling, "I'll get the first-aid kit."

She reached Cutter and put a hand on his neck. No pulse. Hernandez was still putting pressure on the wound.

"Is there just one wound?" she asked him.

His head jerked up at her question. "I don't know."

She did a quick once-over, but couldn't see any others. She checked for a carotid pulse again. Nothing.

"Let me see his back," she said to Hernandez.

He allowed her to put her hands on Cutter's shoulder and bring his body forward enough to see behind him. There was a hole in the right side of his back larger than the size of a golf ball. And blood. So much blood.

Sharp appeared at her shoulder with the first-aid kit. She gave him a tight-lipped glance, then she looked at Hernandez and shook her head.

He shouted something, but she shook her head harder. "He's gone!"

Hernandez stared at her like she'd shot him herself. He jerked his hand away with enough violence to make her rear back. He collapsed onto himself, bowed his head and fisted his hands tight on his thighs.

She glanced at Sharp. He gave her a rigid nod. The other team members were either hiding their faces so they could grieve or staring at her like they couldn't believe it.

Couldn't believe their commander had been killed by their own men.

Grace swallowed the vomit that had risen in her throat and went back to her seat. Marshall had a lot to answer for, and she wasn't going to let him bulldoze his way out of any of it. She put her harness back on, then stared at her bloody hands. Cutter's body was still sitting across from her as if he were asleep. What would his men do with his body? With Marshall no doubt telling everyone they were the worst sort of criminals, they'd have to keep it with them. As if they didn't have enough problems.

They hit some turbulence and the whole aircraft shook like an earthquake registering nine on the Richter scale. It was the last straw for Grace's stomach.

She vomited, managing to miss everything but the floor of the helicopter. Yay her.

A bag was thrust in front of her face and she took it automatically, continuing to fill it with what was left in her stomach. Eventually, her stomach stopped clenching and she was able to hand the bag off to Sharp, who threw it out the open door.

She should be outraged. She should be formulating a plan to bring Cutter's killer, Marshall, to justice. All she felt was tired. So many people had died, so many more were at risk, and now her friend and a man who was the glue to this team was dead.

How on earth were they going to succeed?

How were they going to stay out of jail long enough to prove they weren't the crazy ones?

Marshall had lost his mind. Ordering his men to fire on them—how was murder an acceptable response to soldiers following orders, even if they were someone else's?

Were the men on the ground at the village going to fire on them too?

What about the insurgents who were supposedly firing on the village? Would they even be able to land?

She didn't have her bio-suit. None of them did. How was she going to take samples? The original patrol had contracted the illness, proving to her it had to be airborne.

She glanced up to ask Cutter her questions, to brainstorm a plan...but Cutter was dead.

Sharp had sat down next to her while her thoughts ran wild in her head. He was still and so, so quiet. She hated what she had to do next. He deserved some time to process what had happened, but none of them had time to make sense of any of it.

She put a shaking hand on his arm.

He leaned in close.

"We don't have any protection against the anthrax. For the discovery patrol to get infected, it has to be in the air. How are we going to take samples without putting ourselves at risk?"

"We'll get Leonard to collect some, then land a safe distance away to pick them up."

"Safe distance, huh. How far is that?"

He shrugged, his eyes sunken, his face haggard. "Make an educated guess. We'll land wherever you want."

"Wonderful." If she chose wrong, it could mean all of their deaths.

A hand waving from the front of the aircraft caught their attention. Clark was signaling Sharp to put on a headset. The only one available was the one Cutter was still wearing. Sharp took it off his head and put it on.

He listened for a moment, then started yelling into the mike. Despite the noise from the rotors and engine, she could hear every word Sharp said.

"Commander Cutter is dead, thanks to you." He

paused, then said, "Our bug expert knows what she's doing, and her chain of command supports her. Special Forces soldiers are trained to handle unconventional warfare and think independently. I don't believe *you're* competent to issue orders on the situation. Stop while you still can." He pulled the headset off and threw it on the floor.

"That son of a bitch is trying to blame us for this clusterfuck?" Hernandez asked, his eyes glittering with anger and unshed tears.

"Oh yeah." Sharp's voice sounded as angry and disgusted as she felt. "He's so mad I could hardly understand him, but it's clear. He's going to make the case that we and the doc are at fault for all of it."

"There's just one problem with that," Grace yelled so all of them would hear. "Colonel Maximillian gave me and the A-Team at the village specific orders. I'm sure he contacted Marshall to explain why the site couldn't be cleaned right away."

She made eye contact with Hernandez. "Do you know if Marshall followed Max's orders?"

"I never heard of any orders from anyone else. Cutter didn't mention anything about it either."

Frustration made her want to hit something. "Did he do anything productive while Sharp and I were dying slowly in the desert?"

No one said anything.

She tried a different question. "How long did it take him to send out search-and-rescue after our helicopter went down?"

Hernandez looked like he wanted to punch someone. "About six hours. We didn't even know your bird had gone dark until three or four hours after you took off. Marshall claimed you took the bird against orders to a different location and weren't responding to hails."

"The lying sack of shit," Sharp said. "He's out of his mind."

"We're coming up on the village fast," Hernandez said. "What are we going to do when we get there?"

"Can you get in touch with Leonard?"

Hernandez turned around and yelled at Clark in the copilot seat.

Clark said something back and Hernandez reported back to her. "Clark is talking to him now. We're ten minutes out and clear to land."

"Tell Clark to land at least a quarter mile from the village and the field where the cows died. Ask Leonard to leave the samples then back away."

Hernandez nodded and yelled at Clark.

Now all she had to do was wait to arrive at the village.

Horror crept toward her from every direction. Cutter's body, moving with every jolt and sway of the helicopter, the fear and anger on the faces of the men around her. Nausea threatened to tear her apart from the inside out, her shaking fists clenched so tight the skin over her knuckles was white.

Her hand itched to slide over to Sharp's, to seek out his strength, to have his long, strong fingers entwined with hers. Holding hands was inappropriate for so many reasons. She was the ranking soldier. Cutter's death was her responsibility and hers alone.

Cutter had died doing the right thing. Sharp had been shot, more than once, beaten and a higher-ranking officer had betrayed his trust. All of which happened because of her. Was she going to get all of them killed? Sharp killed?

No. She couldn't allow herself to think that way.

What did she need to complete the mission?

Samples of the bacteria.

Safe transport to Max's lab at the naval base in Bahrain.

Corroboration of her version of events.

She needed to make sure her friends, these men who were doing their best to help her do the right thing, the only thing that could save so many more lives, left this situation with their records clean and reputations shiny. And alive.

Marshall was going to do everything he could to bring her down and Sharp's A-Team with her.

She couldn't let that happen.

Grace closed her eyes, breathed deep for a few seconds then forced her hands to open. She poked Sharp's arm and waved him close so she didn't have to yell so loud. "I need to talk to Max. Colonel Maximillian. He needs to be aware of what's happened, and Marshall's role in screwing this up."

"We can try," Sharp said, bending over and picking up the headset off the floor of the helicopter. He handed it to her.

It still had Cutter's blood on it.

Her stomach rolled, but she stuck it on her head and asked, "Smoke?"

"Fire," was his response.

A joke? Now? "I hope that means you're paying attention. I need to get through to my CO. Can you do that?"

"Where is he?"

She told him, then waited while Smoke made the connections happen over the radio. She glanced outside.

Their altitude was dropping. They were almost to the village. She wouldn't have long to talk.

"Dr. Samuels?" Max sounded worried and pissed off at the same time. "Where the hell have you be—?"

"Colonel, there's no time to go into detail," she interrupted. "My helicopter was shot down shortly after we left the site. Only two of us survived, the others died in the crash or were killed shortly after by insurgents. It took us almost a day to make contact with American troops and get back to Bostick."

She sucked in a breath and kept talking before he could interject. "Here's what's really important. Marshall has my original samples, but I don't know what he's done with them. He charged me with a bunch of bogus shit, then threw me in a makeshift brig without allowing me to talk to anyone. He blames me for the death of some of his men. Men who I believe contracted the disease from airborne spores. He didn't even send a search team out to look for us until six hours *after* our helicopter crashed. He's lost his mind. The A-Team I'm working with grabbed another helicopter and we're about to land at the village, but Marshall ordered his men to fire on us as we took off and they killed Commander Cutter." She ran out of air and paused to grab another lungful.

Max spoke in a calm voice. "Slow down. Take it easy. Are you saying Marshall ordered the murder of an American soldier?"

"Someone fired on us from the base... Who else could have ordered it?" Tears threatened to escape her tight control, but if they escaped, everything would, all the terror, fear and frustration of the past two days. Sharp and his team were depending on her. She didn't have time for a nervous breakdown.

"I knew he was a stubborn jackass," Max said, frustration evident in the way he clipped off the ends of his words. "But I didn't realize he would jeopardize the situation because a couple of *quacks* didn't agree with him."

"Is *quack* the worst thing he's called you? It's the nicest thing he's called me," Grace said with a weak laugh. "I think he's determined to make this my fault and, I think by extension, your fault. He's likely to blow the whole place up, and I still don't know how the villagers contacted anthrax. I think it's airborne, but it could also be in the water supply. This bug acts so fast, it's impossible to know from what little investigation that's gone on."

"We need to know that information."

The helicopter landed. A soldier in a bio-suit waited, crouched about twenty feet away. There was no sample container anywhere near him.

"We're here," she told Max. "I'll call you back."

"If you don't," Max said with a steely tone she'd seldom heard from him, "I'll assume the worst and send a new team. That's going to take time we don't have."

"Understood." She took the headset off and dropped it on the floor.

Before she could get out of her harness, Sharp put his hand over hers and leaned close. "The samples are on the ground right next to us." He gave her a hard look. "I'll get them. You stay here."

"But—"

He pointed at her. "Number-one asset, remember?"

She frowned, yanked a pair of gloves out of a side pocket of her pants and smacked them on the palm of his hand. "Until the outside of the container is properly decontaminated, no one touches it without gloves on."

He pulled on the first glove with a snap and saluted. "Yes, ma'am." He grabbed the sample container, identical to the one she'd carried for almost two days, and brought it on board. He stowed it to the interior bulkhead with straps, then turned to her and waggled his hands, silently asking what to do with the gloves.

She had more in her pocket.

She mimed crumpling them up in a ball and throwing them out of the helicopter. So that's what he did.

Smoke turned and waved at her from the pilot's seat, but she wasn't sure what he was trying to say.

"Leonard needs to talk to us," Sharp said. "We're shutting the bird down, okay?"

The level of noise dropped as the engine was turned off.

"Is it really important enough to delay getting the samples to the lab?" she asked.

"He wouldn't have asked if it wasn't."

The rotors slowed down and most of Sharp's team took up defensive positions on either side of the aircraft. Two of them took Cutter's body, wrapped it in a tarp and strapped it to the bulkhead, as well.

Leonard walked toward them, but stopped about ten feet away. As soon as the noise from the helicopter was low enough for him to be heard, he started yelling.

"We're all in deep shit."

That much she knew already. "Can you be a little more specific? Shit is all I've been in lately."

"Marshall has issued an arrest order for all of you. Those of us on the team that came here initially are to be put under arrest as soon as we leave the site. No one is to assist you in any way."

Grace's jaw fell open. "He can't do that."

Leonard looked at Sharp. "Where's Cutter?"

"Dead." Sharp gestured with his head at their commander's body, covered and anchored to the bulkhead.

Leonard stared at them for a moment, then exploded with, "*What the fuck?* When? How?"

"About thirty minutes ago," Sharp answered. "When we were taking off. We took fire from the base."

"Crazy bastard," Leonard said, pacing a few steps away then back again. "What a giant clusterfuck."

"We can't stay here," Sharp told him. "For all we know, Marshall has another bird coming in behind us."

Leonard raised his hands in frustration. "Where the hell are you going to go?"

FOURTEEN

"WE HAVE TO get these samples to the lab in Bahrain yesterday," Grace told Leonard.

"Where are you going to stop for fuel? Every military base between here and Bahrain has probably been alerted."

"Colonel Maximillian will pave the way," she argued. "He—"

"Maybe," Leonard interrupted. "But how fast can he do that? If Marshall's already issued orders and has people looking for you, it's going to take a while for new orders to reach them."

"They'll want to confirm those orders," Sharp added. "That will take even more time."

"We don't have a choice," Grace said between clenched teeth. "Is there nowhere else to get fuel besides American military bases?"

"There aren't any Coalition forces' bases left," Sharp said. "We'd have to stop at a civilian airport or landing field. Anyone with an ax to grind with American military could take a shot at us."

Grace's hopes fell.

"There is one place," Leonard said in a faintly hesitant tone. "A friend of Cutter's set up a not-quite-legal emporium near the border between Afghanistan and Iran at an abandoned military base."

"I hear a *but* in there somewhere," Grace said.

"But this guy is a little on the shady side."

"Do you know the coordinates?"

"No, but Cutter has them in his journal. Do *not* let your guard down around him."

"Journal?" Sharp asked. "What journal?"

"He keeps it with him, usually under his clothes." Leonard backed away a step. "I've got to get back. We've got our hands full with someone taking shots at us everyone once in a while. We had to turn away some family members who wanted to get into the village. Make sure you read through the journal. There might be more info in there you can use."

Sharp waved. "Thanks, man. Take care of yourself."

"Same goes for you." Leonard glanced at Grace and saluted.

She saluted back as Smoke started up the engine again. She made her way back to her seat, but Sharp, Hernandez, Runnel and March went to Cutter's body. Sharp searched his body for the journal and found it under his clothes, in a plastic bag strapped to Cutter's lower back. He handed her the book, then helped the rest of his team rewrap their commander's body in the tarp.

Grace looked at the tattered book in her hands. The plastic covering was coated in blood. Cutter's blood. She ripped the plastic off, unable to look at his blood for another moment more.

The team secured the body to the bulkhead then returned to their seats.

Sharp took the journal and skimmed. About three-quarters of the way through, he stopped to read a couple of pages more thoroughly.

"Fuck." He shook his head.

"Did you find it?" She couldn't tell if he'd found the information or not.

"Yes." He looked around at the team and gave them the coordinates to Cutter's friend's Afghan emporium.

Smoke, who'd turned around in the pilot's seat to listen, asked, "Now give us the bad news."

"Cutter's friend is CIA."

The helicopter was suddenly full of more swear words than she'd ever heard in one place, ever.

Hernandez said it best. "We're fucked. Totally fucked."

The rest of the team seemed to agree, until Sharp put in, "We don't have anywhere else to go."

"We can't stay here," Grace added.

Everyone stopped complaining.

Smoke looked at Grace and Sharp, then at the rest. "Let's hope Cutter's friend is actually friendly." He revved the engines some more and they lifted off.

As soon as they were safely away, Sharp leaned over to talk in her ear. "When we get to the location, I want you to stay out of sight."

"Hide?" she asked.

"Yes. I don't want this guy to know you're with us until I've had a chance to figure out if he's going to help us or bury us."

"Okay, but where are you going to hide me?" She glanced around the aircraft. Every space and crevice was already in use.

"Behind Cutter's body."

She turned her head to look at him so fast, she was sure whiplash was going to be an ongoing problem. "What?"

"It's the least likely place anyone will look."

"It's the *first* place I'd look," she retorted.

His frown was unforgiving. "You got a better idea?"

"Yeah, why don't we pretend I'm one of your guys and I'm injured. I can fake unconsciousness."

His gaze flickered to her chest. "There's just one problem with that, Doc."

"What?"

"You don't look anything like any Green Beret."

She grit her teeth. "So, I've got a chest wound."

"There's no chest wound in the world that could result in your...figure."

"I'll be lying down," she managed to say without punching him in the face. "Cover me up with blankets or something."

"This isn't World War Two. We don't have bulky blankets, just the reflective, emergency kind."

"Then what do you suggest?"

"If you won't hide, you won't hide." He shrugged, a jerky, tense movement. "Just sit there and don't make eye contact with anyone."

"How imaginative. The old *hide in plain sight* plan, eh?"

He didn't respond.

She was going to die. Not from a bullet or bacteria. No, she was going to die of terminal irritation. *Men.*

She crossed her arms over her chest and attempted to relax enough to lower her blood pressure, but her mind wouldn't stop revisiting their impossible situation.

Marshall blamed her for the death of his son. She understood that. She blamed herself for his son's death too. What she didn't understand was his belief that she was somehow culpable for the deaths of his patrol. They hadn't followed procedure. They'd waited too long to put on their protective gear. Yet, he seemed absolutely certain she was at fault. Had his rage compromised his objectivity? That seemed likely. And she'd dragged the A-Team into this mess and now Cutter was dead.

She should tell them all why Marshall had seemingly gone nuts, but she needed them to help her complete the mission.

The mission came first.

Exhaustion weighed her eyelids down, and she didn't have the physical resources to fight the oblivion of sleep.

The rattle and shake of the helicopter kept waking her up to snippets of the conversation around her.

"Why the fuck does Marshall hate her so much?" Hernandez shouted.

"I don't know," Sharp answered. "She didn't buck any of his orders until we got to the village and he wanted to just bomb the place."

"Maybe they'd had an altercation before?" Hernandez's question faded into a fog.

A hard bump of turbulence woke her to hear Runnel saying, "It's like he's gone crazy of the batshit-crazy variety."

She knew why he wasn't acting rationally. The IED explosion two years ago had damaged the living as much as the dead.

Faces slid past her mental eye. People shouting, hiding, shooting. Someone calling out for medical help. She had to get there fast, dodge soldiers taking defensive positions and reach the bloody man on the ground outside of his destroyed vehicle. He was dead. She continued forward. There were two of her nurses, both dead, but the man underneath them was alive. His calls for help spurring her to... A shout from the right and— She heard herself screaming.

Men were yelling, the voices indistinct. The whole room vibrated at a rate that felt wrong and uncomfortable. The discomfort rose, helping her fight her way back to complete consciousness.

"What the fuck happened to her, man?" Hernandez shouted.

"I don't know," Sharp yelled back. "Unlike most women, the doc doesn't talk about personal stuff."

Wonderful, they were talking about her.

"What happened during that convoy attack?" March asked Sharp. "Did you read the entire report?"

"I read the official citation for her medal and talked to one of the men who was there," Sharp answered. "He said she more than earned it."

"So, what is this?" Hernandez demanded of all of them. "Post-traumatic stress?"

"Yes," Grace said, opening her eyes and trying to sit up properly, but Sharp put his hand on her upper back and urged her to keep her head down. As much as it comforted her, as much as she would like to crawl onto his lap and hug him for a year, she waved him off. Not in front of the team. "I started experiencing panic attacks a few months ago in response to specific stimuli."

"You sound like a textbook, Doc," Hernandez said. "PTSD doesn't follow a textbook."

Tears dripped down her face, but she found the strength to smile anyway. "I've discovered that the hard way."

"What's Marshall's problem with you, Doc?" Sharp asked.

She didn't want to remember. "Someone died during that attack. Marshall blames me for that soldier's death."

The men of the A-Team stared at her. They didn't need to give voice to the question on all their faces.

"No," she told them, weary to her bones of carrying the guilt for events out of her control. "I wasn't personally responsible for the death Marshall blames me for. I think I could have prevented it, had I made different decisions, but then other people would likely have died. Hindsight sucks."

Everyone but Sharp nodded. He watched her with narrow eyes and a tilt to his head that told her he knew there was more to the story.

"Nothing about the way he's conducted himself is rational," Sharp said. "Maybe he needs some time stateside, or counseling, or there's something else we don't know about going on, but it's clear he's advocating actions that are questionable, if not illegal."

The face of every Green Beret on the aircraft transformed, becoming cold and calculating. No one said a thing, but they didn't need to.

They were on her side.

Sharp grabbed the headset and handed it to her. "Call your CO. We need info and support."

She wiped the tears off her face and sucked in a deep breath. "Okay." She put the headset on and said, "Smoke?"

"Fire," he replied so fast she had to wonder if that was how he always responded to his name.

"Do you always say that when someone calls your name?"

"Only when things are good."

She waited for him to continue, but he didn't. Curiosity made her ask, "What if things aren't good?"

"I say something else."

Wow, this guy was not a talker. "I need to reach my CO again, Colonel Maximillian."

"Roger that."

She waited, staring at Cutter's blood on the floor of the helicopter. They were lucky only Cutter got hit.

Lucky? That word did not apply. God, the whole situation was messed up. They had a man-manipulated, weaponized bacteria to deal with, and an officer who seemed hell-bent on making it worse.

A click came through the headset and Max's voice filled her ears. "Grace? Dr. Samuels?"

"I'm here, Max."

"What the fuck is going on?"

Grace winced. She'd only ever heard Max swear once, when his ex-wife tried to claim he hit her.

"Nothing good, sir," she replied, trying to remind him to be professional. "Colonel Marshall has lost his mind."

"So, you didn't shoot your way off FOB Bostick?"

"No! Ohmygod, is that what he's saying?"

"He's got two dead bodies for evidence, men who were guarding you. He claims your team of Green Berets killed them getting you out."

"No. That never happened. Those guards were perfectly healthy when we left. If they got shot, someone else shot them. Marshall, on the other hand, ordered his men to fire on us as we took off, and killed Cutter." Her throat closed on his name and she had to focus on breathing for a moment.

Max swore. "I've been talking with General Stone. He's as concerned as I am about the anthrax, but he's also worried about this escalating situation with Marshall. He's determined to nip things in the bud."

"Three men are dead. We're way past bud and into someplace very scary. Look, we're going to try to get to you, but I don't know if we're going to make it. It's a long way from where we are to Bahrain."

"Do you have samples?"

"I picked up new ones from the village, but things aren't looking good there either. There are people trying to get into it. And either locals or insurgents are firing at the Americans trying to maintain the quarantine. They need support. Can you talk to the general about sending them some? They need to be in bio-suits."

"I need those samples."

"This anthrax is so fast, Max. So very fast. I don't know if Cipro is going to stop it. Antibiotics need time to work, but this bug isn't going to give it to them."

"Anyone I send to the site will be given Cipro before they go. That's the best we can do until we have a chance to figure out how this strain is different."

"The men who discovered the dead had been given Cipro. They're dead now too."

"Finding another treatment is going to take time."

They both knew they didn't have time. Whoever designed this anthrax only had to release it again for more people to die.

"Can you get the mobile lab into Afghanistan?" she asked.

"I'll make the request. It's a good idea and will certainly expedite matters with providing treatment to anyone exposed to the bacteria." He didn't say it would also make it easier for him to help her, but she heard it in his tone. "Where are you going?"

"I'm not certain. We need somewhere we can stay out of sight until you and the general can clear things up."

"If it looks like it's going to take more than six hours to rescue you and your team, I'll come to you with the new level three mobile lab Dr. Martin has developed. It fits inside three duffel bags."

"I'll give you to the pilot, Smoke. I think he can give you coordinates of the location we're heading to now."

"Take care of yourself. You're a damn good doctor. Don't get yourself killed."

"I'll do my best, sir." She pointed at the headset and Smoke.

Hernandez tapped Smoke on the shoulder and she heard him join the conversation. He gave Max the co-ordinates they were on their way toward.

"Maximillian out." The line went dead.

Grace took her headset off and handed it to Sharp.

"Bad news?"

She snorted. "Try the word *disastrous* or maybe the word *horrific*." She had to make herself meet his gaze. "You know those two guys who were guarding me in Marshall's little brig?"

"Yeah."

"Well, they're dead. Marshall is saying you guys or me, I'm not sure which, killed them while breaking me out of jail."

For the first time since she'd met him, Sharp's jaw hung open.

"So, basically, if Marshall's got compelling evidence," she said, "we're screwed."

FIFTEEN

SHARP STARED AT Grace's pale face and tight fists and couldn't think of a damn thing to say.

The entire team had noted early on that Marshall liked playing the game of *fuck you* with anyone who came onto his base. But this...this took it into deadly territory. In his ten years wearing the beret, Sharp had never seen anything like it.

There was always someone, usually an old-school officer, who pushed back when Special Forces came in to tell them how to handle their locals, how to train them and have everyone get along.

That was the problem with regular army. They wanted things done their way. Period.

Green Berets went in a different direction. They often operated from the inside of another nation's military, trained them to use their own skills, weapons or hell, even their geography as a tool in their arsenal to keep the peace and uphold the law of the land.

Marshall had gone insane.

"Hey, boss." Hernandez yelled it loud enough that everyone heard.

Sharp looked at him, then the other men in the bird. "I'm not the boss." He jerked a thumb at Grace. "She is."

"Understood, but Cutter's dead and Leonard isn't here. We need a team lead. That's you."

Sharp glanced at the other men. Smoke, Runnel and

Clark both had their thumbs up. So did March. Beside him, Grace too.

Fuck, one more thing he didn't need today, but Hernandez was right, they needed someone to give the final word.

He threw his hands up in the air, surrendering to their unanimous vote.

"So, what's up?" Hernandez said. "Whatever the doc said gave you the worst case of indigestion I've ever seen."

"Things have gone from worse to completely fucked," he yelled so everyone would hear. "The two soldiers who were guarding the doc at the base are dead. We've been accused of murdering them when we broke her out."

"And people believe that shit?" Runnel asked.

"They've got two bodies and we're not around to say different, so yeah, people believe it."

"My CO is working on getting the truth out there," Grace added, shouting. "But Marshall's actions are above and beyond anything sane. We're currently under an arrest-on-sight order."

"You're just telling us this now?" Sharp asked. He couldn't believe she hadn't mentioned it. What was she waiting for, the bullets to fly?

"Sorry, I just remembered."

That's when he saw it. The lines bracketing her eyes, the white line of lips pressed too tightly together and the paleness of her skin. She was holding it together, but only just.

He remembered seeing that expression on his mother's face, right before she died. Stress was an illness for which the patient had to want the cure. His mom had been a nurse and the most generous and giving woman he'd ever met.

Her generosity led to her death of a stroke at forty.

High blood pressure had been blamed, but he knew the real cause. She'd worked herself to death. Wore herself out caring for other people, most of whom never thought about her again after they left the hospital.

Yeah, Grace was a doctor, was used to seeing the uglier side of life, but what she'd been through in the last few days was something else. This was combat, physical and psychological, and at least one of the perpetrators of the violence was someone she should have been able to trust with her safety.

They didn't teach doctors how to deal with that in medical school. Nope, for that you needed to go through Special Forces Training.

"Well, we're not dead yet and we're still in the air, so..." He shrugged. "Next time tell me...us, sooner."

"I should have told you immediately." She punched her thigh with a shaking fist. "But I...I'm tired and if one more thing happens I feel like I'm going to fall apart." The half smile she showed him looked forced. "I probably shouldn't tell you that, but you need to know."

"Doc," he said, nudging her with one shoulder. "Sometimes the only reason I remember my name is because Hernandez yells it at me so often."

An angry furrow dug its way between her eyes. "Don't pity me."

He laughed. "Pity is the last thing I think of where you're concerned. Geez, Doc, you survived a helicopter crash, shot a bunch of insurgents and saved my life. You kept up with me when we went to ground, saved me again and if that wasn't enough, kept your shit together while being accused of God knows what by a tyrannical asshole. I'd say you've damn near earned your Green Beret."

She stared at him for a moment, as if unsure of his sincerity, then rolled her eyes. "Make sure you tell Max. Maybe I'll get a raise."

He chuckled and said, "It's going to take some time for us to get to Cutter's friend. Grab some sleep while you can." He tapped his shoulder as an invitation to her to lean her head on him.

He couldn't hold her, not with others watching, but he could do this much.

"If things don't get cleared up in less than six hours, Max is going to come to us with a mobile lab capable of handling anthrax."

"Okay, that might work. If it doesn't, we'll figure it out. Go to sleep."

"What about you?"

"I'm going to keep watch, but Hernandez, Runnel and March are heading toward dreamland." He angled his chin toward his teammates, who had put their heads back.

She looked at them, then nodded. "Okay. Wake me when we get...wherever." She leaned against him, the top of her head reaching just over his shoulder.

She was such a tiny thing, hard to believe she'd kept up with him the way she did. Damn, if that didn't make him hotter for her than ever.

Her breathing evened out within a minute or two. She was wiped out.

He glanced up and caught Hernandez grinning at him. Then the bastard winked. Sharp flipped him the finger. Hernandez closed his eyes and let his head fall back.

He'd better not tease Grace. He'd have a chat with his team first chance and tell them not to make her feel uncomfortable. He didn't give a shit if they gave him a hard time, but she wasn't him. In order for her to come out of this disaster with her career intact, she needed to have a spotless reputation.

That much, he'd try to give her.

Cutter's journal rested next to him. He picked it up and began reading through it, attempting to locate any information that might be useful in their current situation.

Cutter had a lot of training notes, names and descriptions of Afghans who he felt were safe to approach for information and a few hand-drawn maps of different areas of the country. Areas that didn't have much in the way of official maps.

Sharp went back to the info on Cutter's CIA friend. The guy was an American, the son of Afghanis who'd immigrated to the States fifteen years ago. He spoke three languages without accent, had a degree in power engineering and a journeyman's ticket in automobile mechanics. He'd been in Afghanistan for the last three years, running a sort of general store and fix-it shop in an abandoned military base the Soviets used in the northern part of the country.

He traded in information, supplies and repairs. The Taliban left him alone because he could get almost anything from anywhere and he fixed up their cars. The CIA used him for information and occasionally a place to hide people they didn't want anyone to find.

Cutter had gone to university with him and graduated in the same class. On Cutter's first deployment, he'd saved his CIA buddy's life. Sharp just hoped the guy had aviation fuel in that store of his.

Then he found the notes on Marshall. There was a question mark near the name Joseph Cranston. Who was that? Then he got to the interesting part.

Cranston was credited with saving Grace's life in the same incident where she earned her Bronze Star, but there was also a sealed note on Cranston's record. Cutter hadn't been able to access it. Most of the time, when a portion of a record was sealed, it was bad news. What had happened that day?

He went back to reread the info about Cutter's friend. Going there was a risk. There wasn't anyone to support them if any unfriendlies were around. Unfortunately, going anywhere else was even more hazardous thanks to Marshall's bullshit story about them murdering fellow soldiers.

They'd just have to stay alert and keep Grace out of sight as much as possible.

Fuck. She wasn't going to like that.

Clark waved at him from the copilot's seat, so Sharp put the headset on.

"We're five minutes out," he said.

"Roger." He used one foot to nudge Hernandez. He woke up and Sharp pointed at his watch then five fingers. Hernandez kicked March and Runnel, and gave them the same message.

Sharp put a hand on Grace's shoulder and gave her a gentle shake. She woke with a start, but recovered quickly enough, blinking at him with her big blue eyes. She glanced around, then gave him a weak smile.

"Are we there?" she asked, not loud enough to be heard over the engine, but he could read her lips just fine.

"Almost. I want everyone alert."

She nodded, straightened up and yelled out, "I need a weapon."

She did.

He caught March's eye and shouted, "Find her a weapon."

March got up and opened the rear storage unit. He came back with a Beretta and two additional magazines of ammo for it.

She took them with a grim expression and steady hands. As tired as she had to be, she was holding herself together and he was so fucking *proud* of her.

"What else is in there?" Sharp asked March.

"A couple more Berettas and one more clip." He glanced at Grace, who was loading her weapon. "There's also a couple of first-aid kits and some MREs."

"Give that stuff to Grace."

Clark nodded and went back to the unit. He returned with his arms full and placed it all on Grace's lap. He made one more trip to the storage unit and handed her a backpack.

She looked at it for a second, then turned to Sharp and yelled, "Is this how you plan to keep me out of sight? Hide me behind a backpack?"

"Got a better idea?"

She hesitated for a moment and he could almost see the gears turning in her head. "Unfortunately, no." She opened the pack and dumped everything inside.

Sharp glanced out and saw that they were losing altitude near a group of buildings nestled in some rough and tumble hills. He turned back to Grace. "Keep your head down and don't say anything unless I tell you it's safe. If this guy isn't alone or I don't like the looks of him, we may have to leave in a hurry and I don't want anyone trying to grab you. Okay?"

She raised her chin and nodded. Goddamn, she was trying so hard to be brave, to hold herself together, but her sunken eyes and stressed mouth told him she needed a whole lot more sleep, food and safety before it was anything more than an act.

Sharp looked at his team and knew they'd do everything they could to help him provide all that and get her where she needed to go. He shouted, "Eyes open. Stay frosty."

They all nodded.

As the helicopter descended, Sharp took in as much of the surroundings as possible. There were a couple dozen buildings, some were missing a roof or walls, others looked like they could be useable. A number of vehicles were strewn around, some nothing more than rusted hulks, while others looked like they were running, all of them decorated in various amounts of dirt and rust.

Three people stood in the shade crated by an overhang of a large building set into a hill. One man and two teenage boys, it looked like from their heights and builds. All three had Soviet-made rifles in their hands.

The wind and dirt the helicopter kicked up didn't seem to bother them as they set down to one side of the building.

Sharp got out first, alone, then approached the man. Behind him, Smoke kept the engine on just in case they had to take off in a hurry. Not that it would do them much good. They were nearly out of fuel.

Sharp stopped about ten feet away from the man and gave him a respectful nod. "I'm looking for someone," he said in Dari.

The man didn't say anything.

"A friend of a friend."

Finally the man said, "Who is this friend?"

"Cutter, Geoffry Cutter."

The man's expression didn't change. "I don't know any Cutter."

Sharp held up the journal with its hand-drawn cover. "Are you sure?"

The man frowned at him, then glanced at the helicopter. He met Sharp's gaze again. "Come inside. Bring your people." He turned and yelled at the two teens in Dari, telling them to cover up the bird, then bring fresh water for coffee.

They ran off to one of the other buildings.

Sharp turned so he could see both the man waiting for him and the helicopter. He waved at them and Smoke cut the engine.

They got out of the machine, the Berets casually keeping Grace in the middle of their formation. Grace had the smarts to do as he ordered and carried the pack in front of her like a shield, hiding her figure and part of her face from sight.

The man waved at them. "Come in out of the sun." He disappeared into the building.

Sharp nodded at the team, then led the way. He took his time, looking around, making note of the piles of parts for cars, trucks and tanks. Mostly Soviet.

Inside the building looked like a cross between a set from *Lawrence of Arabia* and someone's living room. There were several couches arranged in a rough circle around a large hookah. Next to that was a small, clay cooking stove with a coffeepot sitting on the ground next to it. The man had taken a seat on one of the couches around the hookah. He reclined, seeming at ease, and asked in English, "Where did you get that book?"

Sharp took a seat on an adjacent couch, put his rifle butt down on the rough wooden floor and let out a sigh. "From Cutter."

The man tilted his head to one side. "I thought you said you were looking for Cutter?"

"I lied. He's in the helicopter."

The man stared at Sharp, his gaze hard and unrelenting. "Why isn't he here with us?"

"Because he's dead."

"His body is in the helicopter?" The question was asked with an edge sharp enough to flay skin off bone. "How did he die?"

"Friendly fire." Sharp didn't want to explain further, but was prepared to give what information he could.

The man was on his feet, out the front door and yelling in Dari to the two teens who were still outside, to get their asses back. He turned to Sharp. "You will have his body brought here. Now."

Sharp nodded at Hernandez, who went out with Clark. Smoke, Runnel and March stayed right where they were next to Grace. She was standing a couple of feet away from the odd collection of seating around the hookah.

The man marched up to Sharp and demanded, "Explain his death to me."

Like that was going to happen. "Are you his friend from university?"

"Why should I tell you anything?"

"Because he was my commander *and* my friend," Sharp snarled, taking a step toward the other man. "And the only way I can be sure the man responsible is going to pay is with help."

"Who's responsible?"

Sharp shook his head. "I'm not one hundred percent sure, but so far Colonel Marshall, FOB Bostick, is on the top of my suspect list."

The man's eyes narrowed. "Who are you?"

"We're—"

"No. You. Who are *you*?"

"I'm..." About to say his name, he realized the guy wasn't looking for that either. He wanted to know who Sharp was to Cutter. "...a sniper. Everyone calls me Sharp."

The man rocked back on his feet. He looked at Smoke, who stared at him with his pale blue eyes, in a face carrying the strong bones of his Navajo ancestors.

Hernandez and Clark came in with Cutter's body and laid it carefully on the floor.

The man studied them carefully, then moved on to Grace.

As soon as the CIA's gaze landed on her, Sharp asked, "You know of us, yes?"

The man pulled his gaze off Grace a little too slowly for Sharp's piece of mind. "Most of you, yes. Who is this?" He pointed at Grace.

Sharp went with the truth. "New team member."

The man narrowed his eyes, then nodded. "My name is Aaron Jamal and Cutter is...was one of my best friends."

"I didn't know CIA agents had friends," Hernandez said.

Jamal glanced at the body on the floor. "Well, I have one less." He looked at Sharp. "Can we speak plainly now? What do you want?"

"Aviation fuel."

"For your helicopter?" Jamal shook his head. "Impossible."

SIXTEEN

GRACE PEEKED OVER the top of the backpack at Sharp's unhappy expression. He was either going to argue with Cutter's friend or he was going to force the issue. Neither was going to improve their situation.

She must have made a noise because both men turned to look at her, but before anyone could say anything the two teen boys came back in with a bucket full of water and a radio squawking with a man's voice in Dari.

Everyone in the room besides her must speak the language because they all froze, then tensed.

Cutter's friend glared at Sharp, then yelled at the two teens, gesturing with his hands at them.

They rushed out again.

"Thank you," Sharp said to him.

"I'm not doing it for you," Jamal said.

Doing what? Grace could only watch the faces of the men around her for a clue as to what was going on. None of it looked good.

"I'm doing it to save my own skin and the skin of the people living here." Jamal glared at everyone, but seemed to stare a little longer at her. "What trouble have you brought with you?"

"Fuel us up and we're out of here," Sharp suggested softly. "The danger's gone."

"It's not that easy," Jamal said, pacing away. "Aviation fuel is hard to get. I don't have a lot and what I do have is spoken for." He turned and paced back toward Sharp. He stopped suddenly and pointed at her. "Who or what is that?"

"A team member."

"I've never met a Green Beret who hid behind a bag."

Yeah, hiding behind a backpack never was much of plan. She sighed, leaned over and put it on the floor.

Sharp's gaze jerked in her direction. His eyes narrow and jaw clenched, he shook his head, but it was already too late.

Jamal stared at her like he couldn't believe his eyes. If she thought he looked angry before, he looked furious now.

Wonderful, Sharp looked ready to strangle her, and the only person who could help them was about to shout and call names and probably order them to leave.

But they still needed his help.

"I'm a doctor," she said calmly, pulling the cloak of her profession around her, letting it straighten her back and lift her chin. "An infectious disease specialist."

At her words, Jamal paused, confusion joining the anger on his face. She could almost see the thoughts playing through his head. "What is that to me?"

"A great deal."

"Grace," Sharp growled. He took a step toward her.

"He needs to know," she argued softly. "He might even be able to give us good advice regarding our next steps."

"What is it you think I need to know?" Jamal asked crossing his arms over his chest.

Grace glanced at Sharp, and though his nostrils flared and he grit his teeth, he nodded once.

"Approximately two days ago," Grace began, "someone released weaponized anthrax on a small village near the Afghan/Pakistan border. Everyone, *every single person* in that village was dead less than a day later."

Jamal's jaw dropped open.

"The strain kills incredibly quickly, like nothing I've ever seen. This was not an accident. Someone designed, weaponized and tested this strain for a purpose." She paused for a moment. "That someone has managed to sabotage our efforts to get this strain to a lab where it can be properly identified and a treatment plan created."

"What?" Jamal's hands fluttered about aimlessly. "Why are you *here*? I don't understand how I—"

She held up the sample container. "We need fuel to leave, or a safe place to hide."

Jamal stared at the package like she was holding an armed nuclear bomb. "A...a bounty has been placed on all of you," he stuttered. "One million American dollars. You can't stay here." He backed away, closer to Sharp. "The boys have covered your aircraft with tarps, but this compound is frequented by several different parties. Some of them hostile to Americans." He swallowed hard, still staring at Grace like she was the grim reaper. "I would give you the fuel, but it's been paid for and the people who bought it are not ones to cross." He stared at his feet for a moment. "I can hide you, at least for the time being."

"Thank you," Sharp said in a tone so devoid of emotion, she knew he was furious.

"Wait here." Jamal scurried out, casting frightened looks over his shoulder.

"What?" Grace asked the guys. "Do I glow in the dark or something now?"

"Nah," Hernandez said. "You looked pretty serious and tough telling him all that stuff, though."

"His advice sucked," Clark said. "He didn't give us any new ideas. I thought dudes in his line of work were good at that."

"I doubt he's had a container full of a deadly organism displayed in his..." Grace glanced around the building. "Store before."

"You did cut through the normal bullshit in record time," Sharp said. "Maybe I should let you do all the talking from now on." The words should have sounded complimentary, but his tone hadn't changed.

She was so tired of male bullshit. "He needed to know," she told him though gritted teeth. "How can we expect him to help us if we don't share all the information?"

"I didn't stop you, did I?"

"No, but you sure didn't like it and you made that very clear." She wished she could wipe the intractable expression off his face. "There's protective and then there's getting in the way of me doing my job."

His brows rose.

Jamal came back inside, a cell phone at his ear. He nodded as he listened, then hung up without saying a word. "I've received instructions to hide you. The doctor and the container are not to leave this compound."

Sharp pointed at the sample container. "We have to get that stuff to a lab."

"The lab, with military support, is coming here, but..." He held up a hand. "I have to keep you completely out of sight. There are too many people looking for you. At least five different groups are hunting you now and all of them want what she's carrying."

"So maybe we should keep on the move," Hernandez suggested.

"No, you don't understand. These are dangerous men, insurgents, extremists and even terrorists from all over this part of the world. They want the container...and the doctor."

Someone swore, Grace wasn't sure who.

No, oh no. She wouldn't last long in the hands of any the men Jamal described. She'd rather die.

"If you run, they will force you to land, then they will kill you, and take the doctor and the anthrax," Jamal continued. "Your only hope is to hide."

"What about the helicopter?" Hernandez asked. "It's too big to hide."

"I'm going to say you landed and took one of my trucks in exchange for the helicopter."

"Finally," Clark said. "Some useful advice."

"That's not a bad idea, taking a truck," Runnel said. "Maybe we should do that?"

Sharp shook his head. "We'd be an easy target on the ground." He turned to Jamal. "But if we're going to hide, it needs to be a really good place."

"Yes, yes, I have the perfect spot." He rushed to the other side of the building, calling, "Come, come."

Hernandez took point while everyone else followed with Sharp covering their rear. Grace glanced at him with a questioning look.

His answer was a shrug, but the lingering traces of anger on his face told her he'd have a few not-fun words to say to her as soon as there were fewer ears to listen in.

Yes, she'd tipped their hand to Jamal before he was ready, but things were moving so fast, there wasn't time for all the normal testosterone-fueled male posturing.

Jamal brought them to the back wall of the building and cleared away several piles of parts, plumbing, electronics and other stuff until he revealed a wood floor. He pulled up one end to reveal a set of steep stairs. "A bunker," he said.

"Is this the only way in?" Sharp asked.

"No there's another exit some distance away from the compound on the other side of these hills. It overlooks a deep ravine and is meant as an escape for me if things go very bad."

Hernandez snorted as he went down the stairs and into the darkness. "Yeah, I suppose we qualify as very bad."

Grace moved to follow him, but Sharp held her back. After a few seconds, Hernandez called out, "All clear."

Sharp took his hand off her shoulder and she descended into the dark.

At first she couldn't see much, but as her eyes adjusted to the lack of light, after a few seconds she was able to make out the shape of the walls and floor. The tunnel was surprisingly roomy, and she could almost stand up in it. The Berets were all going to have to bend over, but at least no one had to crawl. It went forward for some distance and had a variety of odds and ends lining the walls. Pieces of wood, tools, and even weapons.

She followed Hernandez with Clark and Smoke right behind her. Clark touched her shoulder and moved past her to take the position behind Hernandez. About a minute of walking later, both men stopped and picked something up off the ground. She craned her neck around them to see what had caught their attention.

A tidy pile of grenades.

"Are you two paying cash for those or putting it on credit?" she asked.

"What are you talking about, Doc?" Hernandez asked. "We just gave that guy a helicopter. We've got plenty of credit."

"Shut the fuck up." Sharp's voice floated past them and the guys got moving again.

Behind them, there were a couple of bangs as the cover to the entrance was put back in place and the tunnel got much darker. The men wearing helmets turned on their lights.

No one said anything for a long time as they kept moving through the tunnel. Grace found herself getting drowsy, the lack of sleep catching up to her in a big way. She blinked her eyes to keep them open, but she was afraid that as soon as they came to a stop she was going to want to crash.

She stumbled and Smoke put his hand under her arm to help her up. "Doc?"

It was amazing to her how much the man could ask with one word. "I'm okay, just really, *really* tired."

Ahead of her Hernandez and Clark had stopped moving and were looking at her with concern on their faces.

"Doc," Smoke said. "You can sleep soon."

"Sounds good." She smiled at Smoke and patted him on the hand holding her up. When Hernandez and Clark advanced down the tunnel again, she followed, putting her hands on the walls to help keep herself from tripping.

After another five minutes or so, light filtered its way into the tunnel from somewhere up ahead. The men in front of her suddenly stopped and crouched down on the floor, with Clark holding up a closed fist.

She knelt before anyone had to tell her to and waited

while the men traded more hand signals back and forth. After a moment a decision seemed to have been made, as Smoke slipped past her and Clark.

Sharp came up behind her and whispered in that oddly dead tone that didn't carry more than a couple of inches in her ear. "The tunnel ends not far ahead. They're checking to make sure it's clear."

She nodded.

And waited.

Finally, Clark got out of his crouch and waved at her, March, Runnel and Sharp. They walked slowly into an open room that had probably started as a cave, but had been enlarged and shaped by man. Some of the walls had stones laid in them, forming benches and shelves, along with alcoves for storage. Near the far end of the room was a well. The light came from past it, filtered as if it had to travel through an obstacle course.

Hernandez came toward them from beyond the well. "The exit is camouflaged, but useable."

"Camouflaged as what?" Sharp asked.

"A garbage dump."

Grace's tired mind could hardly string two thoughts together, but hiding in a dump seemed oddly appropriate. "Sounds like home to me," she said plunking herself down on one of the stone benches.

"Anyone around?" Sharp asked.

"Nope. We're outside of the compound and the exit opens out onto a steep slope. It's covered by lots of old timber, rusted metal car parts, scrub brush and debris the wind has deposited. Nothing useable."

"Does it look like it's been disturbed recently?"

"No. I'd say we're good in here, for now at least."

"Did you find a bathroom out there?" Grace asked.

Hernandez grinned at her. "Yep, it's a little old-fashioned, ah...I don't think there's any toilet paper, but—" he angled his thumb over his shoulder "—head left before the exit."

"The doc and I need to rest," Sharp said, his voice tired. "You guys set up rotating watches, one for each entrance."

"You got it, boss." The men broke up into two groups, Smoke, Runnel and Clark hunkered down while Hernandez went back down the dark tunnel toward the compound and March moved to keep watch on the garbage dump exit.

Sharp knelt down next to her and she had to refrain from asking to use him as a warm blanket. "Time to crash, Doc. Keep all your gear on in case we have to leave in a hurry."

"I need to use the little girl's room."

"Okay, just be careful and quiet."

Like she didn't know that.

Grace got to her feet, leaving the sample container where it was resting on the stone bench, and walked past the well, looking for this rustic bathroom.

It was a hole in the dirt floor.

She stared at the urine and fecal stains all around the hole and swallowed a mouthful of bile.

This obviously wasn't the ladies' room.

She pulled a biodegradable tissue from one of the pockets on her pants legs, pulled down her pants and squatted over the hole. As she pulled her pants up, she caught herself falling forward.

Get yourself horizontal.

Grace pulled up her pants and stumbled her way back to where she'd left her pack and sample container. Sharp was sitting next to her stuff, drinking some water. He held out the bottle and she swallowed three times.

"I have to sleep now," she mumbled to him as she handed the water back and crawled a few more inches to collapse on the floor.

"Not there, Doc." Sharp's hands slipped under her shoulders and pulled her forward. God, they felt good. Too bad they weren't alone. "How about here?" He let her collapse on the ground, only it wasn't as hard as it should be. It was lumpy and...

SEVENTEEN

SHARP WATCHED SLEEP take Grace between one second and the next.

"She's out?" Runnel asked from where he sat a few feet away.

"Yep, like a switch."

"Cool," Clark said. A couple seconds later he asked, "What the fuck are we gonna do now?"

"Option one," Sharp said, sitting on the stone bench next to Grace. He leaned forward to rest his elbows on his knees. "We wait here for the situation to be cleared by a higher authority and head back to Bostick. Two, we wait here for the doc's boss, Max, to come to us with more gear. Three, we split up, draw attention away from the doc, so she can get the samples to Max."

"I don't like the idea of leaving her without protection," Clark said. "Splitting up might work for a little while, but once it's out that she's not with us..." He shook his head. "She'd be even more vulnerable."

"Together we're a larger target," Smoke added.

Sharp frowned. "Those samples need to be processed. Whoever created this bug could use it anywhere on anyone. That's our number-one priority."

"This mission has been fucked up since go," Runnel said in his deep drawl. "Too many coincidences."

"That's been worrying me too," Sharp said. "I wonder if our helicopter getting shot down was more than just a lucky shot."

"A traitor?" Clark asked.

"Or an infiltrator maybe."

"Marshall?"

"No, he's got a history with Grace. But maybe someone who knows that history took advantage of it to create confusion and conflict to keep everyone from dealing with the big problem."

"Anthrax." Smoke sounded like the voice of doom.

"I think the picture is a lot bigger than anyone knows."

No one said anything for a couple of minutes. Sharp gave them a chance to think on things. He wasn't Cutter, and he wasn't going to make decisions that could get them killed all by himself.

"The doc is stubborn," Clark said. "She's going to keep the pressure on. It'll make her an even bigger target."

Sharp nodded. "As soon as she was ordered to investigate the deaths at the village, she became a primary target of whoever wants to use the anthrax as a weapon."

"I vote option two, boss," Clark said. "I don't trust Marshall to not fuck this up even more."

Sharp looked at Smoke, who nodded, and Runnel, who grinned.

"Hernandez and March will be on board," Clark said.

"Give them the heads-up," Sharp instructed. Clark and Runnel split up to carry out his order.

"Smoke, go talk to our CIA friend, find out how he plans to deal with our incoming visitors."

Smoke nodded and got to his feet.

"I'm grabbing a few minutes of sleep," Sharp said.

Smoke smiled and headed back into the tunnel.

Sharp rubbed his eyes and glanced at Grace. She was snoring softly and looked so damn peaceful and cute that, had they been alone, he would have curled up on the floor with her. His hands itched to hold her, to feel her softness, to capture a piece of home.

But they weren't alone and he couldn't afford to have the team question his objectivity. If they knew how deep his need to protect her ran, they'd question it now.

He moved to sit next to her on the floor of the cave, leaned his head back and closed his eyes. One of the tricks all Special Forces soldiers learned was how to put themselves asleep in a few seconds, in order to take short naps whenever needed. This allowed them to stay awake without a long period of sleep, for up to several days at a time.

He sank into the breathing pattern that would trigger sleep.

"SHARP."

He jolted awake at the sound of his name.

Smoke crouched in front of him and their CIA friend, Jamal, stood a few feet behind with Clark. But it was the item in Smoke's hand that caught his attention. A satellite phone. He glanced at Grace, but she was still out cold.

Sharp took the phone and stood, waving at the men to back away from the sleeping doctor.

Everyone moved until they were just inside the tunnel.

"Got any intel for us?" Sharp asked Jamal.

"Too much," he said, his tone sardonic. "*Everyone* is looking for you and your doctor. I've had two armed groups of extremists come through my compound already. I told them the story you made up about the helicopter, but I think they're suspicious. The arrival of more Americans will attract even more attention. Dangerous attention."

"How long until nightfall?"

"Three or four hours until full dark."

"Okay. I'll see if I can work some magic."

"I have to go watch the store," Jamal said. "Stay quiet." He headed back through the tunnel.

Sharp went to where Grace was sleeping and shook her until she complained. "Bug off," she said, her eyes still closed.

Sharp ruthlessly controlled the spike of need her grumpy complaint shot through him. *Fuck, he had it bad.* "Grace, do you have a personal cell phone number for Max?"

She lifted her head an inch, squinted at him and gave him the number. "Can I go back to sleep now?"

"Yep."

Her head dropped and her snoring purr resumed as if it hadn't been interrupted at all.

The ease of it hit him between the eyes.

Trust. The level of trust it took for her to sleep now, in the middle of a life-or-death situation, with only a word from him humbled the shit out of him. It was going to kill him to go back to life at a base, where he couldn't touch her and had to pretend his feelings didn't exist.

Fuck, he needed to sleep some more or he'd be crying on Runnel's shoulder. Ick.

Sharp sat down a few feet away and punched in the number.

A cautious male voice answered, "Hello."

"Hey, Max," Sharp said keeping his tone light, almost cheerful. "This is Grace's friend Sharp. Can you talk?"

A couple of seconds of silence passed before Max replied, "Just a moment."

The sound of someone walking and a door closing. "How is she?" Max asked in a quiet tone.

"Sleeping. She's good."

"I have transport arranged," Max explained. "I'll be flying by helicopter to a spot in Iraq, then transferring to a truck so I shouldn't raise too many eyebrows."

Sharp stomped on disappointment. "Alone?"

"No, I have another A-Team coming in with me."

"Okay, that will help. How soon can you get here?"

"An hour or two after dusk." He paused for a moment. "I've argued with Marshall to the point where he won't take my calls. At the moment his orders are to arrest you on sight. General Stone is coming from Germany to take over the situation, and I've talked to him at length regarding this entire fuckup. He wants to get to the bottom of all this and has countermanded Marshall's orders, but there seems to be a communication problem. Stone's orders haven't been passed along to everyone."

"Figures. Nothing has gone right since the anthrax attack."

"Be ready for my arrival, and Sharp?"

"Yeah?"

"Take good care of Grace. She's one of my best doctors and a good friend."

Something in Max's tone told him there was more to the story. "Any special reason for that request?"

"Things have not been easy for her since she won the Star," Max said.

"How bad is it?"

"I don't know. See you soon."

Max hung up.

Sharp walked around to talk to each of his men, letting them know the plan and the timetable. Hopefully lying low would get them out of this ridiculous situation without any more trouble.

Like his grandma always said, plan for the worst, hope for the best.

At best they all got out with no one getting killed or going to jail.

At worst, they all died, and there were way too many possibilities in between. He went back to where Grace was sleeping and put his head back for another power nap. No telling when he'd sleep next.

GRACE WOKE FEELING like she'd been run over by a herd of cows. Every muscle group she had ached. Even the insides of her eyelids. She lifted her head and turned to see what was going on.

Sharp was seated a couple of feet away, his head back and eyes closed. His breathing was deep and slow.

Behind her, she caught movement out of the corner of her eye.

Smoke, Runnel and Clark sat on the ground in the center of the cavern. At the moment, they were watching her, but it was obvious by how they situated themselves that they were watching the entire space.

Clark caught her gaze and put sleepy hands by his head, then he pointed at her and nodded.

She dearly wished she could follow his suggestion and get some more rest, but her head was too full of the danger they were in, the problems they were facing and the stacked odds against them.

Her stomach growled. Loud enough that all three men heard it.

Runnel laughed silently, and Clark threw up his hands and motioned her to come over. Smoke just smiled, his white teeth bright against the backdrop of his tanned face and scraggly beard.

Grace pushed herself up onto her hands and knees and crawled over to the three soldiers. They were all grinning at her.

"Stuff it," she whispered to them.

That just made them laugh. Even silent Smoke. He held out a bottle of water to her and she plopped herself on the ground so she could take it.

Warm water had never tasted so good.

Clark handed her a MRE, which she devoured. The three men watched her like they'd never seen anyone eat before.

"I haven't eaten a meal in..." She had to think about it. "Days."

"You still haven't," Runnel said.

Grace rolled her eyes at him. "Funny." She finished eating without any further commentary from the guys and drank some more water before looking at them, hoping for an update on their situation.

"You should get some more sleep, Doc," Clark told her. "We might be busy in a few hours."

Well, that was unhelpful.

The anthrax samples sat only feet away.

They'd been accused of murder and their commander had been murdered.

On top of all of that, a despot masquerading as an army officer was trying to find a way to punish her for something she couldn't have prevented.

Would he stop if she told him she punished herself daily for it?

Sleep. Ha. She snorted softly. "I've got so much adrenaline in my system right now I could power a small town. What's the poop?"

"Poop?" Clark asked, as if he'd never heard the word.

"You know, the latest, the situation, the status, the sticky wicket, the—"

"Stop," Smoke said, holding up his palm and shaking his head. He transferred his gaze from her face to Clark's. "Give her the *poop*."

Clark struggled not to laugh. Runnel looked like he was going to bust something if he didn't let out his laughter.

She gave them a look. "You need to get out more, with, you know, people who don't swear all the time."

"Doc," Runnel said, unable to keep the grin off his face. "Those people are a long way from here."

"I realize that, but think of them once in a while, please."

"Yes, ma'am. The poop is, we're waiting for *your* Max to get here."

Was she hearing attitude?

"He's not *my* Max. He's my boss and a good friend."

"Whatever." Clark shrugged, and didn't look the least bit sorry. "Sharp talked to him while you were out cold. He's coming with another A-Team, all disguised as extremists."

"That's not a bad idea."

"Yeah." Clark gave her a sidelong glance. "You planning on playing with that bug in here?"

She looked around the cave. "Since this place is mostly underground, the temperature is moderate. We're protected from wind and any odd idiots who might get curious and want to investigate what we're doing." There was enough space, even with another dozen men, as long as they made an effort to stay out of the way.

"Odd idiots?" Clark asked, laughing again.

"You know what I mean."

"The sad thing is, I do know what you mean. And you're right, there are no eyes on us in here."

She glanced around the cave again, trying to pick out the best area to set up the mobile lab. The stone benches along the wall where Sharp was sleeping were probably best. They would need to move some stuff around.

"Uh-oh," Clark said to Smoke. "I know that look on her face. It's the one that says we're going to be moving furniture."

When she turned to give the two men a piece of her mind, Smoke pointed at Clark and said, "Odd idiot."

Clark looked at his friend sourly. "Thanks, man."

"What's with all the noise?"

Sharp's voice brought Grace's head around. "I'm sorry, I thought we were being quiet enough."

He glanced at his watch, then at her with a frown. "You should still be sleeping."

"I've got too many thoughts racing around in my head."

"Grace," he said, his voice heavy with disapproval. "You won't be good for anything if you don't get more sleep."

"I had a great cat nap." She stood and put her hands on her hips. "When I was doing my residency I had to work thirty-six hour shifts. I know what my limits are." She grabbed her pack and pulled out the medical supplies. "Speaking of limits, I'd like to examine your various wounds to make sure none of them reopened over the last few hours."

Sharp watched her face for a couple seconds more before he stood. He grinned and started unbuckling his pants.

Clark, Runnel and Smoke got up at the same time.

"We're going to relieve Hernandez and March," Clark told Sharp, waving his hand around in Sharp's general direction. "And, uh, give you some time to do that."

Clark and Smoke split up, one going to the tunnel, the other out toward the hillside exit. Runnel nodded at them. "Yeah, so, I'm going weapons shopping in the grenade aisle."

She watched them all but run away. "That's not necessary." But they were gone. She turned back to Sharp and asked, "What do they think we're going to do, have sex?"

Sharp shrugged. "Probably."

EIGHTEEN

"They know you've been shot a couple of times, right?" Grace asked with a touch of disbelief as she grabbed her pack and began pulling out fresh bandages.

Sharp snorted. "Like that would stop me."

"Excuse me?" Grace froze and stared at him with her eyes wide.

He gave her a mischievous grin. "For you, two measly bullet wounds are nothing."

"Be serious," she said, sounding impatient. Like every irritated woman talking to a man she was comfortable with. "A rumor like that could ruin both our careers."

Except, her hands were shaking.

"Grace—" he began.

"Sharp," she interrupted. "Take your goddamn pants off."

Her hands might be shaking, but her voice was rock solid.

"Yes, ma'am." He shucked his pants, got on the ground, stretched out his legs and reclined on his elbows so he could watch.

She looked him over, starting from the pants wrapped around his ankles to his face. Whatever she saw there made her shake her head. "You're such a guy." She grabbed a pair of gloves, snapped them on and went after the bandages over his latest wound. "How does this one feel?"

"Okay. No worse than before."

She peeled the last layer off and leaned forward to get a better look. Dirt streaked her face, her short hair was messy and there was blood splattered all over her uniform.

He had never seen a more beautiful woman. Ever.

What kind of degenerate moron gets a hard-on in this crummy situation?

Him, obviously.

She poked at the wound and made a happy noise at the back of her throat. A little antibiotic ointment smeared over the stitches, new nonstick pads and more bandages secured it all to his leg.

She switched to the wound on his thigh, leaning over him further in order to reach, and he had to force himself not to grab her and pull her across his lap.

Her hands brushed the skin of his inner thigh as she took the bandage off and he nearly came in his underwear.

Once the bandage was off, she removed the pads and pushed his leg up, so she could see, and prod, both entry and exit wounds.

"How bad is the pain?" she asked, her hands handling him with confident care. No hesitation, just the competence only experience and knowledge gives a person.

Fuck, that was hot.

He let his head fall back and said, "I'm going to hell."

"What?"

He brought his head up and let her see the need on his face. The kind a man never gets over, never lets go.

She glanced at the erection the size of a canoe in his underwear, rolled her eyes and said, "Put that thing away before someone sees it."

Sharp had to choke down a belly laugh that would have alerted anyone within a mile of where they were. It shook his body so hard tears leaked out of his eyes and he collapsed on the ground.

"Goddamn, Doc, I love your mouth," he managed to wheeze out.

When she looked at him like he was the dirty-minded man he was, he added, "But I love your brain even more."

"Stop with the sucking up," she said as she gave his thigh the same TLC as his other leg, then wrapped it all up with another bandage. Again, she seemed fine, until you looked at her mouth and the white lines of strain around it.

Great job, dickhead. Was he determined to fuck everything up today?

He wiped the stupid grin off his face. "I'm sorry."

She glanced at him as she collected all the dirty bandages and moved back so he could pull up his pants. "Okay."

The word sounded forced to him, and she headed toward the hillside exit a little too fast. If he'd thought he'd gotten himself out of the doghouse with that sorry excuse for an apology he was wrong.

"Shit," he said, jumping as he tried to get his pants over his butt. "Grace, wait."

She paused, but only for a second.

"Grace." He finally wrestled his fatigues up and leaped forward to catch her arm in a careful grip. "I really am. Sorry, I mean."

Her blank face didn't change.

"Fuck, I'm no good at this touchy-feely stuff." He ran a hand over his face. "I shouldn't have acted like a sailor who hasn't seen port in months. I'm such an asshole to even think that shit. How can I make things right between us?"

Her shoulders relaxed and she blinked fast a few times, like she was trying not to cry. "You just did it."

"What are you apologizing for?" a voice said from behind Sharp.

Hernandez. Just what he needed, a peanut gallery. Not.

Sharp turned to head off anything else the moron was going to say. "Being an asshole. Your turn is next." Out of the corner of his eye, he saw Grace keep going toward the exit with the garbage.

Hernandez grinned at him. "Making time with the doc?" he asked in a confidential speaking tone of voice.

Sharp's reply wasn't any louder, but it had a backbone of cold steel. "Fuck you." He glared at his friend. "Say whatever you want about me, but do not disrespect the doc."

"Ah, shit, sorry, Sharp." Hernandez looked genuinely hang-dogged. "I wasn't thinking."

"Yeah, well, start, will ya? We've got to be on top of this and back her up all the way or we might all be dead."

"You bozos are too hardheaded for dead," Grace said, coming back into the main cave. "I bet you'd even argue with Saint Peter at the Gates about being a wrong delivery."

"Us?" Sharp said, turning to include her in their conversation. "Argue? Never."

Hernandez held out his hand to her. "I'm really sorry, Doc."

After a brief hesitation, she took it. "We're good." She turned her intelligent gaze on Sharp's face. "I've heard this kind of thing before in the heat of the moment."

"Oh yeah?" Hernandez asked.

Sharp was going to kick his ass. He opened his mouth to start the beating, but Grace got there first.

"Two years ago I ended up in the middle of a fire-fight. There was this one marine sergeant who kept yelling at me to get my, and I quote, 'sweet American ass back inside the armored vehicle.' I told him he could go fuck himself, but I wasn't going without my wounded." She laughed softly. "I thought he was going to strangle me, but after it was all over, you know what he did?"

Sharp and Hernandez shook their heads.

"He came up to me and said, 'Good job, Sweet. Good job. *Oorah!*'" She smiled at both men. "Best compliment I've ever been paid." She headed for her pack and began putting things away.

"That was when she won the Star?" Hernandez asked quietly.

"Yeah."

"I'm going to take that as a win," Hernandez said. "*Oorah.*"

GRACE GLANCED OVER her shoulder at the two soldiers standing several feet behind her. They were both looking at her with identical proud expressions on their faces, like she was important to them.

Tears prickled the corners of her eyes, and she had to pretend interest in organizing her pack in order to hide how much it meant. How much it helped with the difficult job ahead of her. Because the really hard part hadn't even started yet.

Max would be here soon, maybe in as few as a couple of hours, and the work to identify how this strain of anthrax had been altered, magnified and weaponized was going to take some time. Then they had to test the bacteria against all known antibiotics to discover if any of them could kill the bacteria, or even slow it down. Again, taking up more time they didn't have.

Given the deaths of the discovery patrol members, finding a quick answer didn't seem likely. In the meantime, they had to pray the creator of the anthrax wouldn't use it before they were ready. Even less likely.

She glanced around the cave, trying to picture how the equipment might fit into the space.

"How can we help?" Sharp asked, coming over to stand next to her. Hernandez flanked her on the other side.

"Well," she began, "I think these stone benches will make the best working surface, but we'll need to put down plastic sheeting in order to remove the possibility of dust contamination. If our CIA friend has some we could do that before Max and his team arrives."

Hernandez nodded. "I'll ask him. How much do you need?"

"I don't know, guesstimating stuff like this isn't a skill of mine, but it's got to cover from here—" she moved to stand at the end of one bench, then walked about twenty feet down the wall and stood at the end of another one "—to about here, but a few extra feet wouldn't hurt."

"About seven or eight yards. Got it." He headed out, entering the tunnel and disappearing into the dark.

"What's the next job on your list?" Sharp asked.

She handed him a bottle of water. "You're going to drink all of this while I talk."

"They gave me a unit of blood in the medical center

at Bostick," Sharp told her softly even as he opened the bottle and took several swallows.

"Not nearly enough. Did they give you any saline or other fluids?"

"Saline, I think, while I waited for the blood to arrive, and an electrolyte drink right after, but I don't know how much."

She harrumphed. "You need to eat too."

"We've got MREs, is that okay?"

Why was he asking so carefully? "It's better than nothing." She frowned at him. "Is something wrong?"

He shook his head, then finished the water and grabbed an MRE and another bottle of water.

He wasn't arguing with her and seemed genuinely interested in preparing for Max's arrival, so why did she feel like something was wrong?

"So, what's the next job?" he asked, a pleasant, cooperative smile on his face.

She didn't trust that expression at all. "We could move everything, so nothing is in the way when the team gets here. Thirteen more people occupying this space."

"Might get a bit cozy," Sharp remarked, looking around.

"We're going to need to work and sleep in shifts, so setting aside an area for sleeping would be useful too."

"Good idea. There was a smaller room off to the right just as the tunnel starts. That might work. Is Max bringing anyone besides his A-Team?"

"I don't think so."

"Then you'll be the only woman." It was a statement of fact. An irrelevant fact in her opinion, but the way he said it, with just a touch of extra stress on the word *only* made her wonder why it was relevant to him.

"So?" she asked.

"So, stay within sight of one our guys, okay? Until I have a chance to see who's on Max's team."

Her jaw dropped open and for several seconds she couldn't even breathe, let alone articulate how ridiculous his request sounded.

"You," she said, "are paranoid."

"I'm cautious. It's my job to prote—"

"Shut up," she interrupted, tapping his meal with one finger. "And eat your food. Maybe a little sugar in the bloodstream will aid your thinking."

"When did you eat last?"

"While you were sleeping." Sick of his overbearing taking-care-of-the-little-woman attitude, she deliberately left him and began moving things away from the area she wanted for the lab.

He ate his food, drank the sports drink included and another bottle of water before going in search of the trash inside this camouflaged garbage heap.

She was alone for the first time in days.

The starch went out of her legs and she plopped onto the bench she'd been sweeping rocks off of.

Fear was exhausting. It took a lot of energy to remain in a constant state of terror, and every time she thought she and Sharp were out of danger, something else would happen to make things worse.

Unfortunately, worse seemed to be coming at them from every direction.

Her emotions were all tangled up and not only that, but physically, she was at her limit. At some point soon, her body was going to shut down whether she wanted it to or not.

"Hey, you okay?"

She pulled her hands away from her face. Sharp was crouched on the ground in front of her.

"Just running out of gas. I thought medical school was bad, but this is...worse by an order of magnitude."

He nodded. "Yeah, this kind of constant-alert shit will kick your ass in short order. Have another nap before this place gets busy."

"I thought I was okay, until I had more than two seconds of quiet, then I couldn't even stand anymore." Tears leaked out to wet her face, which made her feel even more inadequate and weak.

One of his big hands reached out to brush the wetness off her cheeks.

He frowned and felt her forehead. "Grace, you're burning up."

NINETEEN

It took Grace a couple of seconds to process what Sharp was saying. Burning up? One hand sought out her sore leg. Pain radiated from the wound.

"Shit. I need to see." Hands jerking on her belt and the fastening on her pants, she jerked them down and bent to examine her leg. "Damn it." The wound was puffy, red and hot to the touch.

"How long has this been going on?" Sharp leaned down to look, then speared her with a furious glance. "Could you try to *not* die in front of me?"

A kernel of anger flared inside her tired mind. "Could you try to *not* be an asshole? This—" she pointed at her infected wound "—is not my fault. You want to blame someone? Blame Marshall."

Footsteps approached, but Grace didn't bother looking up. There weren't enough of them for the men to be Max and his team. That left her guys and she wasn't worried about them witnessing an argument.

"Whoa," Hernandez said. "What's with the lack of pants?" He stopped several feet away, March next to him.

"It looks like the doc's leg is infected," Sharp told them, his voice still tight with fury. "She's got a fever."

"That's a problem we didn't need," March said.

"I don't have any antibiotics with me," she said, her own anger already burned out. All she felt now was tired and light-headed.

"Will Max?" Sharp asked.

"Probably Cipro, but I'm not sure what else."

"Here's what you're going to do," Sharp told her in a tone allowing no questions or disagreement. "You're going to grab that nap, stay hydrated and eat more often so you don't fall over once the work starts."

Did he think she was going to protest? She tried to dredge up some energy to tell him he was acting like a jerk, but there wasn't anything left. "Yes, Dad."

"There's one other important thing the doc needs to do," Hernandez said.

"What's that?" she asked.

His face looked pained. "Pull up your pants."

March's expression matched Hernandez's and she couldn't help laughing. She tried to pull up her pants, as requested, but wobbled on her feet. That made her laugh harder.

"You look fucking drunk, Doc," Sharp said, pushing her hands out of the way, putting his on her waistband and getting her fatigues all the way up.

She sat down and fastened her pants. "I wish I were drunk. That would be kinda nice about now."

Sharp helped her back to her feet and guided her with a hand on her lower back toward the alcove they were going to use as a crash pad. She loved his hands. His big, warm, wonderful hands. If only he trusted her a little more. She lay down on the cool ground. "Night," she said, closing her eyes.

SHARP STARED DOWN at Grace, who looked too pale in the washed-out light of the cave. He stepped away from the sleeping area and waved at his team to follow.

"She looks like shit," Hernandez said without fanfare. "You sure she's going to be okay?"

"I'm not sure about much right now," Sharp said. "Other than the fact that we'll be up shit creek if things don't go like clockwork from now on."

"Right." March snorted. "Like that's going to happen."

"Exactly, so we need to be on top of our game." He looked at each man for a moment. "Be ready to help however you can, don't wait to be asked. We also need to be ready in case this place gets stormed by any unfriendlies."

"I'll work on a run-and-gun strategy if we have to get out of here fast," March said.

"We could booby-trap the tunnel and the other exit," Hernandez said.

"A firefight here would be..." Smoke let his voice trail off.

"Suicide?" Sharp asked.

"Likely," Smoke replied.

"Let's get it done, gentlemen," Sharp ordered. "Stay frosty."

His team dispersed while he went to have a chat with their CIA friend. Hopefully, Grace would get enough sleep to help her think with a clear head despite the infection in her leg.

He took his time with the trip through the tunnel, taking note of the condition of the stone all around, the items sitting on the ground lining the walls. They could certainly put more stuff in the way, make the tunnel look unused and impassable.

First line of defense.

He arrived at the ladder leading up to the wooden

hatch, then slowly lifted it up so he could see if anyone was around.

No feet in evidence.

Sharp slipped through the hatch and lowered it silently. He stood and listened for voices, but didn't hear anything, so he moved forward through the building to the next room. Again, it was empty.

The sound of men talking finally reached him just outside the main room with the seating area around the fire. CIA was speaking in Dari to someone, maybe the two teens he had working for him. He gave instructions for the arrival of the truck. Some of the men would be interested in buying a couple of the rusting hulks of vehicles for parts. They were to show them around and make sure they were given every courtesy, but they weren't to be allowed to go into any other buildings.

Some of the men were coming to trade and negotiate for more costly items. They might stay a couple of days.

The boys affirmed their understanding of their instructions and went outside to watch for the truck.

CIA came around the corner and stopped dead when he saw Sharp waiting for him.

"One of my men asked about some plastic sheeting," he said in an even tone to give no hint he'd overheard a thing. "Did you find any?"

"Yes, I put it over here." CIA didn't hesitate to lead the way.

He was a cool one, Sharp had to give him that.

Sharp grabbed the roll of plastic and gave CIA a nod. "Anything else I should know?"

"I believe your friends will be here in less than an hour. Some of them are pretending to be buyers while the others will join you in the cave."

"Have you been made aware of what we'll be doing down there?"

"Testing a cure for the anthrax?"

"Hopefully we'll get to that point. First they have to do analysis, then they start looking for an antibiotic that will kill it. It's precise, dangerous work that could kill us all. I just wonder if you should send your two young helpers home until we know what we've got."

"If I send them away, the people who come through here might ask questions, become suspicious."

Sharp thought about it for a minute, then the perfect reason occurred to him.

"Tell everyone the truth, sort of. Tell them you found out the strangers who arrived in the helicopter all died and you're scared the boys were going to be next. Tell everyone to stay away for a couple of days until you know if you're sick or not."

"And the men arriving today?"

"If you wait to send the boys home until tomorrow morning, you can say one of your good customers got sick too."

CIA thought about that for a few seconds before, finally, nodding. "Yes, that might work. The threat of illness is one thing most won't ignore."

"Good." Sharp gave him a respectful nod and made his way to the hatch over the tunnel. His last view of the room above was of CIA staring after him with a thoughtful look on his face.

The team had already changed the topography of the tunnel. They'd moved in several long lengths of wood and other debris. It wasn't finished, but it was looking promising. He entered the main cave and rested the plastic sheeting against the wall. The team had finished moving everything out of the way and the place looked ready to be occupied by whatever equipment Max brought.

He moved toward the hillside exit and liked what Smoke and March were doing with it. They'd added a few things to the inside side of the debris cover without changing anything else. One of the things they'd added was a long beam of wood they could use to bulldoze a quick route out.

Now all they needed was Max and his escort of a dozen Special Forces soldiers.

GRACE WOKE TO the sound of men.

Some were quietly talking, others were moving around. The sound of plastic wrinkling, a lot of plastic, stirred her interest. There was a reason why that was important.

Max was here.

Grace tried to sit up, but found it more difficult than it should have been. Cramped muscles shook, but she forced her way vertical, then slowly, with all the grace of a drunk elephant, got to her feet.

The room spun, so she braced her hand on the nearest wall and used it to keep herself upright. Though she'd just woken up, she felt exhausted, her brain running on half speed while her whole body ached. Even her breathing was labored.

Why was this so hard?

Her first step was mostly stumble, the second and third not much better. She stopped, gathered her strength and wits and carefully set her feet, one in front of the other.

When she emerged from the sleeping alcove, she glanced left, the tunnel looked dark, then right. Sharp stood about six feet from her position, his back to her, with Max facing him. The two men were talking, and Max looked way too serious.

Nothing new there, he always looked serious, even when most people were laughing. Always a little out of step in social situations was Max.

He saw her over Sharp's shoulder and moved to go around the bigger soldier, but Sharp was faster, and blocked his path.

"Grace," Max said, frowning and glancing at Sharp like he wasn't sure why the other man would get in his way.

Sharp shifted slightly so he could look over his shoulder, yet still keep Max in his peripheral vision. "Doc, you okay?"

Grace tried to smile, but it took up energy she didn't have and she gave up on it almost immediately. "Not really." She looked at Max. "I think I need some antibiotics."

Max's nostrils flared, as if he could scent any sickness she might emote from where he stood. "Anthrax?"

"No." She shook her head slowly. "I think this is your everyday average wound infection."

"Let me see it," he demanded in his normal bossy tone of voice, and took a step toward her.

Sharp did not get out of his way. "Just so we're clear, Doctor," he said low and slow. "Grace's well-being is my number-one priority."

"Ah, so that's what this is about," Max said nodding. "I assure you, I will never do anything to jeopardize her health." He paused as if carefully considering his next words. "Or happiness."

She couldn't see Sharp's face, but some of the tension went out of his shoulders. "Awesome."

She frowned. She was missing something here, she just couldn't figure out what. She did know she was going to have to have a talk with Sharp about his attitude.

"Grace," Max said to her. "Where's that wound?"

"On my leg."

He shifted his attention to below her waist. "Take off your pants."

SHARP WANTED TO wrap his hands around Max's neck and choke the living shit out of him. Did the guy have any common sense? You didn't order a woman in an enclosed space this small to take off her pants and expect to get no attention. Not when there were eighteen other guys in there with her.

It didn't help that after about two incredulous seconds, Grace started to laugh, and kept on laughing until she fell on her ass.

"What's so funny?" Max asked, tilting his head to look at her sideways, like she was some kind of problem he wanted to fix.

"Pants," she said, continuing to laugh.

Max crouched next to her and stuck an electronic thermometer into her ear. It beeped and he didn't look happy with the result.

"How high is it?" Sharp asked.

"One hundred and four." Max put the thermometer into a pocket, grabbed Grace under her elbow and tried to haul her to her feet. "I need to look at that wound."

Sharp strode over and scooped Grace off the ground, her laughter dissolving into giggling and hiccups. He went into the alcove and laid her on the makeshift bed she'd just been sleeping on and began working on her belt and the fastening on her pants. He managed to pull them down and reveal the bandaged wound.

Max cut it off with a pair of scissors he fished out of another pocket.

Red, puffy skin, even worse than before, with each stitch now weeping a yellowish discharge, made Sharp glad the doctor was here for the first time since he arrived.

Grace hadn't warned him that Max had no bedside manner to speak of.

"*Fuck*," the doctor said. "Who put these stitches in?" he demanded of no one in particular. "A baboon? A crackhead? A drunk?" Max stood and walked to the pile of equipment bags not far away in the main cave muttering, "Incompetent morons think they can just throw something together out of dental floss and duct tape and expect it to heal fine."

He returned with an IV set, a bag of saline and another smaller bag of fluid. "I need something to hang these bags from," Max told Sharp. "Preferably a couple of feet above her."

Sharp had seen something that might work lying on the ground in the tunnel. A metal pole, one end twisted and bent. He grabbed it, and by the time he got back to the alcove, Max had the IV needle in the back of Grace's hand and saline dripping through the line.

Sharp worked the unbent end into the ground and hung the saline from it. He gave it a shake. It seemed sturdy enough.

Max attached the smaller bag to Grace's IV line and began feeding her the antibiotic.

"Do you have enough for her?" he asked her boss.

"Yes, this isn't Cipro. What she's got is a staph infection, not anthrax." Max stood. "She's going to need a few hours of sleep before the fever breaks. She looks like shit."

"It's been a shitty couple of days."

Max snorted, but he seemed content enough.

"What do you need?" Sharp asked.

"I need to do my work uninterrupted. Can you ensure that?"

"I'll coordinate with A-Team Commander Faulkner."

"You'd be doing me a favor if you kept him on the other side of the room...cave from me."

"Is there a problem?" The last thing this mission needed was people arguing with each other.

"Several. We've disagreed on nearly every decision since we left Bahrain. I can't work with people who won't listen to reason."

"Whose reason?"

"Mine," Max said like the answer should be obvious.

"Have you worked with Faulkner before?"

"No."

"Faulkner is damn good at his job. Probably as good as you are at yours. You need to give a little, Max," Sharp said to him. "Sometimes it's about staying alive long enough to find the cure."

Max didn't hide his expression of distaste for that idea. "You Special Forces soldiers always think you have the answer."

"That's because we do."

Max grumbled something under his breath, then turned and began unpacking his equipment.

Faulkner waved at Sharp from across the room.

"Good to see you, Falcon," Sharp said with a salute. "I wish I had better news to report."

"Cutter's dead?"

"Yeah. Marshall is more than one brick short of an outhouse. We were fired upon from the base."

"Well, you did steal a helicopter."

"We were following Max's orders," Sharp explained. "And Marshall was, in no way, making rational decisions. He'd thrown Grace into some kind of gulag without allowing her to get all the medical care she needed, which is probably the reason she's got an infection now."

"Grace, is it?" Faulkner studied Sharp with eyes that missed nothing.

"She's earned her place on our team," Sharp told him. "Ask the rest of them. She's even got Smoke speaking in complete sentences."

Faulkner grunted and a smile came and went on his face. Getting him to smile was a tough job. "Why don't you start from the beginning and tell me the whole story?"

"Yeah, that would be the moment we stepped onto FOB Bostick about two weeks ago. No, it's pushing two and a half weeks now." He shook his head. "Marshall took one look at Grace, confirmed her name, then devolved into a dictator on the spot."

TWENTY

Faulkner crossed his arms over his chest and shook his head. "He called Max and yelled like a madman at him."

"I can't see Max taking that without comment."

"Nope. It was a fun phone fight to watch. Neither one of them listened to a word the other said."

"Even the word *anthrax*?"

"They threatened each other with it." Faulkner shrugged, disgust wrinkling his nose. "Like a couple of screaming little kids."

"Things have been FUBAR since we got to Bostick, but it wasn't until we got sent out to investigate the deaths of a village full of people over the span of less than twenty-four hours that things went completely to hell." Sharp looked Faulkner in the eyes. "Someone shot our aircraft down and I don't think it was an accident."

"How so?"

"At the time the crash didn't seem connected to the anthrax, but now...there are too many coincidences. Too much of the wrong information getting out and not enough of the right info." Sharp glanced at the alcove where Grace was sleeping. "The only reason I'm still alive is because she stepped it up and shot three extremists before they could kill me."

"I heard you got shot."

Sharp found himself reluctant to take his gaze off

Grace. "Yeah, that and shrapnel from the crash, but I'm okay."

"If Marshall did intentionally kill Cutter," Faulkner said slowly, "the shitstorm has only started."

"Isn't General Stone coming to relieve Marshall of his command?" Sharp asked.

"Not exactly." Faulkner smiled ruefully. "He'll arrive at Bostick tomorrow morning, and plans to straighten all this out, but he isn't taking sides until he hears from everyone. Marshall will still be in command of the base."

"Well, that's just fucking perfect. Grace is scared to death of him."

"Why?"

"She wouldn't tell me."

Faulkner watched Max move around, preparing his equipment and directing a couple of soldiers as they created a clean room with the plastic sheeting.

"So, we have two volatile situations," Faulkner said slowly. "One is the threat of someone using this anthrax as a weapon, and the other is a bunch of officers who hate each other's guts and are possibly willing to kill because of it."

"I think we need more hazard pay," Sharp said.

Faulkner grinned at him. "Now, there's a request I'd love to see you make in person."

"You just want to see someone kick my ass," Sharp said with a smirk. He moved off to check the alcove and was happy to see Grace still sleeping. Her IV antibiotic bag was nearly empty, so he mentioned it to Max.

Max glanced at him in a way that made it clear he'd forgotten all about Sharp already. "Don't touch anything," he said as he disappeared into the alcove. He came back a few seconds later and continued to set up his work area and equipment. "Her fever is down a little, but she needs more sleep."

"How long until you've done what you need to do?" Sharp asked him.

Max snorted. "I have no idea, but I've been given a thirty-six-hour deadline to deliver a report with recommendations to General Stone."

Sharp grunted. "I didn't think you had that much time."

Max turned to stare at him. "I hope you're wrong."

"So do I."

Max continued to stare.

"What?" Sharp asked.

"You're the sniper, right?"

"Yeah."

Max nodded. "She trusts you, which is why I'm going to give you a direct order."

Sharp couldn't keep his eyebrows down.

Max didn't seem to notice. "Whatever happens with this situation, don't leave her alone with Colonel Marshall."

"Yes, sir."

"Good. Now, I'm going to begin some delicate work. Please tell the others to make every effort to be quiet."

"Colonel," Sharp said. "We're hiding from an awful lot of people who would love to kill us. Quiet is our first order of business."

GRACE WOKE FEELING hungry and in desperate need of the cave's inadequate bathroom facilities.

She put out a hand so she could leverage her body into a sitting position and noticed the IV in the vein on the back of her hand. She followed the tubing up to a couple of bags hanging off a pole above her head. After maneuvering herself onto her knees, she was able to read the labels on the bags.

Saline and *clindamycin*.

Memories from the past few hours rose hesitantly. Max arriving. Her infected wound. Max putting in an IV. Several times Sharp's hands and voice reassuring her she was going to be okay.

No one was around, so she pulled her pants down, peeked under the bandage and looked at her sore leg. It was red and inflamed, but not quite as bad as she remembered. She felt less foggy too. Maybe her fever had gone down enough for her to think clearly.

Redressing, she got up, grabbed her IV bags and left the alcove.

Darkness had fallen and the cave was lit in strategic places only. Those light sources were carefully shielded so no light could make it through the patchwork of debris and garbage camouflaging the hillside exit of the cave.

Max was inside a do-it-yourself clean room fashioned out of clear plastic. He was wearing a full bio-suit and was seated at a microscope viewing something through the lens.

The Special Forces soldiers were scattered around the rest of the cave, playing cards, sleeping or watching Max. Until she came into view.

Sharp got to his feet and walked over to her, putting one finger over his lips to tell her to be quiet. As soon as he was close enough, he leaned down to whisper in her ear, "A group of twenty men are camped about fifty feet away, along the edge of the garbage dump. They're not carrying a lot of firepower and look like locals, so I don't think they're here for us." He paused then asked, "How are you feeling?"

"Like crap," she whispered back. "But better than a little while ago. My head is clear."

Even in the near darkness, she could make out a relieved smile on his face. "Good. Why don't you sleep some more?"

"Can't," she said, wincing. "I need to use the ladies' room again."

"Okay. You remember where it is?"

She nodded. "I don't remember if there's somewhere to hang these, though." She lifted the IV bags.

"Let's take a look," Sharp said and led the way to the hole in the ground.

She smiled at Smoke, Hernandez and the other soldiers she knew as she walked by. They smiled or gave her thumbs up in return. The ones she didn't know nodded respectfully to her, which surprised her enough that her nods back were probably more than a little wobbly.

As soon as she and Sharp were away from the lit area of the cave, darkness made walking difficult and she found herself standing alone, trying to see where Sharp went. He surfaced out of the dark, took her hand and tugged her along behind him.

Then she realized he must be wearing his night vision goggles. "Hey," she whispered. "Got a pair of those goggles for me?"

He didn't answer audibly, just squeezed her hand, but she figured that was a yes. They slowed, then he put the goggles in her hand.

She got them on and slid past him and around a short corner of the rock wall to the hole in the floor of the cave. Ugh.

There was however, a ridge of rock she was able to hook her IV bags to. Yay.

Sharp didn't say a thing when she gave him back the goggles and he led her back to the main room of the cave. She expected him to drop her hand as soon as it was safe, but he didn't. He kept hold of hers until she stopped in front of the plastic clean room. She tugged and Sharp set her free with a shake of his head.

What was his problem?

"How are you feeling?" Max stood on the other side of the plastic.

"Better." She smiled. "Have you made progress?"

"Some. I think I know how this anthrax strain kills so fast."

That was incredible news, so why did he look and sound so glum?

"And?" she prompted.

"And I don't know if any known antibiotic will have any effect. I'm setting up a sensitivity test right now."

"What mechanism makes this bug so deadly?"

"There seems to be an affinity for red blood cells, lysing them like a hemolytic streptococcus would. It might be leading to a rapid onset of sepsis that kills the patient."

"So rapid the antibiotic can't keep up?"

"That's what I'm afraid of. If those first soldiers died of the anthrax infection despite the fact that they'd been given Cipro prior to deployment, we have a big problem here."

"Have you tried mixing Cipro with other antibiotics? If it's behaving like a strep, try penicillin boosted by a beta-lactamase inhibitor along with it."

"An interesting approach. One worth investigating."

"Working with anthrax requires level-three containment facilities," Grace observed. "Who could have made it?"

Max looked grim. "There are no official labs of that level in Afghanistan. The closest ones are in India. Anyone crazy enough to release this bacteria into a village to see what it would do, isn't interested in proper procedure or safety."

"What can I do to help?" she asked. She wanted to get in there and assist. She was feeling better despite the exhaustion pulling at her and making her knees wobble.

Max's gaze shifted, following the small movement. "You can get some more sleep," he told her, turning away to go back to the microscope.

"But—"

"Grace," Max said, his impatience all but shouting at her from his partially turned body, as if he had to force himself to stop and talk to her. "I need you healthy, not on the verge of collapse. Have something to eat and let your sharpshooter and his *pals* take care of you."

The room full of men behind her went graveyard quiet.

"For a smart guy, Max," she said, forcing a sunny tone into her voice that didn't agree with her clenched hands on her hips, "you say the dumbest things. Do not shove *my* soldiers into that cramped *barely necessary item* box in the back of your head. These aren't some uneducated grunts. They're highly trained and very intelligent." She lifted her chin. "Now, apologize."

"Apple what?" Max asked as if he'd never heard the word before.

"Apologize, Max. Sharp and the others deserve it."

Max finally looked past Grace to the men behind her. He paused, then blew out a breath and said, "I'm sorry, gentlemen. I tend to think my work is more important than everyone else's."

"Don't sweat it, Max," Sharp said. Grace realized he was standing right behind her. "I intend to take care of her...and you."

Grace looked up at Sharp's impassive face. He wasn't kidding.

She stifled a laugh. It could be fun to see him boss Max around when it came time for the colonel to get some sleep or eat.

"Come on, Doc," Sharp said to her. "Time for another MRE."

"Oh, joy," she said, but followed him over to an unoccupied spot on the floor not far from where Smoke sat watching Max work.

His large hand covered her forehead.

She stared at him and the hand disappeared.

"You don't feel hot," Smoke said to her.

Wow, four whole words strung together. Usually, she had to work hard to get that many out of him. "I think my fever is gone."

A shadow fell over her and Sharp bent down with another MRE and a spork to eat it with.

"Thanks," she said as she took the food from him. The warmer around the meal was already doing its job and she found the heat reassuring and comforting. Once the sun went down, the temperature did, as well.

"He doesn't have much of a bedside manner, does he?" Sharp asked.

"No," Grace agreed. "He's pretty focused on the work. People usually come second with him, until you prove you're smart enough to be useful. Once he considers you part of his team, he'll take care of you whether you like it or not." She took a bite of her food, then added, "Sort of like you."

"He is pretty protective of you. Falcon said he pushed hard to get here. Used up a couple of favors and now owes a couple more. Are you sure he doesn't have a thing for you?"

"I'm sure." Was Sharp jealous? She leaned in close and said in that tone he'd taught her that didn't carry at all, "He's head over heels for someone else."

"You sure?"

"Yep. I'm on his team, which means he's like an older brother. There's a gal who works with us sometimes who has him tied up in knots. I don't think he even realizes he's crazy about her." She ate another couple of bites. "He's protective, but he's also really good at pushing me to do things that might be a stretch."

"Like the training we've been doing together for the last year?"

She froze for part of a second, then forced herself to carry on. "Yes, like that."

Sharp leaned close this time and whispered, "You'd better not be thinking of me as a brother."

From the way the men around them glanced at her with smiles on their faces, he hadn't whispered quietly enough.

She focused on her food, shoving a large bite into her mouth so she couldn't answer.

Smoke nudged her with one shoulder.

Her face grew hot as she finally swallowed down the food. Why had she stood up for Sharp again?

"Oh no," she said with mock seriousness. "I think of you as irritating, bossy and occasionally dense, but never as a brother."

TWENTY-ONE

"Now, Doc, no need to be like that," Sharp said to her.

What was that smile doing on his face? The one that made him look like he'd won a lottery.

"I'm sick, remember?" she said, and worked on finishing her food. Right now, sleep sounded like the safest thing she could do for her mental health.

Sharp suddenly straightened and turned to face the tunnel. The other soldiers quickly followed suit and within a second or two, all of them were on full alert, weapons in hand.

CIA emerged out of the dark, breathing a little too fast, his face a little too pale.

"Are we blown?" Sharp asked him, getting to his feet.

"No," CIA panted. "Worse. The dead village your men were guarding came under attack by a large group of extremists. We're not clear on which group it is, but all contact has been lost."

"Fuck," Sharp swore. "Leonard was there with Bart and Lee, along with some of Marshall's men."

"A group of Afghan soldiers has also gone missing."

"Missing?"

"There's been no contact from them in more than twenty-four hours."

"Why is that relevant?" Falcon asked.

"Their last known check-in was only about forty kilometers from the village, farther north and west toward Tajikistan."

"I don't understand," Grace said, unable to read from the expressions on the men's faces what was going on.

"Extremists have been moving around that part of the world," Sharp explained. "From Syria east through Iraq, Iran and toward Afghanistan. They're gathering strength in Turkmenistan, Uzbekistan and Tajikistan."

"If a group came into Afghanistan from Tajikistan, hit that Afghan patrol and your village, it could mean the beginning of a new offensive of extremists."

"They sure as heck don't want the current government to succeed," Sharp agreed. "Killing a bunch of American soldiers and making Afghans disappear gives them credibility and power with locals and other groups." He turned to CIA. "Has anyone or any group claimed responsibility for any of this?"

"No, but an unknown militant group has demanded that all American troops leave the country immediately or the Afghan troops will be executed."

Grace listened to the men discussing these latest developments, but remained confused by them. The anthrax attack seemed unconnected to these acts. They were days apart, for one thing. The disappearance of the Afghans appeared to be politically motivated, while no one had even mentioned the anthrax attack, for another.

So why did something about all of this feel off?

"Who's in command of American troops in this part of the world?" she asked of no one in particular.

"General Stone," Sharp said.

"The same General Stone who is enroute to FOB Bostick?" she asked. "To straighten out the communication mess between me, Max, Marshall and the Special Forces?"

"He's there now," Falcon said. "Arrived about two hours ago if he kept to his schedule."

"And what would his first priority be once he got there?" Grace asked.

"He'd send more men to reinforce our military presence at the village," Falcon responded.

"And if a bunch of our allied soldiers just happened to disappear? What would he do?"

"He'd send out search-and-rescue."

"Holy shit," Sharp said, staring at Grace like he'd never seen her before. "You think Bostick is going to be the next anthrax target."

Max stopped pretending to work and walked up to the plastic wall separating him from the rest of the cave. He stared at Grace with a horrified expression. "What better way to demoralize our troops than to take out a large number, along with their commanding officer?"

"It makes sense. Sick sense, but still..." Falcon said.

"Grace," Max ordered. "You need to take your men and few of mine and go to Bostick to either stop that attack or get everyone out. General Stone will listen to you."

"I thought I was too sick?" she asked. Either she was useful or not. This business of being around only when someone wanted her did not sit well with her.

"You *are* too sick, but you're the only one with the knowledge to convince General Stone, and I think, to talk Marshall off of the ledge he's put himself on."

"Marshall tried to kill her and the rest of us. Why the hell would you want to help him?" Sharp demanded.

"Because he's a victim, just like the rest of us. Right

now, he's in a place where the pain is constant and he can't see a way out, so he's not thinking clearly," Max replied. He glanced at Grace again. "I think Dr. Samuels can patch up some of those wounds, if she's given a chance."

"So, you know what caused his—" she searched for the right word to describe Marshall's behavior "—fury?"

"I haven't come right out and asked him, but I did do a more thorough look into all of the personnel present two years ago," Max said.

"I wish I had done that before I went to Bostick," she said. "I would have dealt with him differently. I don't think I can salvage the situation."

"What the fuck are you talking about?" Sharp asked her and Max, his voice a cool growl that made her wince.

"It's a long story," Grace said, "but the short version is, Marshall blames me for the death of his son. And—" she took in a deep breath "—he might be right."

Everyone stared at her for a long moment.

"Bullshit," Smoke said, the word slicing through the silence.

"Smoke's right," Sharp said. "There's no way. You're one of those people who wouldn't think twice about throwing themselves on a grenade to save someone else."

"Two years ago," Hernandez said, joining the conversation for the first time, "when you earned your Star?"

She nodded, but didn't say anything further.

"She saved two men who were bleeding out, and shot two extremists who were taking turns shooting anyone who moved," Max said. "What most people don't know is that she was also shot during the event."

"It was just a scratch," she said, her teeth clenched

so tight together her jaw hurt. "And I'm no hero, I was doing my job. If I could give that medal back, I would."

She turned to Max. "What should we do?"

He glanced behind him at the equipment. "I've started the sensitivity testing and it's got to cook for at least several hours. I can't go, but you can."

Sharp pushed his way between Grace and the plastic wall Max was behind.

Was he trying to protect her?

"And do what?" he asked. "We don't know if our situation has changed."

"We brought enough aviation fuel to get your helicopter to Bostick. So get going and call on the way. If General Stone has been there a couple of hours already, that arrest order has been rescinded."

"Jamal?" Falcon said to CIA. Only his name.

"Officially, the arrest order is gone, but unofficially—" CIA looked at Grace "—there's still a price for her."

Max mused, "Interesting."

"That's not what I'd call it," Sharp growled, still staring at her like it was all her fault.

"Stop staring at me like I'm some sort of evil genius. I didn't ask for all this."

"Sharpshooter," Max barked.

Sharp responded, "Yes, sir."

"Stop arguing and start moving. You and the men you choose to take with you, along with Grace, have two objectives. One, warn General Stone. He and the base are the most likely targets of our bug baker. Two, find the damn cook and kill him."

Sharp smiled a shark's smile. "Yes, sir." That grin died as he glanced at Grace. "Sir, about Grace—"

"She goes with you. Not negotiable. You may need her, and we both shouldn't be in the same place in case things go...bad here."

"Understood."

"Grace, I left some oral antibiotics for you on your pack."

"Wonderful. I hate IVs." She got up and went to the alcove where her pack rested and found the pills.

Movement behind her caught her attention.

Sharp crouched in front of her. "I'll take your IV out."

She held out her arm silently and he pulled the plastic catheter out of the vein on the back of her hand. His thumb pressed a piece of gauze down on her tender flesh, then he put a Band-Aid over it to hold it in place.

"Let's see your leg." His tone allowed for no argument.

She silently pulled off her pants. Again. "I should have listened to my grandmother," she muttered. "She always told me to stash a clean pair of underwear in one of my pockets in case shit hits the fan."

"Really?"

"She was a WASP, an Air Force service pilot during World War Two. It's how she met my granddad. She'd be disappointed in my lack of preparedness. But it's not like I've had time to change my underwear, and far too many people have seen...mine."

He leaned close and said quietly, "The only people who've seen your underwear are Max, me and our guys, and they were very careful not to look."

She froze and slowly met his gaze.

His grin was pure sin. "I'm becoming enamored with the color pink."

"Isn't that against the Special Forces soldier rules?"

"Not when that's the color of your girl's panties."

"Your girl?"

His grin got wider and he said, "Let's see those stitches."

She slid her pants down and exposed the wound.

He reached out with his hands to remove the bandage.

"Gloves," she reminded him.

He grabbed a pair from her pack and peeled the bandage away. While still red and puffy, the swelling had gone down and the stitches seemed to have stopped weeping and were scabbed over.

"How many doses have I had of antibiotic?" she asked. She could have slept through one or two depending on how often Max had ordered them.

"Two."

"This looks good, then. The pills should be all I need."

"How do you feel?" Sharp asked as he took off the gloves and threw them in a makeshift garbage can.

"Tired, but not light-headed or achy like I did before."

He stared at her hard, like he was trying to decide if she was telling the truth or not.

"I'm okay," she told him, putting her hand on his, which still rested on her leg. "I'm not great, but I'm okay."

"You *will* tell me if you feel any worse than okay." It was an order.

"Of course, and I'd like you to do the same. Don't ignore it if the pain in any of your wounds gets worse. Pain is the body's way of telling you there's a problem."

"Deal," he said, holding out his hand.

She took it, expecting a professional, impersonal handshake.

What he did was yank her up against him and kiss her. Hard. His lips gave no quarter, his tongue no escape.

She didn't want to escape. Her heart sped up and her breathing got choppy, and all she wanted to do was get closer to him. When he kissed her no pain could reach her, and no memory could destroy the pleasure and peace his touch inspired.

What was she doing? Anyone could walk past and catch them. It could ruin both of their careers.

When he pulled away, he rested his forehead against hers, his eyes closed, like he needed time to collect himself before facing anyone else. Had they kissed for two seconds, two minutes or two hours?

His eyes opened and he stared at her, the expression on his face changing from dangerously hot to plain dangerous. "When I get you naked, you're going to stay that way for a month."

"We shouldn't do that anymore," she whispered. "It's not...professional." Though the idea was shockingly tempting. She could picture herself and Sharp, naked and wrapped around each other in a bed, the pillows and sheets spilled onto the floor. She breathed out a shaky breath and said, "No, we can't." She waved a hand between them. "Isn't a good idea."

He snorted. "None of this is a good idea."

She opened her mouth to explain further, but he shook his head. "No, I get you. Regulations and common sense say not to go there. The thing is, I'm not sure I care what the rules say."

"I care," she said in a very small voice.

He stared at her, his gaze so deep he had to be seeing all the way to the bottom of her soul.

"We'll be heading out in a couple of minutes," he said

as if the last few minutes of their conversation hadn't happened. "Remember, you're human and you're not indestructible."

There was so much they needed to talk about, but there wasn't time. As she finished getting her pants on, she said, "Pot. Kettle. Black." She grabbed her antibiotics, her pack and moved to get up, but Sharp hadn't moved and didn't seem interested in getting out of her way. "Sergeant, do I have to order you to stand down?"

"No, ma'am." His face was shuttered, but there was an edge of violence in the set of his jaw and narrowed eyes.

She put a tentative hand on his shoulder, met his formidable gaze and said for him alone, "I promise I won't do anything to jeopardize myself or anyone else unless I have to. I'll be careful and I'll be smart."

"It's killing me knowing the danger that's ahead. The guy behind this biological weapon is nuts. He's like a loaded handgun with no safety. One squeeze and there's no calling the bullet back."

"Are you saying I'm not capable of doing what might be needed?"

"No, that's the problem," he said in a tone that sounded casual when the words were the opposite. "How fine is the line between a situation you can salvage and one you can't?" He stood and left her considering her answer.

She didn't know.

TWENTY-TWO

Someone found Sharp a backpack and he jammed in every weapon he could get his hands on, along with extra water and energy bars.

He found himself wishing Grace wasn't the damn good soldier she was.

Then there was her tendency to do practically *anything* to save another person.

He'd seen her, goddamn it, seen her leave a place of safety and put herself in harm's way to save another soldier. Him. She'd do it again. She'd do it over and over. It was the way she was built, for service and sacrifice.

If she were a man, she'd have made an excellent Special Forces soldier.

Green Berets were trained to get the job done and to think outside standard warfare tactics. Grace and Max were the only two people who understood the weapon their enemy was using, and neither of them were disposable. Max, at least, was doing the smart thing by staying out of sight and getting the lab work done. Where he wasn't smart was sending Grace to do the fieldwork.

She was a wild card. She didn't think in terms of warfare, she thought in terms of life and death.

Black and white.

No compromise. No surrender.

It hit him like a two-by-four to the back of his head. She thought like their enemy thought, in terms of all or nothing. She was willing to die to defend her people, like their enemy was willing to die to kill them.

If only Marshall knew he had the perfect weapon in the woman he seemed to be trying to destroy.

She also probably saw them as friends with benefits. Could he be satisfied with a pseudo-relationship? A part-time girlfriend, a woman not totally his own?

No way in hell.

He wanted her, all of her, twenty-four-seven, no holding back, no hiding anything. He wanted to shout to the world that she belonged to him and he belonged to her. She was the best partner he'd ever worked with at anything. Her laughter, her smile, her gorgeous eyes. He couldn't imagine a future without her in it.

Oh *fuck*. He *loved* her.

Smoke appeared in front of him. "You ready?"

Sharp jerked his stunned brain back to earth, gave his pack one last look, decided it was full and closed it up. "Yeah."

He found Grace outside the plastic wall, talking to Max. He wanted to kiss her, hold her and order her to stay here in the relative safety of this disguised garbage dump. He could do none of those things.

"Are you sure there isn't anything else I can do?" she asked her commanding officer.

Max shook his head.

"Grace," Sharp said. "Can I have a word?"

"Of course." She followed him a short distance way. "What is it?"

"We're missing some vital intel." He hoped what he was about to ask her wouldn't blow up in his face. "What happened two years ago to make Marshall think you're responsible for the death of his son? Which brings up my next question. He had a son?"

Grace stared at him for a moment, the color draining from her face.

"I know you don't want to talk about it, but it's impacting everything we're trying to do." He glanced around at the men in the cave. "We're all soldiers here and you won a Star for what you did then. Whatever it is that's tearing you up inside, we *understand*."

"Yeah." She nodded and seemed to deflate, her shoulders hunching. "I'm sorry. I should have told you a long time ago, right after the night he confronted me. I don't like thinking about it, let alone talking about it." She shook her head. "I've tried to forget that day, but it's a part of me now." She glanced around, blew out a breath and said, "I need a place where I can sit down."

Smoke gestured at the rock he'd been sitting on earlier and she sat. "Okay." She took a couple of moments to get settled. "The convoy had a dozen trucks in it. We were moving our combat support hospital to one of the forward bases seeing a lot of injuries. We were supported by armored vehicles with mounted guns. You know, the big ones." She'd spoken to Sharp, but all around him, he could see heads nodding.

"I don't remember how long we'd been driving when the IED went off. Maybe two or three hours? The explosion took out the first vehicle entirely, and no one survived. The second truck was badly damaged, and the third was disabled by enough shrapnel from the blast to make it mechanically unsound.

"There had been six people in the second truck. Two died right away, the other four sustained injuries. Only two people in the third truck were injured. The other four escaped immediate injury.

"My surgical team was split up between three trucks in the middle of the convoy. We grabbed first-aid kits, jumped out and ran toward the blast zone. That's when we started taking fire. I don't know how many people were shooting at us, but it seemed like the bullets were coming from everywhere." She stopped to catch her breath, but she couldn't seem to slow her breathing down.

Sharp crouched next to her rock and put a hand on her shoulder. She relaxed a little. This was going to be bad. Really bad.

"I don't remember how I ended up there, but the next thing I knew, I was behind the door of another armored truck, a marine crowding me into the corner as he fired again and again at whoever was firing on us. A bullet took him in the neck. I tried to stop the bleeding, but it ripped his carotid artery apart and there was nothing I could do." She sort of smiled, but not really. It was the kind of thing a person did when they felt they'd done a particularly stupid thing.

"It made me angry, so I grabbed my weapon and began firing myself. I shot at every target I could see until I ran out of ammunition. For a second or two I thought the weapon had jammed, then I realized I was out of bullets. Shouting for help from farther forward in the convoy got me moving again, but without anyone firing at me. I figured I'd scared off whoever had been responsible for the shooting." She twisted her fingers together, pulling at them as if there was something wrong with them.

"When I got to the third truck, I was waved forward

by the lead surgeon. He couldn't go as he had his hand inside a man's chest, probably trying to control a bleeder. I rushed up to the second vehicle and found two of our trauma nurses dead. Shot in the back of their heads while trying to triage the dead and wounded inside, I think. At first I thought everyone was dead, then I heard moans and knew someone was alive inside."

She swallowed hard and continued. "I pulled the bodies of the nurses aside and discovered two men alive. One was even conscious. I began triaging them, but someone started shooting at us again. One of the wounded's sidearm was only inches from my hand. I grabbed it, turned and aimed over the edge of the door. The shooter was only about twenty feet from me and couldn't have been older than nine or ten years. He looked terrified and was shouting at me in Arabic or Dari, but I don't speak either one, so I didn't know what he was saying."

She glanced at Sharp. "How could I kill a child?" She looked away before he could answer and continued. "I hesitated, certain that if I just stayed still and let the boy calm down, he wouldn't shoot."

Tears dripped down her cheeks, but she didn't seem to notice. "There was a shout from down the convoy and a marine ran toward me, firing at the boy. He missed. The boy didn't. It was a head shot and the marine went down fast. So fast. The boy turned his weapon on me, but I shot him first. Twice in the chest. More extremists came toward the convoy and I kept shooting."

"Marshall's son was the marine who tried to help you? The one the kid shot?" Sharp asked.

"Yes. I hesitated to kill that boy, and Marshall's son paid the price for my mistake."

"They don't share a name."

"No. Marshall told me he'd only become aware of his son's existence when the soldier tracked his father down after his mother died. He found his birth certificate with her papers with Marshall's name on it. Marshall told me, he'd never been prouder of anything or anyone than he was of his son. He'd only known him a year."

"Grief is one thing," Sharp said slowly. "But blaming you for the death of a soldier—"

"They gave me a medal," she interrupted. "If he had been your son, how would you have felt?"

"Proud," Sharp said. "He drew fire from you and gave you the chance to defend yourself and the wounded."

All around the room, men nodded in agreement.

She stared at them, her hands opening and closing, like she wanted to hit someone. "He should have gotten the medal, not me."

"Several someones thought differently," Sharp said, keeping his tone as solid and sure as tempered steel. "We're fighting people who use terror as their primary weapon. They want you to feel guilty. They want you to feel afraid. Don't rent them space in your head."

"Oh," she said, partly laughing and partly crying. "They've got a mortgage on the whole thing. I'm going to need a good therapist after all this is over."

"Get evicting already, we've got a job to do," Sharp told her in his best drill sergeant voice.

"But, Marshall—"

"You let me worry about him. You've got to get your head back in the game. Get your stuff together. Wheels up in ten."

Her mouth opened and closed a couple of times before she visibly pulled herself together and stood.

Max pointed at a stack of crates. "There's ten percent formaldehyde solution. Take as much as you can."

"Formaldehyde?" Sharp asked.

"It's one of the better disinfectants for anthrax spores," Grace explained.

"How else do you kill them?"

"Heat works, but it needs to be a controlled burn."

"So blowing shit up is out?"

"That would be my last choice. Surfaces contaminated with spores might be moved or thrown clear of any resulting fire before the spores are destroyed. Spores can be viable even after forty years in soil. No viability range has been established for surfaces exposed to air, but I would err on the side of caution and assume years." She began sorting through the supplies Max brought and seemed fine enough to leave alone for a few minutes.

Sharp walked to the other side of the plastic room Max worked in and waved the doctor over. "I don't have time to convince you she's safer with me than anyone else."

Max didn't say anything, just watched him with careful eyes.

"You're her commanding officer and her friend. How do I help her?"

"That was the right question." Max smiled at him, the ruthless sort of smile a brother might wear when he's about to irritate his little sister for her own good. "She's intelligent and fearless when it comes to the safety of other people. It's herself she's not so good at looking after," Max said in a low, rushed voice. "Become her shadow. Support her decisions. If she tells you to run, grab her and take her with you."

Sharp let out a breath. "Thanks." He turned, gathered up her pack and his, grabbed his loaned sniper rifle and flashed the hand signal for a huddle with his team.

"You can come with Grace and me to Bostick or stay here. What's it going to be?"

Hernandez spoke first. "We're with you and the doc."

The others nodded.

Sharp looked at them all in return. "Okay. Let's get moving." He headed toward the stockpile of supplies with his men a step behind him.

Grace looked up from an open box filled with what looked like spray bottles. "We need this case of disinfectant."

"There is more in the truck," Max told them without looking up from the microscope. "In buckets. Take what you need."

"There aren't enough bio-suits for everyone," she said, her lips pressed together tight. "Only me."

"You're the most likely person to come in contact with the spores, so that makes sense," Sharp said.

She bit her bottom lip. "Maybe we should limit the number of people who come on this trip."

Sharp smiled gently. "You're going to need all of us, darling. You're the bug expert, but we're the bad-guy exterminators."

She glanced behind him and the team and said, "But—"

"You can't talk us out of this," Sharp explained. "We don't know how Marshall is going to react when we get there. You need backup."

"What about General Stone?"

"We're going to recommend he leaves as soon as possible after we land." Sharp waved a hand at the case of spray bottles, and Hernandez stepped forward to pick it up.

"Are you ready?" Sharp asked her.

"No," she told him with a sigh. "But I guess I'm going anyway."

Sharp offered her pack to her and she took it with a wry grimace. "I think I'm going to burn this when I get home."

"There you go," Sharp said, nudging her a little with one elbow. "Now you're thinking ahead." He led the way into the tunnel and they began the trek toward the hatch at the other end. She fell in behind him.

"Why are you so cheerful?" she asked, frowning at him.

"It's just nice to get out of the cave for a little while," he said like he was some 1950s housewife.

She rolled her eyes. "Why is it, that when the danger is the highest, you get really silly? Like when you had to slap me out of my hysterics after our helicopter crash."

"Dude," Hernandez said, disapproval coloring his tone. "You slapped her?"

"No. I slipped a spare magazine for her Beretta into her back pocket."

"Huh," Smoke grunted. "Is that what we're calling it these days?"

For a moment no one said anything, then Grace began to laugh. So hard she stopped walking, slapped a hand over her mouth and had to lean one hand against the tunnel wall to keep from sliding down to her knees.

Sharp grinned at Smoke, the sly devil, and winked at the other man.

Smoke gave him a brief smile in return, his straight

white teeth gleaming in the darkness and against his tanned skin.

Grace stopped laughing and smacked Smoke on the shoulder. "You ought to come with a warning label."

"What, like slippery when wet?" Hernandez asked.

Smoke appeared to give it some serious thought. "Smoke. Fire. Boom," he said.

"Yours would read, 'out for lunch,' Hernandez," Sharp said as he started walking again.

Very quietly behind him, Grace said, "I shouldn't be laughing. Our situation is so...terrible. Is it okay to laugh?"

Sharp glanced at her over his shoulder. She sounded so tentative, so uncertain, he wondered if her fever had come back.

"Doc, we don't have time for the sniffles now. We've got to use every weapon we've got to stay focused and alive. We'll cry together later, when it's safe," Hernandez answered her.

"Humor," she said slowly, "is a weapon?"

"Damn straight."

"You cry together?"

"Laugh, cry, get drunk and generally lose track of a couple of days. If you don't find a way to vent the crap you pick up when you're on a mission, you'll go *loco*."

"Well, I sure wish someone had told me that a couple of years ago."

"Someone should have," Sharp said. "You're welcome to our decompression party."

"Ooh." Hernandez coughed. "That means we'll have to keep our clothes on."

"You are the only one who feels he has to be completely free, Hernandez," Sharp said.

Grace choked and snorted.

Up ahead, the hatch to the room above came into view. Sharp held up a hand and any noise anyone was making disappeared. Even Grace went quiet.

She knew what their hand signals meant. Hell, he shouldn't be so damn surprised, he'd been using them in front of her and with her almost constantly for the last few days.

He knelt at the base of the ladder that ended at the hatch and waved Hernandez forward.

He went up the ladder and cautiously lifted the wooden door. He used a small dental mirror to scan the room above, then disappeared up into it with no sound at all.

TWENTY-THREE

A FEW SECONDS LATER, the hatch opened and Hernandez gave the all-clear signal.

Sharp went up next, then Smoke slipped past Grace to wait at the bottom of the ladder. After a few moments, he urged her to follow Sharp.

The room above was dark, and she realized she was going to have to ask someone if it was night or early morning. She didn't even know what day it was.

Shadows moved and Sharp was suddenly there, a firm, strong hand under her elbow as he guided her away from the hatch and toward the front of the building. Hernandez was there, talking softly to two men dressed in traditional Afghan clothing. They nodded and moved off before she was close enough to make out what language they were speaking.

CIA was there too, and for once he looked calm. Their leaving was probably the best thing he'd heard of in a couple of days.

Sharp leaned down to whisper in her ear, "This place is being watched, so when we go, we're going to go fast. It might be a bumpy ride at first."

"Bumpy because of the helicopter's engines or because people will be shooting bullets and rockets at us?"

"Yes."

She waited for him to pick one. It took her a moment

to understand he meant yes to both. "Better get me a barf bag," she said with a sigh.

Movement behind her grabbed her attention. Smoke, Clark and March joined them, and she found herself dragged into a football huddle.

"We're leaving hot. Smoke, you and Clark take first and second seats. Hernandez, Runnel, the doc, March and I will strap down in the back. Is the formaldehyde and the crate of supplies the doc wants in the bird?"

"In and secure," Hernandez said.

"Smoke, Clark, go."

They disappeared into the darkness.

The men rearranged themselves to surround her, Sharp in front, Hernandez, Runnel and March on either side and behind her. She missed the signal they had to have been given, because they moved as one, almost carrying her along in their rapid walk to the helicopter.

She got in and sat when one of the men pushed at her to do so. Buckling up her harness took only a few seconds, but the machine was still silent.

A few seconds later, the engine started up, its high-pitched whine a shock in the velvet quiet of the night. Normally, it would take a few minutes before they would take off, but not this time.

The whine rose and rose, until she feared her ears would burst. Then the entire machine shook with enough force to make her cling to her jump seat, her harness unable to protect her from shudders groaning through the metal.

Grace clenched her teeth and prayed they didn't take off, just to fall out of the air and crash.

Someone grabbed one of her hands, forced it to let go of her seat and shoved something plastic in it.

She brought it closer to her face. A barf bag.

Funny.

The whole aircraft shuddered hard. Again, and again. Something pinged not far from her head.

"We're taking fire," Sharp yelled in her ear. A hand pressed against the back of her neck, forcing her to put her head over her knees. "Head down."

The helicopter flinched from several more blasts and gunfire.

On the other side of her, someone grunted in pain.

She turned her head, but it was too dark to see who'd been hit. She turned the other way and yelled at Sharp, "Who's sitting on the other side of me?"

"March."

"I think he's been hit."

Sharp swore and unclipped his harness. He went around her and reached out to the man next to her.

Grace put her hand on March's shoulder so she could at least feel if he was responding to Sharp. Beneath her hand, he took in a breath and she could feel the vibration of his diaphragm as he answered Sharp's questions.

Sometime during their conversation, the noise and vibration of artillery and bullets disappeared.

"How bad is it?" she yelled in March's general direction.

"It feels like a laceration," Sharp told her. "Not a bullet wound. He took it across the shoulder."

"Can we turn on some lights now? I could bandage him up if I could see what I was doing."

"Sorry, Doc, we've got to run dark or risk getting fired on again."

"Isn't that illegal?"

There was a pause. "Back home it sure is, but this isn't Kansas, Doc."

Well, she certainly felt like a fool. "Right. Sorry."

"Never apologize for being a law-abiding citizen," Sharp said. "We all wish we were home."

"How long are we running dark?"

"About thirty minutes."

Grace reached out and squeezed March's uninjured shoulder. When he leaned closer to her, she said to him, "You let me know if the bleeding doesn't stop or gets worse. I'll try to bandage you up blind."

"I'm putting pressure on it, Doc," he said. "It should be fine."

When she didn't let go, he added, "I promise to tell you if it doesn't stop bleeding."

"Good."

Somewhat mollified, she settled back in her seat.

Huh. For once, she didn't feel airsick.

The men around her stirred a long time later. The lights all came on and when Grace looked out the side of the helicopter, FOB Bostick was below them.

The engine slowed and they dropped onto the same pad as the one they'd departed only two days ago. This time no one was shooting at them, but there was a strong force of soldiers surrounding the area. For their protection or other reasons?

Smoke shut down the engine and Sharp got up first. "Stay here," he said to her on his way past her and onto the tarmac.

Grace resisted the urge to shake her head and spoke to March first. "Let me see your shoulder."

He held still while she got some of the gear off of him, tore open his uniform and slapped a nonstick pad on the wound then used a self-adhering bandage to keep it in place.

She kept glancing out to check on Sharp, but he hadn't gone alone. Hernandez stood just behind him and to his left. She picked Marshall out of the crowd as well, but he wasn't the man Sharp was talking to.

General Stone?

Sharp nodded and gestured at the helicopter. Marshall turned his gaze on the aircraft and even though March was blocking the colonel's view, she felt as if his gaze was a laser, targeting her for his next shot.

Finally, after what felt like an hour, Hernandez jogged back to them.

"We're good," he said as he gave the all-clear signal to everyone in the cargo section of the bird. He moved to tell Smoke and Clark, and within moments they were disembarking and walking toward the knot of officers waiting with Sharp.

Her feet weighed twenty pounds each and she had to force herself to keep walking. She couldn't believe Marshall would give up his anger just because a superior officer ordered him to. No, he'd suffered a loss that had wounded him in ways most people couldn't even see, let alone understand.

She was responsible for that loss.

Sharp turned and stepped out of the way, revealing a man in his fifties, his salt-and-pepper hair buzz-cut short, with a face set in stone.

She saluted along with the rest of the team.

He returned the salute and never looked away from her face. "Major Samuels."

"Sir."

"You look like shit."

"Yes, sir." Why argue with the truth?

He regarded her coldly for several seconds, then asked, "Did you order, request or beg Commander Cutter to release you from Colonel Marshall's custody?"

"No, sir. I called them a bunch of idiots."

Stone grunted.

"To be fair, sir," she continued, "once I realized they weren't going to revise their plan to leave the base, I agreed to go. Reaching Colonel Maximillian with samples could not wait."

Stone's expression didn't change. "All of you," he said looking at the members of the A-Team, Marshall and Grace, "come with me."

He walked with them to the closest building, the one the team had used as their personal base, and turned to face everyone.

"I've had this conversation with Marshall already, but you need to hear it too." Still, he looked at Marshall, who nodded in return.

"Two years ago, Major, you won the Bronze Star for your actions during an IED attack. During that attack, Joseph Cranston, part of your CASH unit's escort, broke cover and rushed a child insurgent he believed was going to shoot you."

"Yes, sir. I saw it happen."

"What you don't know," Stone said as if she hadn't spoken, "is that sending out a kid like that is a common tactic. Usually, a larger group of men wait for the kid to get close to their target, maybe even get a shot or two off, then rush the target while you're distracted by the whole kill-a-kid-or-die moral dilemma going on in your head."

She frowned. How did that change anything?

"Cranston had been ordered to stay where he was.

Told in no uncertain words to not break cover, that it was a trap. He disobeyed orders anyway."

"Because of me."

"No, because he wasn't using his head. His CO knew your record, knew you were a crack shot too. You were semi-sheltered by the vehicle, treating the wounded, not out in the open where anyone could pick you off." Stone sounded even colder than he looked. "Cranston made a decision that killed him."

Grace couldn't stop herself from protesting the general's uncompromising assessment of the event. "I don't agree, sir. I believe he chose to help in the only way he could. He acted as a distraction for the enemy, one I needed because I hesitated to shoot that boy. I hesitated, and I would have been killed if Joseph Cranston hadn't drawn the kid's fire away from me." She had to blink fast or let the tears in her eyes fall. "He was brave and he should have gotten the medal, not me."

"You believe that?" Marshall asked into the dead silence following her statement.

She turned to look at him. For the first time since she'd met him, he didn't look as if he was seconds from erupting. "Yes."

He stared at her for several moments, then nodded, though his lips quivered. "I did *not* order anyone to fire on your helicopter when you left here. I wanted to. I'd just found the two marines who were guarding you dead and believed Cutter and his men were responsible."

"We left them alive and well, if tied up," Sharp told him. "I've got a question. If you didn't order your men to fire on us, who did? Cutter was killed in that exchange of fire."

"I don't know. I ordered everyone to stand down, but

someone started shooting, and you know what happens after that. Once the first shot is fired, the battle is started whether you want it or not."

"You don't know who took the first shot?" Sharp asked, accusation and disbelief making his tone a blunt instrument.

"No." Marshall was back to looking angry again.

"Someone is working hard to make trouble," Grace said.

The general didn't reply verbally, but one eyebrow rose enough that she continued.

"The biological agent that killed the villagers has been confirmed as weaponized anthrax spores. The village was a test, to see the weapon at work, to gauge our response, and, as soon as I left with samples to be confirmed, my helicopter was shot down. We weren't on the ground for long before extremists arrived and began killing any and all survivors. I don't believe anyone was supposed to survive that crash."

"All part of the same attack?" General Stone asked.

"I suspect so." She turned to Marshall. "Did anyone talk to you about me? Maybe say things to make you believe I was at fault during the incident two years ago?"

Marshall frowned, but didn't answer. He glanced away, and she could almost hear the gears turning in his head.

"When were you notified of the helicopter crash?" she asked him.

"I was told there was a glitch with the radio on the bird, but that it was in the air and on its way to Colonel Maximillian's lab. I didn't find out it had crashed until several hours later."

"Who told you about the glitch?" Sharp asked, his voice rough with anger.

"One of the men who was killed when you escaped."

"An infiltrator?" Sharp asked.

"From Iowa?" Marshall shook his head. "I have spoken about the death of my son to one person. A trusted ally."

"Ally?" Grace asked. "He's not an American?"

"No. He's Afghani, assigned by the Afghan government to liaise with us. I've known him for two years. His intel has been responsible for saving a lot of lives. I wouldn't hesitate to have him at my back."

"Why would you talk about losing your son to him?" Grace asked.

"He lost his own family three years ago in an Islamic State attack in Syria." Marshall stopped talking for a moment to clear his throat.

"His name?" Stone demanded.

"Mohammad Asil Akbar."

"I want everything you have on him, including the man himself, brought here to me right now," General Stone ordered.

"Here, as in this building?" the general's aide asked, eyeing the piles of stuff littering the corners.

"Here. If we do have an infiltrator among us, this is not where he'd expect to be questioned."

"Yes, sir." The aide and a couple of other soldiers hurried off to carry out his orders.

Marshall walked over to talk to the general softly, and Grace found herself wilting under an exhaustion that seemed to weigh a thousand pounds. Her head pounded in time with her pulse.

Sharp was watching her, and when she made eye contact with him, he walked over. "What's up?"

"I need some water."

He handed her a bottle of water from his pack.

She took it, downed a few swallows, then took an antibiotic with a few more swallows.

The general's aide came in at a run. "Sir, Akbar is gone." The soldier held out an envelope with Marshall's name on it. "This was left in his quarters."

TWENTY-FOUR

STONE REACHED OUT to take the envelope, and Sharp sucked in a breath to stop him, but Grace hollered first.

"Don't touch it!"

Everyone froze.

"Anthrax. Envelopes." She nodded at a table that stood against the nearest wall.

The general's aide walked over, gently set the envelope down and backed away with his hands in the air.

"Sir," Grace said. "We brought an effective disinfectant with us, wash your hands in it." She turned to the general. "I recommend you seal off Akbar's quarters and work area."

"Contaminated?" Marshall asked.

"I won't know until I can test for anthrax, but it's better to be safe rather than sorry."

Marshall ordered a man to bring some of the disinfectant from the helicopter.

"What would it look like?" Sharp asked. "If there was anthrax planted there."

"That's the problem," Grace said to everyone. "The spores are so small, you'd think it was a little bit of dust." She sounded as worried as he felt. Dust? How were they supposed to fight that? With vacuum cleaners?

"General Stone," Sharp said. "This attack could be aimed against you or whichever high-ranking officer it would require to clean up this messy situation. Respectfully recommend you leave the base."

"Or, the people behind this attack could be waiting for me to leave," he said. "It would be relatively easy to take me out in a helicopter."

"Not if one left before yours as a decoy."

The general grunted and considered the floor for a moment. "Major, could this anthrax be produced anywhere?"

"I've been thinking about that. Some mobile labs are fully equipped for anthrax. Max is working in a portable isolation chamber in a cave at this moment. And, if you're not too concerned with safety, all you really need is power and privacy."

"Afghanistan is riddled with caves."

"For a lab to be operating for any length of time, they would need to bring in fuel for the generators."

"And other supplies, as well." Stone nodded and turned to Marshall. "Have your people review satellite pictures of the region from the past month. Look for fuel and other supplies going into the mountains, or vehicles leaving full and returning empty."

"Yes, sir." Marshall turned and nodded at a man, who ran off to carry out the orders.

"I've got a bio-suit, but I'll need a Sandwich," Grace told the general.

"I can have one here in three hours," Stone said. "Colonel Maximillian organized resupply for this eventuality."

"Excellent."

"Until it gets here," the general said, pointing a finger at her, "you are to report to the base hospital. You will follow any recommendations the ranking doctor might make. Understood?"

"But, sir, Akbar's quarters?"

"There are people on base who can take care of that. Hospital. Now."

Grace looked like she'd just sucked on a lemon. "Yes, sir." She turned her sour expression on Sharp, but all he did was smile back. She needed care and he was willing to play dirty to make sure she got it.

Grace saluted the general and left to follow her orders, he hoped.

"You." The general looked at him with a scowl on his face. "You've made yourself responsible for the major?"

It wasn't exactly a question, but he answered it anyway. "Yes, sir."

"Commander Cutter was your CO and now he's dead." The general shook his head. "What a goddamn mess." He looked at Smoke, March, Clark, Runnel and Hernandez. "Is this all that's left of your team?"

"No, sir. Our second in command, Leonard, is at the village north of here where the anthrax first appeared, with the other two surviving members of the team."

"I've sent reinforcements up there and ordered anyone healthy to return here. They should be joining you soon enough."

"Yes, sir."

"Your job is to dog the major's steps. Never let her out of your sight. Understand?"

"Yes, sir.

"I don't care if she squawks loud enough to raise the dead, you men go where she goes."

"She's that important?" Marshall asked, his own expression sour.

"People with her skills don't grow on trees. We've got less than a dozen specialists like her in the army," the general said. "But she's also reckless. You boys keep her out of trouble or I'll have your asses over a hot fire. Understood?"

"Sir, yes, sir," they responded together.

"Go," he ordered.

They went.

Marshall raised a hand, as if to stop them from leaving. "Sergeant, I..." He stopped with a faintly surprised look on his face, as if it were the first time in his life he didn't know what to say.

Sharp didn't need to hear the words. "I'll tell her, sir."

Marshall's face turned red, but he met Sharp's gaze with a steady one of his own. "See that you do."

Sharp saluted and led his team out into the sunshine.

It looked like a beautiful day. Quiet and peaceful.

He'd learned not to trust either.

The walk to the base infirmary didn't take long, but Grace was already lying down on a gurney, a doctor and a nurse talking to her while they worked.

The nurse glanced up and saw him and his guys walking their way and pulled the curtain to block their view.

As if that would stop him.

He flashed a hand signal at his men to stay where they were and ducked around the curtain.

"Out," the nurse ordered as soon as she caught sight of him.

He looked at Grace.

She rolled her eyes. "He can stay. I have the feeling General Stone ordered him to stick close."

"You sure?" the doctor said.

"Yeah, he was the first one to patch up my leg. I don't

think the sight of my underwear is going to incite him into unbridled lust."

Someone outside the curtain coughed.

Sharp grinned, but kept his mouth shut.

"Who's out there?" she asked.

"Who do you think?"

"All of them? Huh, I guess I scared someone pretty bad."

"Several someones." Including him. Sharp shook his head. "You've got a nose for trouble, Doc."

She winced at something the doctor or the nurse was doing. "I wish I didn't."

"How's her infection looking?" Sharp asked the doctor. "She had a fever before."

"It looks okay," the doctor said after a glance at Grace's face and her nod. "I'm going to give you a liter of saline to get you rehydrated," he said to Grace. "Keep taking those antibiotics."

"Of course," she replied. "Can I go back on duty as soon as that liter is infused and I've had something to eat?"

"No," Sharp said. "You need eight hours of rest, minimum."

"He's right, Grace," the doctor said. "Sleep is your next order of business."

She looked from Sharp to the doctor and back, then rolled her eyes again. "Fine."

The doctor walked away from Grace and stripped off his gloves. "Angie is going to put a new dressing on that and get the IV started."

"Thanks, Ted," Grace said. She looked at Sharp. "Could you hunt down some food? You should eat too."

"Sure."

Sharp sent Hernandez and March to get MREs for everyone while the nurse got the IV running in the back of Grace's hand.

Sharp pulled the curtain aside so Smoke and Clark could join them. A few minutes later, March came back with five MREs and Sharp took way too much satisfaction in watching Grace eat.

He was such a Neanderthal.

"March, how's your shoulder?" Grace asked while they ate.

March paused in his shoveling of food into his mouth. "Fine. Doc cleared me for duty."

Grace frowned at him, but didn't say anything more.

When Hernandez came back, his face was so carefully blank Sharp knew shit had hit the fan somehow.

"What?" Sharp asked them, setting his meal aside.

"Her bio-suit has been punctured in multiple places," Hernandez said. "It's useless."

"Marshall hid ours somewhere, track those down."

"They've been destroyed too."

"Fuck me," Sharp hissed. When were they going to catch a break with this bug baker?

Grace looked pale. "Sabotaged? When?"

"Don't know," March answered.

"General Stone and Colonel Marshall need to know."

"Fill them in, Hernandez, then get your butt back here."

Hernandez saluted and jogged away.

Sharp studied Grace's expression. She was staring into space, her mind obviously working.

"What next?" he asked her.

"I think we can safely say someone doesn't want any of us to have the proper isolation equipment available."

"Agreed."

"If it were you," Grace asked him, "revenge on your mind, and you wanted to kill a bunch of American soldiers, including a general, what would you do with a baseball-sized amount of anthrax spores?"

Scary question.

"I'd probably put a plan A and B into motion. Plant some inside the base and throw some at the base."

"Plant some," she muttered under her breath. "Like in a workspace or gathering place?"

"Nope, if it were me that lost my family and I was wanting to kill those I decided were responsible, I'd take out the highest-ranking person in the organization by making sure my weapon was targeted at him. The throw-and-run type of weapon, I'd use on the grunts taking orders."

She nodded. "I agree. Please send someone to tell General Stone and Colonel Marshall not to go back to their quarters until they've been checked for spores."

"Yup," Sharp said, nodding at Clark.

"Next, we need to evacuate the base. Get all the grunts out of here."

"Hmm, I don't think that's going to work, sweetheart," Sharp said.

"Why not?"

"If everyone leaves before the designer has released his pestilence on everyone here, he'll just change his plans and target another base. One we might not know about. Now is the time to find him and stop him. Before he initiates his attack."

"How are we going to do that?" She shook her head. "It won't work. I'm not willing to sacrifice a few hundred soldiers like they're nothing more than fish bait."

"That's not what I'm saying. I want to hunt this fucker down and kill him before he has a chance to do anything else."

"Hunt him where?"

"That's what all those satellite pictures are going to help with. We should be able to narrow down the possible locations."

"And if you're wrong?"

"We move on to the next location."

"What if that's wrong?"

"Grace," Sharp said, smiling at her. "This is part of the job we're actually good at."

"Why don't I feel reassured?"

He shrugged.

Clark came back at a run. "I was too late."

"What?" Grace asked sharply.

"Marshall went to his quarters. When he opened the door, a light bulb fell on the floor and shattered, releasing a cloud of fine dust." Clark stopped to take in a breath. "He closed the door right away, but some of the spores could be hanging around, right?"

TWENTY-FIVE

GRACE RAN. BLOOD DRIBBLED down the back of her hand and off the end of her middle finger. When had she taken the IV out?

Someone bellowed her name behind her, but she ignored it. The clatter of footfalls, many of them, chased her, but she ignored them too.

She wasn't going to lose the father like she'd lost the son.

A hand wrapped itself around her arm just south of her shoulder and tried to pull her to a stop.

She abruptly switched directions, throwing her weight onto the man who'd grabbed her, pushing him to the ground. She twisted her arm to get him to let go, but his grip was strong and sure, and she found herself hauled down on top of him.

She bared her teeth at the one man she trusted to let her do her job and snarled, "Let me go."

"Doc," Sharp growled back at her. "You can't go in there."

She met him glare for glare. "I can't let him die."

Sharp's voice was hard, cold and unrelenting. "He's dead already."

A cold chill abraded her exposed skin, and a broken sound of protest escaped her tight throat. "We don't know that for sure."

"Lying to yourself never works out. I know, I've tried."

His shot hit home and she sucked in a painful breath and pushed at his chest with both palms. "We can't do nothing."

He scanned her face with an intent gaze then let her go with slow deliberation. "We can't run willy-nilly into danger either."

She had run off without thinking. The bio-suit was damaged. No one should go anywhere near Marshall's room until the air and surfaces within twenty feet of the doorway had been tested for spores.

How the hell was she supposed to do anything to help anyone without a way to protect herself?

Anger's heat suffused her body, curling her hands into fists. Helpless—she was helpless to stop this weapon, to stop the man behind the weapon.

Helpless was one thing she refused to accept.

She forced herself to engage her brain. She needed information. "Does Marshall have a phone or radio with him?"

"Yeah."

"I need to talk to him. I need to know exactly what happened."

Sharp's gaze didn't waver, but he nodded. "It's this way." He led her to another set of prefab buildings, these devoted to communications.

He left her standing in the middle of the room to talk to the soldier manning a computer and wearing a Bluetooth headset.

She turned and found the way out blocked by Smoke and Clark. "I'm not going to run away."

Clark shrugged while Smoke didn't reply at all except to glance at Sharp once, then back at her.

"Doc?"

Sharp's voice brought her attention back to him, and she walked toward the phone he held out to her.

"Colonel Marshall?"

A man coughed. "Here," he said, his voice so rough it sounded like it had been torn to shreds.

"Can you tell me what happened?"

He made an impatient sound.

"I'm sorry if this is getting repetitious, but I need to hear it from you, not second—or third-hand."

"Understood. I opened the door to my quarters and a light bulb fell from somewhere above me, smashed on the floor, releasing a cloud of fine dust." He paused to cough for several seconds. "As soon as I saw that cloud of shit, I knew. The son of a bitch had put a trap in my room. I know I'm dead, but I didn't want to take anyone with me, so I slammed the door."

"How long after the dust was released into the air did you shut the door?"

"A second, maybe two."

"It's only been a few minutes since it happened, yet you sound very ill. Can you describe your symptoms for me?"

"Sore throat, watery eyes, difficulty breathing."

"When did those start?"

"Within a couple minutes of breathing in that crap."

"I'd like your input on our next steps. My bio-suit has been damaged beyond repair. This reduces our ability to investigate what's happened and assist you."

Marshall laughed. "I've heard you talk like that before, and I always thought you were a cold fish, Doctor, but now I realize you're so angry you've got yourself on lockdown."

She had no response for that.

"Here's what you're going to do." His voice changed from amused to steel-strength hardness. "You're going to find the fucker who's fucking with us and kill him."

"But..."

"No buts, Doctor. Those are your orders."

It took her two whole breaths to calm herself enough to attempt speech again. "There has to be a way to help you."

"I'm dead. Make it worth something."

"I don't think I can do it. Leave you to die, I mean."

Marshall didn't say anything for a few moments. "You never let Joe go, did you?"

A sob burst out of her, and she sucked the rest back until her whole chest hurt from keeping them in. "No. I see his face in my mind every day. When I wake up, when I doubt myself, and before every decision."

"My son acted without thinking and it got him killed," Marshall said in a tone she'd heard him use for his own soldiers, but never with her. "He fell for the distraction. Don't make the same mistake. Find the *real* enemy. He's probably not far. Men like him want to watch their handiwork in motion. Figure it out, Major Samuels. Kill the asshole before he kills again."

"Yes, sir." She swallowed hard and said, "It's been an honor serving with you."

The line went dead.

Grace put the phone down gently and turned to face Sharp. "He said this is all a distraction and we're falling for it. We need to find the real enemy. Marshall thought he wouldn't be far."

"What about Marshall?" Sharp asked.

She couldn't stop the tears from rolling down her face. "He's already feeling sick. He inhaled a huge amount of spores. I don't think...he'll last long."

General Stone spoke from where he sat, unnoticed, on the far side of the room. "Marshall's right. Go find me that bugger," he said to Sharp. "But don't kill him, not unless you have to. I want to have a little chat with him."

"Yes, sir."

"Doctor," Stone said to Grace. "You're going with the Berets. They may need your expertise."

"Understood, sir."

"However—" he pointed a finger at her "—no heroics."

"Sir, I believe Sergeant Foster will sit on me if I try to do something noble like trying to save someone's life in the middle of a firefight."

"And take care of that hand."

She glanced down. The back of her hand was covered in blood and big scab had formed where the IV had been inserted into a vein.

"I will, sir."

Stone grunted and waved a hand at them.

Sharp took Grace by the arm again and walked her out of the communications building and into supply with Hernandez, March, Runnel and Smoke trailing behind. He loaded her up with clean clothing, body armor, a Beretta and extra clips of ammunition.

He marched her to the nearest bathroom, where she washed her hand and put a Band-Aid over the puncture hole.

She disappeared into another female soldier's quarters and changed clothes. When she came out, she felt almost human again. "I'm ready," she told Sharp.

"That makes one of us," he muttered, then added in a louder tone, "We're expected in the War Room. Those satellite pictures should be ready now."

She glanced at him while he spoke and watched the muscle in his jaw bunch. "You're angry?"

He didn't answer.

She put her hand on his arm and pulled him to a stop. "Talk to me."

Hernandez coughed. "We'll meet you there." He patted Sharp on the shoulder. "Good luck, buddy." March, Runnel and Smoke followed him.

Sharp scowled at the men, then met Grace's gaze and crossed his arms over his chest.

"What?" she asked, matching his posture.

"This is going to be a bitch of a mission, and I don't want you..."

"There?" she finished.

"In harm's way," he corrected.

"I've been doing that since I took the Hippocratic Oath. There's a part that goes, *I will prevent disease whenever I can, for prevention is preferable to cure.* This is prevention."

"You're equating disease prevention to taking out a terrorist?"

"Yes." She shook her head. "Jerk." She continued walking to the War Room, Sharp grumbling behind her all the way.

Stone was in the War Room and examining a number of satellite photos. As soon as she and Sharp walked in, Stone gestured at Sharp to join him.

She glanced at the photos on the table, but they all

looked the same to her. This part, she wasn't going to have much input in. She just hoped Sharp wouldn't do anything to make her job harder in the name of protecting her.

She moved around the table to look at the photos from a different perspective. At first they seemed so alike, studying them would be a waste of time. As she looked at them, though, individual elements began to pop out of them. At first it was the rutted lines of roads and buildings, or their remains, crafted by man. She found one with three trucks headed down the same rough country road.

Hadn't Sharp said to look for a spot with a lot of truck traffic in and out?

She picked up the picture and studied it closer. The trucks appeared to be heading to...nowhere?

"Where is this?" she asked out loud.

The room went silent, and she glanced up. Sharp was on his way around the table to her.

She handed him the photo, then he looked at it and nodded.

"Here it is, sir. Sixteen hours before that one." He pointed at the photo Stone was currently looking at. He strode around the table and put the picture in front of the general.

Stone stared at the photo. "I agree. Get out there and find out if this is our traitor's home base."

Sharp glanced at the men in his team and said, "Saddle up."

HE DIDN'T WANT her on this mission. Damn it, she'd been through hell already and she didn't need to get beat up, shot or infected with anything else. Unfortunately, they also needed her on this mission.

It was the only reason he hadn't duct-taped her to a wall in her quarters.

He led his men and Grace back to their staging area to get geared up and remembered she didn't have a bio-suit. Fuck.

"You don't have a suit."

"No. I don't."

Shit, she wasn't going to let that stop her, she of the Hippocratic Oath.

"I'm not about to throw my life away," she said in a softer tone. "I won't take any unnecessary risks."

"Who gets to define what *unnecessary risk* means?"

She sighed. "Both of us."

He stopped and pointed a finger in her face, when what he really wanted to do was kiss the fight right out of her. "If things go to shit, you follow my commands. No arguing or hanging back."

"As long as you let me do what I need to, no problem."

He held out his hand and she shook it.

"Jesus Christ, I'm outta my fucking mind," Sharp muttered as he resumed their journey to the staging area. *And in love with a fucking angel.* That, he didn't say out loud. She'd run like hell if he did.

A helicopter was waiting for them, fueled and rotors turning when they hit the helicopter pad twenty minutes later. They took off into the setting sun.

The trip wasn't a long one, only forty miles away, but Sharp got their pilot to slow down and fly low as if on a search pattern a couple of miles out from their target. They hopped out as the bird disappeared behind a rise, then the bird popped back up as if nothing had happened.

Sharp's team spread out to watch for incoming threats as they moved closer and closer to their target, likely a cave system.

As darkness fell, they put on their nighttime goggles, Grace too, and continued.

They came across the first roving sentry thirty minutes after departing the helicopter. Smoke took him out quietly with a knife to the throat and hid the body.

They moved forward with more caution and took out two more sentries before having to move down into the rocky gullies in search of the place the road led to.

There was a cave with a mouth about three men wide and two high. Four men, armed with Soviet-made rifles, manned the opening. None of them appeared to be wearing night-vision equipment.

Sharp flashed a signal at Smoke, who moved location slightly, then called out for help in Dari saying he'd twisted his ankle.

Sharp settled into his half-crouch shooting position and found the four in his scope. They were a little too far apart.

The men guarding the cave gathered together, talking about what their response should be, whether one of them should investigate or if two should go.

Sharp couldn't have asked for a better scenario. He let his breath out and fired.

One.

Two.

Three.

Four.

Dead.

Behind him, Grace sucked in a breath.

He waited for her to say or do something to berate

him for shooting the men, but nothing came. No one yelled or moved.

A second later, he and his men were on the move, Grace tucked in behind him. Like she'd been when they'd hightailed it to the hills to hide after the helicopter crash. Her breath came in short pants, just loud enough for him to hear. Just loud enough for him to know exactly where she was even though all his attention appeared to be in front of him.

They moved like a mist, low to the ground in a smooth rush that suddenly contracted and circled the cave's entrance.

Smoke took point, advancing into the cave. Hernandez followed. He gave the all-clear hand signal and Sharp went in with Grace so close he could feel her body heat penetrating his clothing and armor.

Twenty feet in, voices became audible. Men, speaking in Dari.

Smoke slowed their forward momentum, giving everyone enough time to stay in close formation. Darkness faded as gas lights appeared overhead.

Two men suddenly came toward them carrying a crate, headed toward the cave's exit. Smoke let them pass.

Hernandez didn't. He and Clark grabbed a man each and thrust knives into the backs of their skulls. They dropped like dead fish onto the ground.

Smoke and Sharp caught the crate before it could crash on the rocky floor of the cave. They moved it to one wall and went to pry the lid off, but it wasn't nailed down.

Grenade launchers.

Sharp put his mouth to Grace's ear. "Could the spores

be put into a grenade and launched without risk to the person doing the launching?"

"I doubt it, but I don't think that would stop him. Them. Whoever."

He squeezed her shoulder to show his agreement. The asshole behind this insanity didn't give a shit about anyone. Not even himself.

That made him unpredictable. Deadly.

His gut reaction was to grab Grace and get her the hell out of there, but he couldn't do that and not damage the trust he'd built with her.

Trust he needed more than he needed to wrap her in plastic Bubble Wrap and hide her away from the world.

"We're looking for weapons and bad guys," he said almost soundlessly in her ear. "You look for anything that could be used as a spore deployment device."

She nodded.

"Stay right behind me. Put your hand on my back. Remember?" When they'd had to hide to evade capture, she hadn't hesitated to stay in contact, close enough for him to hear her breathing escalate.

She nodded again, and kissed him.

It was nothing more than a quick touch of her lips to his. Over in a second, but that second told him she was good with what they were doing. Good with what they had to do.

It was just his luck she'd toss him on his emotional backside while on a kill-or-be-killed mission.

He picked up his scattered wits and flashed two hand signals at the team, then led them farther into the cave.

TWENTY-SIX

THEY ENCOUNTERED NO resistance in the next twenty feet. No sign or sound of people, though there continued to be gas lanterns hanging every so often from hooks in the ceiling of the cave. They came to a fork. One was lit with more lanterns, but there must be a bend or turn in the cave because they couldn't see more than thirty feet. The other was dark.

Sharp didn't want anyone coming up their asses, so he sent Smoke on reconnaissance while the rest of them continued down the easy path.

They hit the bend, and Clark, who'd taken point, eased around it with the skill of a ghost. Three seconds passed before he returned and gave the all-clear signal.

Sharp went around the corner, Grace right behind, but the gas lights ran out and they switched to night-vision goggles.

This part of the cave appeared unoccupied, as there were only cast-off bits and pieces of wood, metal and wire strewn about.

Those guys with the grenade launchers came from somewhere.

Up ahead, Clark signaled for everyone to stop. Contact. Someone was moving around, but Sharp couldn't make anything out. Maybe the cave turned another corner.

After a few more seconds, Clark signaled the all clear

and they moved forward, but he set the pace even slower than before.

Light teased the edges of his vision, and Sharp realized the cave opened out into a huge room, hundreds of feet in diameter, with more gas lights in use. The room appeared empty until you looked across the space and saw crates stacked, some being used as tabletops, others with their lids off and their contents on display.

As they crept toward what looked more and more like a work area, Sharp figured out what one of the oddly shaped items in plain view on one of the crates was.

A microscope.

Sharp hesitated for a moment. A microscope, but no light source. Wouldn't a generator be needed?

Gas lanterns were in use and no sign of a generator.

He turned to Grace. "Does this setup seem weird to you?"

"As opposed to working in a lab free of dust and contaminants, with good ventilation and a sterile work area?" She grunted and apologized. "Sorry. Yes, it's weird and wrong and I'd like to kick the ass of the idiot who decided he could play weekend microbiologist and create the next deadly plague on earth."

That wasn't what he'd meant.

"Would you work in here? Would it even be possible to do the work required to weaponize anthrax in here?" There were conditions and situations where certain pieces of equipment just didn't function well. Underwater, high winds, long distances.

"Yes. You don't need clean. In fact, an environment where random factors might be introduced to the bacteria might even help the process. Anthrax isn't any more difficult to work with than any other bacteria, it's just more deadly than most."

"No generator," he said.

"If I wasn't actively working on something, I'd shut it off to save fuel."

"He could be out scouting his next target, or firing on his next target. We don't know his timeline."

Clark searched the other side of the crates for unfriendlies and gave the all clear.

Sharp nodded to Grace, and she darted around him to investigate the equipment. He nodded at Clark, who moved forward, following the rock wall of the cave. There was too much air movement for there to be only one entrance and exit.

Hernandez, Runnel and March took up watch positions, facing the way they'd come in, their rifles tucked into their shoulders, ready to fire.

Sharp surveyed the room at the same time as keeping watch on Grace. Her movements were quick and excited, like a predator on the trail of prey. Something snapped, a rubber-bandy sound. She'd put on gloves.

The microscope was given a quick investigation, but she moved on in seconds. The lid of one crate came off and she peered inside. The lid was placed back. Another was opened.

Silence.

Sharp glanced at her. She stared into the box with a horrified expression on her face.

"Grace?"

"It's full of grenades," she whispered.

It took him all of two seconds to reach her. The grenades looked completely normal...for individual devices with the power to tear a person's legs off. If the whole crate detonated, every person within thirty feet would be ripped to shreds.

He reached in with one hand to pick one up for inspection, but Grace stopped him with a softly worded, "No. I'm wearing the gloves." She pointed at the surfaces in clear view. "There's a fine layer of dust."

He withdrew his hand and she plucked one of the grenades out and showed it to him, turning it this way and that so he could see all sides of it.

"It looks undisturbed." He nodded at her to put it back.

"Can you tell if he's in the middle of something or what he's doing with all this stuff?"

"No. Aside from the microscope, there's nothing else here to indicate he's actively using this site as a lab."

"Nothing?"

"Nope."

Men moving munitions. Crates of more munitions and a microscope left where it could draw attention.

"Fuck me," he said as he flashed the get the hell out of Dodge signal. He grabbed Grace by the arm and pulled her into a fast trot toward the way they had come in.

An explosion threw them all on their asses in the dirt.

Sharp's head rang like a church bell on Sunday. He staggered to his feet and bumped into Grace, who'd gotten as far as her knees.

Where were Clark, Runnel and March?

A rock hit his shoulder. From above. Once glance told him the ceiling of the cave was in the process of collapsing.

A muffled yell, and a yank on his arm, brought his attention around to Grace, on her feet now, as she dragged him toward his men, two of whom lay still on the dirt. Where had Runnel gone?

Sharp stumbled after her and grabbed up Clark, who'd taken point. He was out cold, but it looked like he was still breathing. Sharp got him up and over his shoulder in a fireman's carry and walked quickly through the cave as it rained rocks toward the far wall, where he'd felt fresh air flowing.

He was about to put Clark down and go back for March, but when he turned, there was Grace not five feet behind him, dragging March by the heels. He could walk a little farther.

He followed the slight flow of air several more feet and found a narrow opening in the wall.

Thick smoke wafted past him, surrounding his head and making him cough. Smoke?

Adrenaline hit his system like a freight train and he ducked into the opening and walked several feet until the narrow crevice widened into something two men could in walk side by side. He put Clark down and went back for Grace and March.

He found them just as she was dragging the fallen soldier into the slim opening. Sharp didn't say anything, but as soon as he touched her shoulder on his way past her, she let go of March's feet and headed away from the main cave chamber.

Smoke now filled the air three feet up from the ground and up. A fireman's carry wasn't going to work. Sharp grabbed March's feet and dragged him much faster than Grace had been doing. If he lived he was going to have a hell of a headache.

Sharp had to stop a couple of times to cough, and it was getting harder and harder to breathe. Finally, he made it back to Clark and Grace, who was doing a quick triage of the unconscious soldier.

Runnel, he had to find Runnel.

A rumble of rock from the main cave roared through the air like a tsunami wave. Followed by a rapid succession of explosions, one after the other. Smoke, dust and crushing darkness blinded him.

SILENCE.

Sharp lay still. His breathing...odd. What was sitting on his chest?

He tried to lift his right hand to brush the offending object away, but found he couldn't move it. At all.

He sucked in a breath to try again, but all he got was a lungful of dirt and a coughing fit that didn't subside. He struggled to find real oxygen, to sit up and sweep the dirt off his face, but he couldn't do either and his struggles increased. Choking. He couldn't move and he was choking to death.

A wet cloth touched his face and someone yelled in his ear, "Sharp, try to relax." The cloth came back for a second run on his face and he finally took a breath that wasn't filled with dirt.

"We're digging you out," the voice said. Grace. It was Grace's voice. "But it might take a while."

"What?" he croaked out through his irritated throat.

"The cave collapsed," she said. "Some of this part of it too. It nearly buried you alive."

"March, Clark?" he asked hoarsely. "Runnel?"

"March is alive. Unconscious, but alive. Clark...didn't survive the falling rock. I think we lost Runnel in the initial blast."

Fuck. Two more of his men, his friends, *gone*. Anger

surged through his bloodstream, giving him a jolt of energy and strength, but he still couldn't move. The weight on his chest and extremities got heavier and heavier until he found breathing nearly impossible.

Focus, man. *Focus.*

"What about Smoke? Any sign?" he asked.

"Here," said the man himself, appearing on the other side of him. "Took me some time to find my way to you."

"Is there—" Sharp stopped to suck in a couple of breaths "—a way out?"

"Yes." Smoke didn't continue for a couple of seconds. "But not close. Not easy."

"Any escape...is good. Call for...extraction?"

"No signal," Smoke said.

"Stop talking," Grace ordered, reaching across his body to remove a hefty piece of rock. "Conserve your strength while we get you out."

"Were the explosions...accidental?" Sharp asked. She was probably going to get mad at him for not following his instructions, but he needed information.

"Don't think so," Smoke said. "Found wire and grenades."

"I don't like grenades," Grace muttered.

Grief made him nauseous. "Don't like them much either," Sharp whispered.

Grace and Smoke worked silently to remove the rocks and debris from trapping his body. Someone had turned on an LED flashlight, but he still couldn't see much in the dim light. Dust hung in the air like a fog.

When had he lost his night-vision goggles? Probably in the rockfall.

He stared at Grace as she worked and noted she was covered in the fine dust, though a few places on her head, face and neck glistened as she moved around. Blood? Nothing that slowed her down, given her steady movements. If she had died...nope, not going there. He sneezed, which started another coughing fit. This damn dust was going to be the death of him.

Dust.

Spores?

"Doc," he said softly. "Could we be breathing in spores?"

She paused in her rock removal, more of a stutter, a hesitation, before continuing on. "I doubt it."

She didn't sound convinced. "Explain that to me."

"There wasn't any evidence this place was ever used as a lab, not even a crude one. I think the microscope was window dressing. If he had spores to kill us, he'd have booby-trapped his stuff with it. He wouldn't leave it lying around for just anyone to get sick." She paused for a half second longer this time. "He blew us up instead."

Sharp tested the words. "This was a trap." It sounded right, and every one of them had fallen for it, from the general on down.

"I think so."

"Agreed," Smoke rumbled. He rolled a larger rock, the size of a carry-on suitcase, off of Sharp's right leg and suddenly he could move it. The claustrophobia gripping him let go a little and he flexed, trying to wake up his circulation.

Grace and Smoke worked a little faster.

A moan echoed close by and Grace disappeared. "March?" she asked.

He couldn't see her or March, but he could hear the stress in her voice. "How bad is he?"

"Broken arm and concussion. I'm not sure he'll be able to walk on his own."

Smoke moved another large rock from over his torso, and Sharp found he could breathe easier.

"We'll figure something out."

She snorted in obvious disbelief.

"That's what puts the *special* in Special Forces," he told her.

There was no reply for a couple of seconds, then Grace said very clearly, "Fuck. Off."

If she could get angry, she really was okay. "How far away is this exit of yours, Smoke?"

"Not sure. Maybe a quarter mile?"

"Any evidence of more traps?"

"No."

"We weren't meant to survive," Grace said softly. "I'm not sure how we did."

TWENTY-SEVEN

SMOKE ROLLED MORE rocks off Sharp while Grace checked March's arms, legs and torso for any other injuries. He had a couple of bumps on his head. One had bled quite a bit, and while he wasn't really as responsive as she'd like, he was coming around.

"Doc?" he said, his voice as wobbly and frail as that of an old, old man.

"Hi there, big guy, how are you feeling?"

"Headache," he said, confused. "Hurt, everywhere."

"That's 'cause you got hit by rocks, everywhere."

"Rocks?"

"What country are we in, March?"

"Um, the United States."

"How old are you?"

"Eighteen. Did I get drunk and drive?" He sounded worried. "I wouldn't do that." He tried to get up.

"No, no. Lie down, you didn't drink and drive. We're in a cave and there was a cave-in." He was also twenty-six years old, not eighteen. She'd have to watch him close to make sure he didn't develop a bruise on the inside of his skull to match the ones on the outside of it. It didn't take much brain swelling to kill a person.

"Oh." He lapsed into silence. "Where are we?"

"Afghanistan. Do you remember Sharp and Smoke?"

"Yeah, they're on my team."

"Hey, buddy," Sharp said. "Smoke and I are over here."

March tried to get up, but Grace put her hand on his chest and held him down. Normally she wouldn't have had the strength or leverage to do it, but right now, as disoriented as he was, she didn't have to work too hard.

"Sharp is partially buried under rock, and Smoke is digging him out. You just rest until Sharp is free."

"Okay, Doc. I feel kind of sick anyway."

"Sick, like vomiting?"

"Yeah." He closed his eyes and almost immediately dropped into unconsciousness.

"Sharp," she said, letting all of her concern for March filter into her voice. "I think we need to get March out of here and back to the base as fast as possible."

"What's wrong?"

"He's displaying the signs of a severe concussion. Swelling of the brain. If it gets really bad, it could be enough to kill him."

"Can you do anything for him now?"

"No. He's going to need a CT scan and probably surgery."

"You're almost out," Smoke said.

"Be ready to haul ass," Sharp ordered, sounding like he was gritting his teeth.

"Sharp, are you injured?"

"I don't know, but my left arm and leg have fallen asleep. It feels like someone is digging a million needles into me."

"That's normal after having your circulation cut off for a while. I'd be more worried if you felt nothing."

He snorted. "No worries here, then."

As she checked March's pulse again, Smoke got the

last big rock off of Sharp and he pulled himself out from under the rest.

He sat for a second or two, then climbed slowly to his feet, with Smoke lending a hand under Sharp's arm.

"Broken bones?" she asked him.

He bounced a little on his feet and twisted his wrists around. "Don't think so. Everything seems to be working properly. More or less." He bent over and dug through the rock around where he'd been lying.

"What are you looking for?"

"My rifle." He searched for a moment more, before he yanked it out from the debris. He checked it over. "Doesn't look too bad." He turned to Smoke. "Let's get the hell out of here. Lead the way."

Smoke picked up his weapon and nudged March with one foot. "Wake up."

March blinked at him blankly for a moment, then put one hand to his head. "Jesus Christ, who ran me over?"

"A terrorist." Smoke bent down and helped March to his feet.

He swayed. "Can I kill him?" March asked.

"I wish I could let you," Sharp said, limping over to look into March's face. "But General Stone wants to interrogate him."

"How about I shoot him, just a little?"

"How do you shoot someone a little?" Grace asked, not bothering to hide her irritation with the cavalier attitude these men seemed to have toward killing someone.

"In the foot or arm or somewhere not immediately fatal," March explained. His voice was slurring like he was drunk, and when Sharp grabbed him north of his elbow and began towing him along behind Smoke who had already started out, he looked even more unstable.

"Lovely." Grace didn't bother hiding her sarcasm as she picked up her pack, dusted off her uniform and followed the men. "That sounds so much less bad than just shooting *and* killing someone."

"Why are you mad at me?" March wanted to know, a confused expression on his face as he glanced back at her.

"Oh, it's not just you." She looked pointedly at the back of Sharp's head. "I'm mad at a bunch of people."

"But—"

"March," Sharp leaned over to say in his friend's ear. "She's a woman and a superior officer. Don't argue."

"Oh. Right." He put a hand to his head again. "Shit, my head feels like it's about to explode."

Sharp glanced back at her and she gave him a grim look. "We should hurry."

"Yeah." Sharp stepped up the pace and no one said anything for several minutes. It wasn't until Smoke, up ahead, stopped and gave the stop hand signal too.

Sharp left March with her, while he moved ahead to consult with their point man.

"I don't feel so good, Doc," March whispered. There was a glistening sheen of sweat on his face. "Was I drinking last night?"

"No, sorry. Can't blame this on alcohol. It was the rocks."

"Goddamn rocks should have stayed where they were."

"I wish the same thing. I really do."

Sharp came toward them. He leaned in close so they could both hear his barely there voice. "The exit is guarded by at least two men. There may be more."

"Can you get a signal? Call for help?"

"Smoke is talking to the base now. An extraction team could leave at any time, but there's nowhere to set down. The terrain is too rough. We're going to have to travel at least a quarter mile before we get to an area where the bird can land."

Grace looked pointedly at March. "That's a long time to be out in the open, and we need to get back to the base. Now would be good."

Sharp glanced at his buddy and his lips tightened. "Understood." He met her gaze. "You two stay here and guard our backs."

March was in no condition to guard anything, but she nodded. She had a Beretta, she could do the guarding.

Sharp stared at her for a moment then muttered, "Fuck it." He slid a hand behind her head and kissed her. It was quick, hard and thorough. As if he were trying to put a lifetime of need and desire into it. The kiss left no question in her mind that he didn't like this situation any more than she did.

He let her go with the same smooth speed he'd used to kiss her and was gone before she could say or do anything.

"That had better not be a good-bye kiss," she said to herself under her breath.

She helped March to sit down next to a large boulder. He leaned against it and closed his eyes. "I'm not going to be of much use, Sharp," he said, his words slurring a bit. "Everything is blurry."

"He's gone," Grace said in a soft tone. "You and me, we're going to do this together."

"You're a pretty good liar, Doc." March smiled, but it was so sad. "I might be half out of my head, but I'm dying. Those rocks killed me, right?"

"We just have to get you to the base and drill a little hole in your head. Then you'll be fine."

He opened his eyes and stared at her. The smile on his face turned genuine. "That's a pretty fucked-up thing to say."

She opened her mouth to reply, but he sagged, his eyes closing. She put a hand on his shoulder and shook him. "March?" She did it again, then checked his carotid pulse. It was fast and weaker than she would have liked.

Goddamn it, she wasn't going to lose another friend, another *brother*, to these insane people. She didn't know what she could do exactly to expedite the situation, but she was going to do something.

The familiar weight of her Beretta brought with it a strange sort of calm. A surreal peace the eye of a hurricane brings, though you can see the frenzied conflict all around you, and you know it has the power to kill you.

She checked the magazine. Full. Slid the safety off and walked with soft knees toward daylight.

A metallic *pop*, followed by a hailstorm of more, had her crouching down and searching for the source. No one was in sight. No echo. Not in the cave. Outside.

The gunfire continued on and off with small bursts every few seconds. Sharp and Smoke might be moving around, trying to pinpoint where the enemy was. Or the enemy might be trying to pinpoint where they were. Either way, this search-and-destroy was taking up too much time.

She eased over to the narrow mouth of the cave. This entrance wasn't wide, only enough space for a single person to squeeze through sideways. She peered out cautiously, taking her time, letting her gaze check every nook and cranny of the surrounding rocky terrain. No one. Not even her own guys.

She eased out and crouched down to listen.

More gunfire bounced around and she froze in place as it echoed through her brain. Images of the firefight from the IED flashed past and superimposed themselves over her sight.

She wasn't crouched near the mouth of the cave, but behind the open door of an armored vehicle, the bodies of her nurses lay beside her on the ground. Her patient yelled for help, but she was immobile, terrified by what she knew was coming.

The boy soldier.

Killing him had injured her in ways she never expected. A constant acid drip of guilt and self-loathing burning a hole in her soul. She was living it again, powerless to stop it, unless she acted first. Her mind recalled the first moment she saw Joseph Cranston, but instead of his young unlined face, she saw his father's weathered skin and ornery expression.

"You're going to find the fucker who's fucking with us and kill him," he yelled at her, and the mental shout shot adrenaline into her system.

"Yes, sir."

A pebble bounced off the rocks above her and off her shoulder. She glanced up and didn't see anything at first. After a moment, she realized that an outcropping about twenty feet above her was too straight. It was a gun muzzle and the shooter was firing every few seconds or so, in bursts echoing weirdly, making them sound like they came from somewhere else.

She knew Sharp's weapon. She knew Smoke's

too. They looked nothing like the long straight barrel above her.

She had to be sure. She couldn't kill a man without making certain he was the enemy.

Could she get up there without alerting whoever was firing that weapon?

Grace took a few moments and plotted out the likeliest route up and found there were a couple of options. Neither was easy or safe, but she didn't have a choice. If she left the shooter up there and he was an extremist, he was just going to shoot her in the back anyway.

Climbing the rocks was harder than she expected. Her boots were fine, it was her hands that needed protection. She picked up several cuts before she arrived at the top of the outcropping. No time to bandage them.

Out came her Beretta again and she advanced on the man lying prone about fifteen feet away. He was focused on shooting at a target below him.

He wore the traditional clothing of an Afghan male, and the skin of his hands was the color of caramelized sugar.

She needed to see his face. Be certain he wasn't a friend, but foe. "Hey."

The man turned, looked at her, rolled to his side, lifted his weapon and...

She fired. One to the head. One to the heart. Her feet carried her to him and she checked his carotid pulse. Nothing. She'd killed. Again.

Below her in the valley beneath the outcropping, more gunfire echoed.

The extremist had binoculars. She grabbed them and found Sharp. She couldn't see Smoke, but that was no surprise. Sharp was probably drawing fire, so Smoke could circle around and attack from the rear.

Sharp was drawing more fire than he knew. There was a group of three men attempting to come at his position from the rear.

The Afghan man's rifle looked even older than she first thought, but it was firing, so why not use it.

She grabbed the weapon, lay down, checked for ammo and sighted down the scope. It hardly made a difference, but then again, this wasn't a precision instrument like the weapons Special Forces soldiers use. All she really wanted to do was cause some consternation for the men hunting her man.

If she killed one, well, that would be a bonus.

Right?

This old rifle probably didn't shoot so straight, so she aimed high, fired and watched through the scope to see the result.

One of the Afghans dropped. The men with him stared at the body and began gesturing. They turned as one to look at her position.

That's right, assholes. New shooter. New rules.

She had two bullets left. No use saving them. She fired again.

This time her target didn't drop, but he did stumble and do an awkward crab-crawl until he was behind some shelter. Wounded him maybe.

His friend disappeared too, and Grace gave serious thought to leaving her perch for a less-obvious position. Anyone in the vicinity would be able to see her if they had some half-decent binoculars. Not like the piece of crap pair the dead man next to her had.

She sighted down the binoculars to see where she

could help and watched some rapid movement off to the north. A ferocious volley of gunfire began, then ended after about five seconds.

She saw Smoke's head pop up, then immediately drop from sight, but he was moving toward Sharp. She scanned the area for any more unfriendlies, but saw nothing.

She eased back from the edge of the outcropping, keeping her new old rifle with her. She fished some more ammunition off the dead man's belt then headed back down the way she came.

Her hands got cut up a little more.

Grace slid back into the cave and checked on March. He was still unconscious and in the same position as before. His pulse was a little faster and a little weaker, his breathing shallow.

She grit her teeth. He wasn't going to make it to the base.

For a moment, anger and grief blinded her. So tired of seeing men she liked and respected dying. So tired of all the killing. And for what? Power? Control? Terror?

If she could get her hands on the idiot who'd started all this, she'd show him terror. She'd make sure he knew more about it than anyone should.

TWENTY-EIGHT

RAGE GRIPPED SHARP by the throat and threatened to shake him out of his normal calm, professional persona while waiting for his quarry to make a mistake and show himself. Patience had always come easy. Until now. Until Grace decided to do exactly what she'd promised not to do.

It had been impossible to miss. She'd been all too visible standing on the outcropping of stone. He hadn't seen who she was stalking, but he recognized her body language and movements. They'd come straight out of the *how to sneak up on the enemy* US Army handbook. She'd fired twice, then someone began shooting the assholes who thought they were sneaking up on him.

There was no way he could let a woman this perfect for him slip out of his life. There had to be a way for them to be together without it destroying their careers.

If they survived this shit, he was going to find it.

A head popped up, the one he'd been waiting for, and he fired. A hit. There was some frantic movement as the last target moved, but he didn't have a clear shot at this one.

Two shots were fired by someone else from a different direction and the movement stopped.

Smoke's voice whispered over the radio, "Clear."

"Return to Beta position," Sharp said, then started moving himself. He had a doctor to discipline.

On the way back to the cave entrance, he checked on the men Grace had shot. One dead, one wounded. The wounded man lifted his weapon. Sharp shot him before he could fire, but he wasn't happy about that either. He wanted answers and wouldn't get any from a corpse.

He arrived at the cave before Smoke. As he slipped inside, he came face-to-face with Grace lowering her Beretta.

Good. At least she'd been prepared to shoot if he hadn't been friendly.

She ducked her head and walked away, her shoulders hunched like a woman who'd been hit by someone she loved.

Was she hurt?

He lunged after her and pulled her to a stop. "Are you injured?"

Her face was solemn. "Not really." She glanced into the dark interior of the cave. "March...died."

Fuck.

Fuck.

Fuck.

His anger flared again and he squeezed his eyes shut for a moment, wrapping up the rage, frustration and sadness with steel bands of control. He couldn't afford to let his emotions rule him until they were in a safe place.

But he could offer her support. "Come here," he whispered. "Let me hold you."

Yeah, he was an ass, because he was totally taking advantage of her kindness and empathy for him, so he could comfort her.

She came to him without hesitation, without question, wrapping her arms around him and burying her face in the hollow of his shoulder. She didn't cry, but she held on tight. So tight her arms shook.

A crunch on the rocks behind him accompanied by a whisper of sound.

Sharp glanced over his shoulder to find Smoke there, his face set in cold lines.

"March is gone," Sharp told him.

Smoke only nodded, then turned away to stand guard on the entrance.

"I'm so tired of my friends dying," Grace said to him, her voice rough with tears. "So tired of killing people." She pulled away and wiped her face with her sleeve. "No one is going to win. There is *no* win."

He didn't say anything. What was there to say? She was right.

"When did he pass?"

"A few minutes before you got back. I held his hand. I told him he could go, and he went."

He buried his face in her hair and whispered, "Thank you. Thank you for being there for him."

"If it had been you, I'd have yelled and screamed at you to stay." She pulled back far enough to meet his gaze. "I wouldn't have let you go."

A glad sort of fierceness filled him at knowing she would have fought for him. He smiled savagely. "Good."

He hugged for another moment, then pulled away to frown at her. "You promised not to take risks."

"I didn't."

"You climbed a couple stories and anyone looking in your direction would have seen you."

"There was a sniper up there taking shots at you."

"I knew he was there."

"He was trying to flush you out so his friends could kill you."

"I knew that too."

She growled at him. "So, I'm just supposed to stay out of sight, stay safe, while you play hide-and-seek with a bunch of men who are trying their best to kill you?" She poked him in the chest. "Fuck that."

Her growl and willingness to have his back had his cock at fucking attention. If they survived, he wasn't going to let her out of bed for a week. "You promised you'd take no unnecessary risks. That risk was unnecessary."

"I can't read your mind, Sharp. I saw a situation and knew I had to do something. The least you could do is trust me enough to know what I'm doing."

"I do trust you."

"Oh yeah? Then what's with the I'm-the-soldier-you're-the-asset routine?"

"Grace—" He cut himself off. They didn't have time to argue. "Just leave it for now. We've got to get back to the base."

She scowled at him for a second, then nodded her head once in agreement. "I thought a helicopter was going to pick us up?"

"The base came under fire about ten minutes ago. No one can land or take off. We're on our own for now."

"Our friends," Smoke said, "left a couple of trucks."

She stared at him, then at Sharp. "But we didn't accomplish anything here."

"We know this was a trap that almost worked."

"It did work. Clark, Runnel and March are dead."

"Grace. We expected to find a lab here. We didn't. I

think this whole place was intended as a distraction at the least or a deadly trap at best."

"So, if we didn't find the lab here," she said slowly. "Where is it?"

"Exactly."

She looked at him, tilted her head to one side and asked, "If it were you planning this attack with anthrax spores inside grenades, how would you do it?"

Both men froze, their gazes unfocused, considering her question.

Sharp answered first. "The boy who cried wolf."

"Yes," Smoke agreed.

"Distraction. Distraction. Distraction. Direct attack," Sharp explained.

A simple plan.

Simple plans work more often than complicated plans.

"Where are we in the pattern?" Grace asked.

Sharp ticked one finger off. "The attack on the village."

Smoke ticked off the next one. "The deaths of Cutter and the two marines at the base."

Grace ticked off the last one. "This decoy slash trap."

"The direct attack is happening now," Sharp said.

They stared at each other for three long seconds.

Grace swallowed. "Where did you say those trucks are?"

SHARP HUNG ON to the door as Smoke yanked the steering wheel of the ancient half-ton he drove to the right then the left in order to miss a rock that would have hung them up. He followed no road, drove straight across country in a direct line, or as direct as he could manage, toward the base at the fastest speed he dared.

All three of them would be lucky to arrive with their bones intact and their insides not upside down.

Sharp was ready to rearrange the insides of the enlisted moron on the radio. He'd explained that the base was in danger of attack, a second anthrax attack, but the moron kept trying to tell him they had it handled.

"You will do your fucking job," he said into the radio in a tone promising bad, nasty things if his orders weren't followed. "You will inform General Stone of my report and you will do it now."

The moron finally said he'd find someone to report it to and requested Sharp keep the channel open.

"Wow," Grace said to Smoke. She sat between him and Smoke on the torn-up bench seat. "It sounds like Sharp's ready to carve that kid up."

Smoke grunted his agreement, then frowned at the dip in the terrain coming at them and growled, "Hang on."

Grace, unable to reach anything bolted down, grabbed Sharp around the waist. After a couple of hard bounces and a jerk resulting in a metallic *clang*, they headed down into a small valley.

"What was that?" Grace asked.

"Probably the suspension," Sharp said. "Or the muffler." He thought about it some more. "Or it could have been the brakes."

Smoke pumped them and nothing happened. "Brakes."

"No brakes?" Grace yelled.

"Don't need 'em," Sharp said. "We'll be going uphill in a couple seconds."

The truck gave an almighty shake as they started up the other side of the valley. Three seconds up the slope, the drive shaft dropped out like it had only been attached to the vehicle with Silly String.

The engine gave a cough, a wheeze and died altogether.

The truck came to a stop then rolled backward.

"Abandon ship," Sharp said, grabbing his weapon and leaping out the passenger's side. Grace followed him while Smoke went out the driver's side.

His radio squawked.

"Who the fuck am I talking to now?" Sharp snarled into it as if he hadn't just jumped out of a moving vehicle.

"General Stone."

"My apologies, General, I have no patience for stupidity or assholes. The cave was in use by Akbar, but not as his lab. It was a trap. We lost three men inside and had to fight our way out."

"Major Samuels?"

"She's good and keeping up with Smoke and me just fine. Sir, we think Akbar is going to attack the base with grenades containing spores."

"We came under attack, small arms, about thirty minutes ago. I'm preparing to send out units. One to you and one to deal with whoever is shooting at us."

"Don't. I think this is all a distraction to make it easier for Akbar to get his anthrax grenade where he wants it."

There was a two-second pause. "Your dead?"

"Inside the cave. I don't think anyone is going to bother them while we find the fucker responsible for killing them."

"Agreed. Get your asses back here."

"Yes, sir."

With Smoke on his right and Grace behind him, Sharp crested the hill. He took a good look around with binoculars. The base was visible to the northwest, about two miles away, and nothing much between them and it but rocks, brush and a landscape that could easily hide a few men with a grenade launcher.

"What are we doing?" Grace asked.

"Going back to the base. Up for a run?"

"Do I have a choice?"

"Nope."

She shook her head, the picture of female exasperation, but followed him readily enough when he started out.

Smoke took rear guard.

Sharp kept the pace steady as he watched for anything out of place.

A weakly waving arm qualified.

Sharp brought Grace and Smoke to a stop and a crouch with a hand signal. He pulled out his binoculars and scanned the area. The hand wavered like the owner of it didn't have enough strength to keep waving all the time. He could see little else, his view blocked by brush and terrain.

"There's someone ahead with a hand in the air, like they've been wounded," Sharp reported.

"What are the chances they're American?"

"Not very good."

"Another distraction?" Grace asked.

"Or a decoy." Sharp scanned the area again with his binoculars, then went out wider. Could this be another attempt to draw help away from the base or remove defenders from it?

"We can't leave him like that," Grace hissed.

She was right, but probably not for the reason she was thinking.

They couldn't leave a possible hostile in a position where he could approach from behind.

"Smoke," Sharp said. He didn't have to say anything else. The big man moved out, fast and quiet.

"How does he do that?" Grace muttered.

"What?"

"Disappear. I didn't even hear him move."

Sharp shrugged. "We don't call him Smoke just because it's his name."

It took a couple of minutes before Smoke broke radio silence with a single word, "Doc."

Sharp nodded at her and they both headed Smoke's way. What they found chilled Sharp's blood down to the bone.

An Afghan man lay curled up on the ground. The visible parts of his body, hands, face and neck were covered with bloody sores. He was breathing, but it sounded like he was doing it through an old-fashioned coffee percolator. The kind his grandfather used on the stove. The man coughed, and blood droplets appeared on the ground in front of his face.

Grace knelt next to the man, but didn't touch him in any way.

"Anthrax?" Sharp asked.

"Yes." She looked up, glanced at the man on the ground and shook her head.

He wasn't going to make it.

"He was left behind," Smoke said. "Fresh tracks, two men, continue toward the base."

"Shit." A high point in the terrain wasn't far. He jogged over with Smoke beside him and looked around using his scope.

Two men carrying something in a long sack were

within five hundred feet of the base. They didn't need to be close. Anywhere inside four hundred feet would work for what they wanted to do. Including introducing a deadly spore to everyone inside.

TWENTY-NINE

GRACE WANTED TO ease the Afghan man's suffering, but she didn't dare touch him. He could have spores on his skin and clothing.

His face told her more eloquently than words that he was in agony. The coughs racking his body only made things worse. She sighed and was about to move back when his hand snaked out and grabbed her wrist.

She tugged out of his grip fairly easily and crab-crawled backward, until she saw what was in his other hand.

A grenade.

A grenade with its safety pin removed. She had no idea if this grenade had spores in it, but given the condition of the dead man in front of her, the possibility was high.

The man's hand shook and he almost dropped it on the ground. She lunged forward and grabbed it before he could release the safety lever.

No gloves on.

Damn it, wasn't this just lovely.

The man coughed again, then fell silent.

Now, what the hell was she supposed to do? She was holding the worst sort of bomb. The kind that killed slowly.

Sharp and Smoke weren't far away, looking for the

men who'd left this poor man behind. Men with more grenades.

She couldn't ask Sharp and Smoke for help. It would put them at risk, and she wasn't about to endanger them any more than they already managed to do for themselves. Damn Special Forces soldiers thought they were indestructible, until they weren't. Sharp would take the grenade from her and sacrifice himself. It was the way he was built, to protect, to give and give until he had nothing left.

Her body shook with the rejection of that possibility. *No.* This was one sacrifice she couldn't allow him to make.

On the heels of that thought came another. Like a freight train, it smashed through every barrier and fortress she'd ever built around her heart, and for a moment everything stopped. Her breathing, her heartbeat and her perception of the world around her.

She loved him.

Moments of them together flickered through her mind. Sharp smiling and laughing, playing chess and poker, kissing her, touching her, his hands and lips making her feel like she was the only woman in his world.

All of it solidified into one thought, one unalterable truth.

The biological weapon in her fist wasn't going to eat him alive. She couldn't permit it.

She had enough cuts on her hands to make infection likely, and Sharp had lost too much already, too many of the people he cared about. She wasn't going to make him watch her die too.

"I'm so dead." There was no hope. None. Not a single move left open to her.

Except for one. She had to go somewhere where she could throw this death trap away without risk of infecting anyone else.

Anthrax spores were hardy and could survive with all their lethal capabilities intact for decades in some environments.

She couldn't think of a single safe place.

If she threw it down a well, the spores would contaminate the water.

If she threw it into a ravine, the spores would get spread around and picked up by people and wildlife alike.

She needed somewhere isolated. Somewhere people were unlikely to go. Somewhere a sustained, controlled fire could destroy all the spores without spreading them around.

The cave?

It wasn't perfect, but it was the best option she could think of that she could reach on her own without help.

Sharp and Smoke were out of sight behind the brush, but she could hear them speaking softly to each other. Distances. Wind speed. Smoke was acting as Sharp's spotter.

She crept around the plants, kept the hand holding the grenade at her side and out of sight, and waited until Smoke noticed her. It didn't take long.

"He's dead," she said, jerking her head toward the deceased Afghan. "Do you have a target?"

"Yeah."

"You do what you've got to do. I'm going to move back a little ways and keep watch to be sure no one tries to sneak up on us."

"Stay safe," Sharp said in a tone that told her if she didn't, there'd be hell to pay.

She was already paying. Knowing she wasn't going to be able to tell him how she felt about him, how much his trust, respect and desire for her meant to her, was an open, festering wound.

Better than watching him die next to her.

She'd go to the cave and let the grenade destroy its deadly payload and herself quickly.

With one last admiring look at his fabulous ass, she turned and broke into Sharp's ground-eating run.

SHARP'S TARGET WASN'T COOPERATING. "Come on, you fucker. A little to the right." He could see a scrap of cloth from the top of the Afghan's pakol, or hat.

Smoke's whisper was little more than a wisp of fog on a cold day in his ears. "Wind speed steady. Range six hundred yards. Two targets."

Through the scope, Sharp could see the spotter for the shooter clearly, but he wanted them both. Leaving one alive wasn't an option.

A moment later, the tip of the grenade launcher rose into the air. *Come on, fucker, come on.*

The shooter's head rose.

Sharp took the shot. He repositioned for the second target, and fired.

"Both targets down," Smoke reported.

"Look for movement or a secondary team," Sharp ordered.

Smoke was already on it, already scanning the area with his binoculars. "No contact."

Sharp radioed the base. "Targets are down," he said, then repeated it. "Targets are down."

"Can you confirm the kill?" the base radio operator asked. Not the same guy as the moron.

"Not without a bio-suit," Sharp told him. "Advise a one-hundred-yard safe zone around the targets."

"Understood. Return to base, Sergeant."

"Roger." Sharp pulled out of his shooting position. "Fuck, I'm tired."

"The doc is quiet," Smoke observed. "Sleeping?"

"She's been tough to keep up with us this long," Sharp replied. He wasn't going to say a word to anyone if they found her sacked out in a hole.

They walked to their rear, looking for her, but she didn't seem to be about. "You see her, Smoke?" Sharp asked the other man.

"I see her tracks," Smoke answered.

Sharp joined him.

"She walked this far," the big man said. "Then she started running." He pointed in the direction of the route they'd taken from the cave.

"What the *fuck*?" Sharp stared at the deserted landscape between them and the cave. Nothing. *What the hell could she be thinking?*

"Only one reason to go back," Smoke said.

"Fuck me, Smoke, I can't come up with *any*."

"To protect us."

She would too, do anything to protect *her* team. She'd shown her loyalty to them, to *him*, in a thousand ways. She wouldn't think twice.

Frustrated fury made his words come out sounding like they'd been mixed with gravel. "You think that Afghan got her sick?"

"Or had something that could get us sick."

The goddamn woman was doing it again. Taking care

of him by putting herself in harm's way. When he caught up to her, he was going to spank her sweet ass until it was red and she was begging him to fuck her. Sharp radioed the base. "Base, we've lost contact with Major Samuels. We're beginning our search for her."

There was a long pause while Sharp and Smoke began their run to chase down their doctor.

"Say again, Sergeant?"

"We've lost contact with Major Samuels."

This time it was General Stone's voice over the radio. "Explain that to me, soldier."

Smoke had the balls to grunt a laugh.

"Sir, we think she's headed back to the cave."

"Why?"

"I don't know, sir. We're following her trail."

"You sonsabitches don't come back without her. Got that?"

"Understood." It was an order he was happy to comply with. After a few minutes Smoke said, "She's a good runner."

"She found her stride the night we crashed," Sharp said. "Kept up with me and stayed on my six like a tick on a hound."

"When's the wedding?"

Sharp couldn't stop the grin. "Shit, am I that obvious?"

"Yeah."

Sharp let his words rattle around his head for a minute. "She'd better be okay."

GRACE ALMOST STEPPED on one of the men she'd killed earlier, and had to stuff her sleeve in her mouth to keep from screaming. Now that she'd stopped, her legs felt like noodles and her knees were telling her enough was enough. But she wasn't quite done.

She still had to dispose of the grenade in her hand. At least the cave was only a little farther. She could even see the narrow entrance from this angle.

If she didn't do this quick, she might lose her nerve and not do it at all.

The climb up to the entrance was almost more than she could manage, but she got there, glanced over her shoulder and saw the last thing she wanted to see.

Sharp and Smoke running toward her, only a couple hundred yards away.

"No!" She turned and showed them what was in her hand. "It's got no pin."

Did that stop them? No, of course not, not big, bad *extra* Special Forces soldiers. They didn't hesitate as they climbed up to stop only a few feet away.

She stared at them, utterly defeated. "You two are the stupidest people I know."

Sharp looked at the grenade. "I wouldn't throw stones if I were you, princess."

"I didn't pick this up for fun, asshole. That Afghan handed it to me right before he died. It's got no pin, so it's going to go off. I was trying to do it somewhere safe for everyone, but no," she said, trying and failing to stuff the fear and horror overtaking her back inside. "You morons have to run to my rescue." She barely got the last word out around the choke point in her throat.

She wasn't going to make it, wasn't going to be able to stop the tears or the howls of pain for much longer. If she didn't get rid of them, they were going to see everything, *he* was going to see every nightmare and hopeless fantasy she had. She pointed in the general direction of the base. "Not this time. Get lost. Go home, or whatever."

"Either you have a fever again or you're so exhausted you don't know what you're saying," Sharp told her with a shake of his head. "Because we're not leaving without you."

Goddamn stubborn man.

Despair pulled all the starch from her bones and she sagged against the rocks lining one side of the mouth of the cave. A sob escaped its captivity deep in her chest and she hastily slammed the door on the rest. Nothing could stop the tears from coursing down her face.

Sharp took a step toward her and she pushed away. "No, I could be contaminated with spores. Don't touch me."

He froze for a moment, then let his hand drop as he growled, "I'm not leaving you to do this alone."

"Yes, you are."

"No, I'm not."

"I outrank you. I order you to *leave*," she yelled, desperate, willing to do anything to convince him to go.

He snarled at her. "You promised to follow my commands in situations where I'm the expert."

He wasn't going to go. She could see it in his eyes, in the set of his face. He smiled, a long, sad upturn of his lips, and turned to Smoke. "Get us some support here."

"You sure, boss?"

"Never more sure in my life."

Smoke left.

"Okay, sweetheart," Sharp said to her as if they were discussing a plumbing problem and not the instrument of their death. "Let's have a look at this grenade."

She wanted to smack his face. She wanted to kiss the

living daylights out of him. She settled for holding out the grenade and wiping cold tears off her face. "You are so stupid."

"Nope," he said, giving the device a thorough examination, though it was still in her hand. "Just a schmuck in love."

"What?" He couldn't have said what she thought he'd said.

He smiled again. "Speaking of which, will you marry me?"

Speechless, her jaw opened and closed a couple of times, before she managed to snap it closed and say from between her teeth, "Not funny."

"Not joking."

"Ha. We're both going to *die*."

His expression turned serious. "How sure are you of that?"

She lost her righteous anger in a heartbeat. "The possibility is good." She swallowed hard and begged, "Please, I...I love you." The last two words came out as a whisper. She cleared her throat. "Let me finish this alone."

He put his hand over hers on the grenade. "Could you let me do it alone?"

Bastard. Smart, stubborn bastard, he had to know how she felt or he wouldn't have asked the question. "No." Her shoulders sank. "This is going to kill us both."

He didn't respond to her prediction, but asked, "Do you have a plan?"

"Nothing past getting here, throwing the grenade inside and running for my life."

"That's not bad. Let's see if it would work." He moved past her and into the cave. A flashlight came on and he led her inside a few feet until the walls of the cave expanded a bit.

"If we throw it up against that side," he said, pointing to the right. "The blast might deflect off this side and back in on itself rather than funneling outside."

"Okay."

He pointed the light at her, just below her neck, and watched her for a moment. "You look tired, sweetheart."

She was so tired. "Yeah, I'm going to crash soon."

"It's almost over, darlin'."

He made it sound like something was going to change, but they were both inside the nightmare now. "I don't even know what that would feel like."

"We'll both be able to rest soon," he said, coming close and tucking a stray hair behind her ear.

"I've killed you," she whispered, leaning into his hand. "Rest isn't something I'm ever going to have again."

"Won't know until we get there." Sharp took the grenade out of her hand. One second she had it, the next he did. "Out. I'm going to throw this thing in ten, nine, eight..."

She ran.

Seven, six, five, four, three, two, one...

Sharp flew out of the cave and flattened himself over her, huddled against the exterior wall of rock just as an explosion blasted sound, rocks and dirt around them.

Sharp tugged at her and they scrambled down the slope and away as fast as they could go. After a couple of hundred yards, Grace ran out of air, strength and everything else.

"I've got nothing left," she said, folding in on herself and sitting on her butt on the ground.

"Okay," Sharp said, reaching into his pack and pulling out a bottle of water. He took a swig and handed it to her. "We'll wait here for the cavalry."

She nodded, breathing hard. "Make sure they're wearing bio-suits."

"Yes, ma'am." He sat down next to her, then pulled her into his lap, his arms around her, his head resting on top of hers.

She relaxed into his embrace. This might be the last time she had to be close to him, to feel his chest rising and falling with each breath, to hear his heart beating under her ear.

She cried a little more and soaked in the nonsensical words he murmured into her ear. She calmed after a while and he asked, sounding no more curious than if he asked her for the temperature, "How long until we know if we're going to die?"

She sniffed and tightened her arms around him. "A few hours. Not long."

"Don't cry, darlin'. Wherever you go, I go."

THIRTY

THE BAG OF saline hanging above Grace's head was almost empty. She frowned at it. When had she gotten an IV? There were three smaller bags next to it, Cipro, doxycycline and penicillin.

Voices, their volume rising with every word, drew her attention to a knot of uniformed men standing about ten feet away. Though they could have been farther, the room looked a little fuzzy.

"She's been scrubbed head to toe and she's getting massive doses of antibiotics. What more do you want?"

Huh. If that wasn't Sharp, she'd eat her boots.

"She could be infectious and she should be isolated," someone else argued.

"She doesn't even have a cough," Sharp shot back. "*Standard* isolation procedures work just fine."

"You're a sniper, not a doctor."

"I've been working with an infectious disease specialist for months who was happy to share her knowledge. If you'd like more information, why don't you ask her? She's right over there." He pointed at her.

Grace looked at herself. Someone had removed her clothes and dressed her in a hospital-style gown. Her skin looked as if it had been scrubbed hard, the dirt and sand embedded under her fingernails, gone.

No sores visible.

She took in a deep breath and let it out slowly. No coughing either.

"He's right," she said.

The whole group stopped their arguing to look at her.

"I'm asymptomatic. I pose only minimal risk." She smiled at them. "If I start hacking up blood and form bleeding sores on my skin, feel free to stick me in a plastic bubble."

Sharp folded his arms over his chest and gave the officer a *fuck you* grin. "Colonel Maximillian will be here in an hour. You can check with him if you want, but we're following his infection control protocol to the letter."

The officer finally left, the others following him.

Sharp waited until they were gone before walking over to sit on the floor next to her gurney.

They weren't in the infirmary on the base, there was no noise from other medical staff or patients. Someone had set up portable hospital curtains on all four sides of her gurney, making it look like she was inside a box.

"Where, exactly, are we?"

He smiled at her. A much too happy smile. "We're in what used to be the supply room for the infirmary."

"Oh." She studied the grin on his face. Was he high? "How long have I been here?"

"Six hours."

That had her blinking.

He laughed. "After we detonated the grenade, you kind of crashed."

"Oh. Sorry."

"It didn't bother me. You ran out of gas. No shame in that."

His grin was starting to get creepy. "Did you sleep?"

"A couple hours here and there."

"So, what, that fills your gas tank? Find a bed and get some real sleep."

"I will, as soon as Max gets here."

"Why are you waiting for Max?"

Sharp looked at her and raised one eyebrow.

"Oh, for fuck's sake. Paranoid much? No one is going to do anything to me for fear of getting sick."

"Still waiting."

"How's Smoke?"

"He's good. Sleeping."

"Let me guess. As soon as Max gets here, you're going to wake him up while you sleep so I can have a big, scary, silent Special Forces soldier stand guard over me."

"Yep."

She sighed. "How is...Colonel Marshall?"

Sharp's grin drained away. "He didn't make it. Died a couple of hours ago."

"Oh." Sorrow swamped her like a high tide. She hadn't liked him, but she understood his grief for his son. Understood how it could eat at you and change the way you see the world.

"Stop that," Sharp ordered.

"Stop what?"

"Beating yourself up over his death. *You* didn't kill him."

"Doesn't make me feel any better."

"I thought doctors learned to compartmentalize, disengage their emotions so they can treat sick people with objectivity and a clear head?"

"I seem to have lost all my objectivity when I met you."

"Ah, I'm heartbroken."

She was too tired to deal with his shit. "I'm going back to sleep."

"Nighty-night, Grace."

He was smiling again. She could tell from his tone he was damn near gloating.

Asshole. She knew him now. "Just you wait until we play chess. You're going to lose."

His voice followed her into sleep. "Sweetheart, if I lose to you, I win."

"GRACE."

She opened her eyes at her name. "Max." She smiled. "When did you get here?"

"About an hour ago. I had to bribe your watchdog into going to sleep."

"Smoke?"

"No, the other one, the sniper." He snorted. "The silent one didn't require much convincing."

"I think Sharp was overtired."

"His alertness was in no way responsible for his overprotective attitude," Max told her in a tolerant tone. "He follows you around like a puppy."

"He's *not* a puppy."

"The question is, what do you want to do about it?"

The thought of not having Sharp around to talk to, bounce ideas off of, with his strength and calm competence, induced an anxiety she didn't want to entertain at all. "Do I have to do anything?"

Max stared at her, his wise eyes seeing far too much. "What happened?"

She thought back over the last few days. Where did she start? "A lot of things. Awful things. Amazing things." Damn it, she was crying again. She wiped away the tears. "Did you find the man responsible for the anthrax? Was he one of the men with the grenade launcher?"

"No. CIA has confirmed Akbar is responsible, but he's nowhere to be found."

"Is he going to try again?"

"That's what everyone thinks. General Stone has ordered our team to take on some new members. You've been working with your sniper's team to train Afghan forces for almost a year. Would you feel comfortable working with Green Berets as official members of our Biological Response Team? We need men with their training and ability to spot problems from a distance to pair up with our doctors."

"Yes. Absolutely. I trust my guys one hundred percent." More tears. "I just wish I hadn't lost so many of them."

"Sharp? Do you...trust him?"

"With *everything*."

"Everything?" Max approached and asked softly, "Does he know you're in love with him?"

She smiled, but knew it was a weak effort. "It sort of slipped out when I thought I was going to die, but don't worry. We both know where we stand."

"Are you sure?" Max's gaze filled with brotherly concern.

"Yes. He's a good man. The best, we're...good."

"What about this Smoke?"

"Oh, he's a brother. He's harmless."

Max shook his head. "If you believe that, you need a lot more sleep." He got up and took a few steps away.

"Wait," Grace said. "What did you discover about the anthrax? I thought it wasn't susceptible to Cipro."

"It is, just not alone. As you suggested, I tried a cocktail of ciprofloxacin, doxycycline and penicillin boosted with a beta-lactamase inhibitor. The sensitivity test worked, so as soon as you got to the base, I had the doctors here start infusing you with all three. It seems to have worked to prevent the anthrax from getting a foothold in your lungs."

"Did you find spores on my skin? Clothing?"

"Yes."

"Sharp?"

"Far less on him, so he's taking oral Cipro rather than in an IV."

"What about the grenades that Sharp stopped from being lobbed in here?"

"Also tested positive for spores. We found a dozen of them."

"Oh my God. He's insane."

"Yes, and also smart and determined. We haven't seen the last of him." Max fixed her with his best commanding officer glare. "Enough questions. Sleep."

"Yes, sir." Though she didn't really think she was going to, thanks to all the not-so-nice mental images going through her head.

FOUR DAYS LATER, she wished she were back on that gurney asleep.

As soon as Max had declared her fit, which wasn't until her IV antibiotics were done, she was on a helicopter to Kabul, then a plane to the base in Bahrain. Max and a few handpicked doctors were doing their best to predict where Akbar might go next with his anthrax bombs. Max had also requested the assignment of several Green Berets to the Biological Response Team for nine to twelve months, depending on how things went. General Stone green-lighted his request and Grace found herself with a shadow named Smoke.

Sharp was nowhere to be seen. Or heard from.

She'd seen him last at Bostick. He'd waved at her, but hadn't gotten any closer than that. She'd waved back and waited for him to come back, to talk to her, but he never did.

At first, she was irritated, then angry and finally pissed off that he didn't even say goodbye before he left on whatever secret mission he was on. Goddamn SF soldiers and their war games.

Smoke hadn't said more than six words to her since he'd arrived, just stared at her like she was supposed to be doing something other than preparing for another bioterrorism attack.

His silence was driving her crazy.

"What's gotten you so annoyed, Smoke?" she asked on the second day he'd been following her around. "And don't give me any more of your stoic stares. Out with it."

"Sharp," was all he said.

"Sharp?" All her frustration and anger boiled out of her. "You mean the guy who disappeared without a *see you later* or *goodbye*? That Sharp?"

"You know what happened," Smoke said.

"What happened? Of course I know what happened. I tried to save that moron's life by running away with a grenade full of the worst poison known to man and he followed me. He refused to let me—" she choked on a sob "—save him. I thought I killed him, Smoke. I really did. So, you know what I did? I told him I loved him. And after that, he just up and disappeared. He left." She glared.

Smoke frowned back at her. "That's not what happened."

Fabulous. Not even Smoke believed her. "Fuck you and the tank you rode in on." She'd had enough. She'd request a soldier she didn't know, someone who wouldn't make her sad just knowing he was in the room.

She strode away, determined to find Max.

Smoke grabbed her arm. "Wait."

She tugged at her arm and after a moment he let go.

"You didn't know Sharp was arrested?"

"Arrested? For what? When was this?" She advanced on Smoke, poked him in the chest and all but yelled, "Why didn't you tell me?"

"He broke a lot of regulations."

"So what?"

"He made your relationship with him known to...everyone."

"Our relationship?" They hadn't really sat down and figured that out. She loved him, but she didn't know if it was going to go somewhere or not.

"You're engaged."

What? "How can we be engaged when I never gave him an answer!"

Smoke shrugged. "He wasn't going to let some stranger have final say regarding your treatment while you were unconscious."

"Okay." She held up a hand. "Let me think for a minute." She paced back and forth a couple of times. "Sharp was arrested and taken away to face charges for the regulations he broke helping me?"

Smoke nodded once.

"Why the hell wasn't I arrested?"

"He took full responsibility. Said you were acting as

a doctor, which took precedence over military regulations."

He'd saved her. *Again*. "That sneaky bastard."

"Stupid, if you ask me."

She snorted. "Just you wait, Smoke. You're going to meet a woman who makes you sing like a canary someday."

He looked at her with puppy-dog eyes. "That's mean."

Max was arguing with General Stone when she caught up to him. Perfect, two birds she was happy to stone.

"Excuse me, sirs," she said, marching up to them wearing her best *I'm a good girl—no, really* smile. "I have an urgent request for a piece of equipment."

"Equipment?" Max asked.

"Yes, sir." She turned to the general. "It'll require your approval."

"Oh?"

She turned up the wattage on her smile.

"Well, if it's urgent and you can't live without it..." General Stone shrugged.

"What is it?" Max asked.

"Sergeant Jacob Foster." She dropped the smile and fixed both men in place with a glare that would have done Sharp proud. "I absolutely refuse to work without him."

"Well, Major, he's not—"

"Yes, he is," she interrupted. "No insult intended, General Stone, but he's the one man I trust without question. Smoke's like a brother to me, but he asks too many questions."

"*Smoke* asks too many questions?" General Stone sounded like he couldn't believe his ears.

"Yes, sir. He does. Chatters on like a chickadee. Drives me crazy."

Both men stared at her with their mouths hanging open. Finally Stone pulled himself together and said, "The thing is, Major Samuels, Jacob Foster isn't under my—"

"General," Max interrupted. "I think I can deal with the major's request. Thank you, sir."

Stone gave Max a short bark of a laugh and started walking. "I'm happy to turn it over to you."

As soon as he was out of earshot, Grace said, "I don't care what jail or brig you have to spring him from, I want Sharp here."

Max's exasperated expression would have made her laugh if she wasn't so damn angry. "Sometimes, Grace, you need to stop and think."

"What does that mean?"

"Or let people finish their sentences."

"Okay. Sorry. When can Sharp be here?"

"You know what the general and I were arguing about just now?"

"No."

"You and your Sharp."

"Oh."

"Jacob Foster is no longer an active member of the military."

THIRTY-ONE

GRACE STARED AT MAX, her lungs stalled, her heart laboring and pain radiating from her chest throughout her body. "It was my fault. Whatever regulations he might have broken, he broke them for me or because of me. I can't believe how fast this happened. Why didn't anyone talk to me before beginning proceedings against him?"

Max smiled at her. "Slow down. He wasn't officially charged with anything, and no proceedings took place."

"Then why?"

"In order to spare the army the time and expense of a trial on the laundry list of charges he was looking at, he agreed to accept an immediate honorable discharge."

"But there were mitigating circumstances. A trial would have revealed that. Colonel Marshall was responsible for a lot of the miscommunication and—"

"That's why it was an *honorable* discharge," Max interrupted.

"So, he...he's gone?"

"Not exactly."

Grace opened her mouth, then closed it before asking carefully, "What does that mean?"

"The one regulation General Stone wasn't willing to turn a blind eye to was the fraternization regulation."

She opened her mouth again, and again, Max spoke first.

"Sharp made it clear you and he were in a relationship, and he wasn't willing to pretend you're not."

"Oh." There wasn't much she could say to that, though it hurt far more to hear it than she expected. The wound in her chest had gotten a lot wider and bloodier.

"In fact, he told anyone who would listen, loudly, that you were his."

Wait a second. He left, and on the way out the door, he warned everyone away from her? They'd made no promises to each other, other than the kind one lover makes to another. "His what? Doctor? Girl Friday?"

"My everything."

Grace turned.

Sharp stood ten feet away, dressed in his dusty body armor over a clean uniform of the Biological Response Team. He had a full duffel bag slung over one shoulder and a shiny new sniper rifle in one hand. "Hey, Max. Everything squared away?"

"More or less. General Stone wasn't all that happy about your involvement with my team until Grace tore a strip off him and demanded your participation."

"Did he cave?" Sharp asked with a grin.

"Oh yeah," Max said with a chuckle. "Not a peep out of him." He nodded to Grace. "I'll leave you two to get yourselves sorted out. We're heading back to Bostick in about six hours to continue the investigation into Akbar and his anthrax strain. Be packed and ready to leave thirty minutes prior." He walked away, leaving Grace staring at Sharp.

What the hell just happened?

Sharp gestured with his rifle toward her. "Where are your quarters?"

"What?"

"We need to have a conversation."

He was right, they did need to have a talk. Though she might yell more than speak. She spun on her heel and led the way to her private quarters, which was a prefab room about eight by twelve feet. She'd had zero time to do more than to sleep there. As a result, it looked more like the inside of a deep freeze than a bedroom.

As soon as he was inside and the door closed, she started with the list of questions getting longer and longer in her head. "What happened? Where did you—"

Sharp dropped his bag and rifle on the floor, all while staring at her with eyes that damn near lit her on fire. The words coming out of her mouth halted as the intense need on his face ripped the power of speech from her.

Her diaphragm rose and fell like the bellows of a blacksmith while working steel.

He stepped back and, without taking his eyes from her, locked the door.

A sound escaped her throat, lost and mournful. "I thought you left me."

A smile promising sin and sex, enough to feed her addiction for his touch, changed him from a stoic soldier into a man who was made to give pleasure. "You're mine. I'm yours. Not negotiable."

His words spoke to the primitive part of her, the part who wanted to scream to the world that he was hers as much as she was his. *Never negotiable.* "Good."

They launched themselves at each other and somehow ended up on her narrow bed with him on top of her, his hands trying to pull her body armor off, while she attempted the same.

After a couple of seconds he tore himself away from her and attacked his own body armor. "Take it off," he ordered her in a voice so guttural she barely understood him.

She understood what he wanted though. What she wanted.

Skin, warm and smooth, over hard muscles.

She got her body armor off and tossed it to one side. Her shirt and bra went next. By the time she got to her pants, Sharp was back, naked, with shaking hands as he took over from her, yanking her pants down and off so hard they tore.

He kissed her everywhere, his mouth seemingly never satisfied, like hers.

She wanted to taste him everywhere, touch him everywhere, all at the same time.

He put his mouth on one breast, sucked in the nipple and lashed it with his tongue. It sent her into overdrive, a deep groan of need rising from her chest. "Sharp, I need..." She couldn't breathe, couldn't think while his mouth worked her nipple, while his fingers sought out and circled the sensitive entrance to her body.

"What do you need, sweetheart?" he whispered, kissing his way over to her neglected breast. "Say the word and it's yours." His clever fingers dipped inside, then flicked her clit. Back and forth, back and forth, driving her need higher and higher until she felt like she was going to fly apart.

He sucked the nipple in and nipped it lightly with his teeth.

"You!" Good God, she was going to lose her mind. "I need you to fuck me."

His fingers plunged deep, robbing her of words. She was on the precipice, on the very edge, and if he didn't shove her over soon, she was going die.

"Holy fuck," he whispered, pulling his hand away, pushing her onto her back and making room for himself between her thighs. "I can't wait, you're so wet. Tell me it's okay, Grace." He put his forehead against her chest and moaned, "Jesus, tell me to stop."

"No!" If he stopped, she'd fly apart and never find her way home again. "I want you. Please, I need you. I'm yours and you're mine." She wrapped her hand around his cock. Christ, it really was as big as she remembered.

He growled something she didn't understand and let her guide him to her.

He pushed in and her eyes damn near rolled back in her head. He pulled out and pushed in a little further.

Too slow. Too careful.

"Harder," she begged. "Please!"

He lunged into her as far as he could go, pulled out and did it again and again. Every stroke fed the fire inside her. Fed her need.

Her orgasm blasted her from the inside out with a heated pleasure she'd never experienced before. He powered through it, drawing it out until tears of pleasure rolled down her face.

She came back to reality to discover Sharp pistoning into her while he chanted in her ear, "Love you." Over and over again. He groaned, stiffened and shivered over her.

Finally, his body relaxed against hers, though his breathing was still deep and fast. His hands stole around her as he rolled onto his side and he pulled her until she was pressed against him.

"Engaged?" she asked.

He grunted.

"Do I get a ring?"

He pushed himself up on one elbow and leaned over her. He brought her left hand to his lips and kissed her ring finger. "It's in my pants."

She watched him nibble her fingers with all the patience he'd lacked only minutes before. "I'm still...damaged," she told him.

"So am I," he replied. "I'm not scared of your scars, nightmares or your need for touch."

He loved her. She could see it on his face, in his deep eyes and in the way he held her like she was precious.

He *loved* her.

Their next game of chess was going to be very interesting indeed.

She kissed his ring finger. "I'm not scared of your scars, nightmares or your need to protect." She kissed him again. "I love you."

His smile was *happy*. "Do you know when I knew I loved you?"

She shook her head.

"It was in the cave with Max and all those Berets. You were making decisions and planning your strategy to deal with Marshall and the anthrax design like a two-star. Your determination to see the job done and willingness to take the lead. So much compassion and smarts. All I could think was...hot damn, she's the perfect woman."

She remembered. She'd been so scared he was going to try to make her stay behind. "I knew I loved you when I had that grenade in my hand and if I told you I had it, you'd have sacrificed yourself for me. I couldn't let you do it. I couldn't imagine you dead and didn't want to. It was my turn to save you."

"You were *pissed* when Smoke and I turned up to ruin

your plans." His smile made her think wicked, wicked thoughts. "You're sexy when you're all growly and doing the *don't fuck with me* thing."

Her hands skated over his chest and up around his neck. "Love me again?"

"Always, Grace," he whispered against her lips.

EPILOGUE

COLONEL MAXIMILLIAN COMPARED the genetic codes for the various anthrax samples taken from the village, the dead man who'd handed Grace the grenade and the grenades two other men were about to fire into the base before Sharp killed them.

An exact match.

The original strain was a common one found in nature, but it had been taken and its deadly properties magnified until it barely resembled its parent.

Thank God, massive doses of Cipro combined with other antibiotics were able to combat it. If that hadn't worked, Grace and Sharp would be dead. As it was, more doses of the antibiotic cocktail were being stockpiled in military bases all over the Middle East, Asia and Africa.

The threat of an anthrax attack still existed, but the American military and its allies were prepared now.

Akbar wanted more than preparedness. He wanted fear, panic and despair. Something told Max the other man wasn't going to stop until he got it.

* * * * *

*Coming soon from Carina Press and Julie Rowe
Captain Sophia Perry wants to make a difference—
but saving the masses isn't easy when the man tasked
to protect her is so irresistible.*

*Read on for a sneak preview of LETHAL GAME,
the next book in Julie Rowe's*
BIOLOGICAL RESPONSE TEAM SERIES

ABOUT THE AUTHOR

JULIE ROWE'S FIRST career as a medical lab technologist in Canada took her to the Northwest Territories and northern Alberta, where she still resides. She loves to include medical details in her romance novels, but admits she'll never be able to write about all her medical experiences because "No one would believe them!" In addition to writing contemporary and historical medical romance, and fun romantic suspense for Entangled Publishing and Carina Press, Julie has short stories in Fool's Gold, the Mammoth Book of ER Romance, Timeless Keepsakes and Timeless Escapes anthologies. Her book Saving the Rifleman (book #1 of War Girls) won the novella category of the 2013 Gayle Wilson Award of Excellence. Aiding the Enemy (book #3 of War Girls) won the novella category of the 2014 Colorado Romance Writer's Award of Excellence. Her writing has also appeared in several magazines such as *RT Book Reviews, Today's Parent* and *Canadian Living*. You can reach her at julieroweauthor.com, on Twitter, @julieroweauthor, or at her Facebook page, facebook.com/julieroweauthor.

ONE

Security is mostly a superstition.

—Helen Keller

IT HAD TAKEN him three airplanes and over twenty-six hours to travel more than seven thousand miles, and now he was going to have to kill someone.

Ten feet from his hotel room door.

All Special Forces Weapons Sergeant Connor Button wanted was to find a bed and crash for a few hours.

What he did not need was witnessing some idiot striking out with a hot blonde and not taking it well.

She'd just removed his hand from her waist.

The man put it on her shoulder and tried to bring her closer. "Aw, come on, sweetheart."

She slid away, her voice clear across the short distance. "No."

Okay, dude, time to retreat. Only, the guy didn't. He grabbed her by the back of the neck, hard enough to make her gasp in pain, and leaned down, his mouth aimed for hers.

She slapped the moron, but he didn't get that hint either, just grabbed her hand and twisted it behind her back.

Con had to make himself stand still for a second. One second, so he could throttle back the instinct to beat the stupid fuck to death.

Fine. His jaw flexed. He wouldn't kill the asshole, but he could hurt him real bad.

Con dropped his duffel on the floor and stomped toward the woman and the moron whose arm he was about to break.

In several pieces.

Small ones.

The stomping got the moron's attention. He glanced up, saw Con coming and his eyes went wide. He let go of the woman so fast she wobbled, off balance and fell to the floor. Con stopped to help her while moron ran like a track star down the hall and around a corner.

Good call, asshole.

Con bent down and offered his hand to the woman. "Are you okay?"

Her head jerked up and she stared at him with eyes that didn't miss a thing. She scooted away, leaving his hand hanging in the air, then stood. Her shoulders went back and her chin rose.

He almost smiled. She was so not interested in another man getting all up in her business. He'd make sure she was all right, then he'd back off.

"Ma'am, did he hurt you?"

"I'm fine," she said, retreating a step.

Blue-green eyes stood out in a face framed by white-blonde hair hanging in a sheet down to the middle of her back. She was also stacked, though she wasn't showing it off. She was following military clothing requirements, wearing long pants and a collared shirt one size too big, buttoned up to her neck. An asshole had just tried to sexually assault her, but Con would bet a year's pay that had he not come along, moron would have had his hands full of a pissed-off female trying to smash his balls into paste.

He glanced down.

Her mouth was pressed into a thin angry line, but her hands were shaking.

For the first time in months something other than anger or despair slammed into him.

He knew just how she felt. Hyped up on adrenaline and looking for a target.

It surprised him so much he opened his mouth to make some inane comment or other to show her he was no threat, but she raised a hand to stop him.

She spoke a quick, firm "Thank you." And then she was gone, inside the room closest to her. The click of the lock being engaged echoed down the hall.

He blinked at the empty hallway. He wasn't sure she was okay, but those shaking hands and that locked door sent a pretty clear signal that she didn't want another man anywhere near her.

Sometimes other people just made things worse.

He sighed, strode back to his bag, checked his room number again and discovered he was next door to the blonde.

At least he wouldn't have to go far if moron came back.

So much for getting some sleep. He'd lain awake, alert for any noise that might indicate a problem in the room next door, but it had been church-quiet. He got up at zero seven hundred base time, then went in search of his new commanding officer, Colonel Maximillian. The man had an interesting reputation, but he trusted what his buddy, Jacob "Sharp" Foster, a former Special Forces soldier, had to say about him. Everyone else said the colonel was one bullet shy of a magazine. Sharp had warned him that the colonel wasn't exactly regular army, but he gave a shit about his people, and that was number one for Con. If your CO had your six, at least you didn't have to take your attention off what was coming at you.

The colonel had a fancy lab that didn't exist on the base, according to official records. Officially, the lab that did exist on paper was rated for level two containment. Good enough to run the sort of tests any big city hospital conducted. In reality, the lab was capable of level four containment testing. The stuff you needed to wear a bio-suit for and breathe your own oxygen supply.

Con had to pass through two internal checkpoints to gain entry to the nondescript building that was his destination. Colonel Maximillian's office was the first one inside the prefab rectangle that housed the lab and offices. A soldier who didn't look a day over sixteen sat typing on a computer facing the entrance to the building.

The kid's gaze darted over Con's uniform, then he stood and saluted. "Private Eugene Walsh."

"Sergeant Connor Button, Special Forces."

"Yes, sir. Colonel Maximillian is expecting you." Walsh extended his hand in the direction of the first office. "Go right in."

Con gave him a nod, then walked into the office.

He saluted the salt-and-pepper-haired man, who stood and saluted back. "Sir, Sergeant Button reporting for duty."

"Welcome, Sergeant." The colonel came around his desk and offered his hand.

Con shook it once, twice, then released a hand that

hadn't tested him beyond what would be considered polite.

"Take a seat," the colonel said, gesturing at one of the chairs facing his desk. "I'd like to go over your assignment and answer any questions you might have."

"Thank you, sir." Con sat and adopted a neutral body posture, back straight and hands resting lightly on his thighs. It was harder than it should have been.

The last time he'd been in the Middle East he'd been deployed with his unit, attempting to ascertain the military strength of two groups of extremists in Northern Iraq and Syria. Both groups had threatened multiple American and allied targets, as well as calling for sympathetic citizens to carry out terrorist acts inside their own countries.

The last time he'd been in the Middle East, he'd been the only survivor of an IED that took out their vehicle. Fortune had smiled on him that day. He'd been thrown clear.

More and more often, he wished he hadn't been so lucky.

Colonel Maximillian continued to stare at him and seemed content to not say anything for several moments.

Con waited with the patience of a man who'd waited days for just the right moment to take a shot at his target.

Finally, the colonel asked, "How much do you know about your mission here?"

"Probably not enough."

Maximillian's face didn't change. "Sharp said you were smart. Are you, Sergeant Button?"

"That would depend on your definition of smart."

"Observant, creative, organized, able to see unusual relationships between people and information."

"Sir, you're looking for Sherlock Holmes. He's a fictional character."

A brief smile crossed the colonel's face. "How would you describe yourself?"

"Flexible, determined, fuck the box."

Colonel Maximillian's forehead lowered over his eyes. "Were you aware General Stone had some reluctance in assigning you to this mission?"

"Not directly, but it doesn't surprise me."

"Oh?"

How many conversations like this had he had recently? Five, six? "Sir, I received injuries in an attack that killed all the men in the armored vehicle with me. I'd be surprised if he wasn't hesitant." No officer wanted to have a suicidal or homicidal soldier on a mission. Survivor's guilt could lead to either one. Or both.

"Do you consider yourself fit for duty?"

"Yes, sir."

"Why?"

Goddamned why-questions. Why judged, weighed and measured what was in a man's head. What was in his head was not pretty, and not to be shared.

"Sir, I signed on to serve my country. My service isn't done."

Maximillian tilted his head to one side. "That is one of the best non-answers I've ever heard."

Fuck it. Con leaned forward and said in a less civilized tone, "I got thrown off the horse. I need to get back on and finish my ride."

"And if you don't?"

Con's throat closed up. "That thought can't be in my head."

The colonel's face lost its sharp inquisitiveness for a

moment, replaced by a surprising level of comprehension. A second later it was gone and he was flipping through pages on his desk. "You've had some problems with your temper since you returned to duty."

"I'm working on that." Anger was easy. Acting on it was even easier.

The officer considered Con for a couple more seconds, then nodded briskly. "My Biological Response Team is tracking a very dangerous man who's created his own extremely deadly strain of anthrax. We managed to prevent an attack on a base in Afghanistan, but not before nearly one hundred people died of the infection. We think he's not done. We think he'll continue to strike at high-quality American or allied targets, and we don't know where he is or where he will attack next."

Con straightened. Hunting down a homicidal nutcase wasn't the sort of duty he'd taken on before, but it sounded dangerous. Good.

Holy fuck he was messed up.

Maximillian continued. "We were successful in preventing the last attack because we had one of our infectious disease specialists embedded with A-team training members of the Afghan military. General Stone agrees with me—until this man is found, we need more cooperation between my team and army Special Forces. I asked for specific men to work with my people. Men who are not only well-trained and smart, but also creative and who can take a step back and support his teammate or to take charge of a situation if that's what's needed. Jacob Foster says you're that kind of man. Are you?"

Con knew his face didn't show any of the thoughts running through his head.

What kind of monster creates that kind of poison?

It might be nice to have a specific enemy, with a face and a name, rather than a faceless one who could be anyone.

The need to kill, to avenge his dead, was a relentless voice in the back of his head. This mission could get him the opportunity to give himself that, and maybe a measure of peace.

"Sir." He paused, trying hard not to come on too strong. If he lost this chance, he might not get another. "I'm a team player. That means I'll play whatever role is needed by the team."

Colonel Maximillian smiled. "Do you mind working with a woman?"

"No, sir. Sharp mentioned the possibility I'd be paired with a woman." Man, woman, two-headed alien, he didn't care as long as they shared a common enemy.

"You're okay with that? No hesitations?"

The colonel seemed unusually concerned.

What the hell? While he might smack down a fellow Special Forces soldier, he'd never lay a hand on a woman.

"Sir, I'm the youngest of five children with four older sisters. Working with or for a woman is nothing new to me."

"Good." Maximillian nodded. "I don't mean to sound paranoid, but the doctor you're going to be working with is somewhat...high strung."

"High strung?"

The colonel shook his head. "That's the wrong description. She's young, she's a genius and she has absolutely no idea how to talk to anyone who isn't a scientist or doctor."

That didn't leave a whole lot of people. "Genius, as in graduated from medical school really young?"

"She's twenty-four and is the youngest physician in the USA to have a double speciality in virology and hematology."

"Virology, I get. Hematology?"

"The study of blood cells."

If she was an overachiever, he could work with that. "So, work is her life, and before that, it was school?"

"Exactly."

"S'okay. My second-oldest sister is married to a physicist. He speaks math, and we get along just fine."

Maximillian quirked an eyebrow. "You speak math?"

"Nope. I speak barbeque. Everyone has something to say about properly grilling a steak."

The colonel laughed. "You'll do. Time to meet her." He stepped out of his office and led the way down a hall. "Oh, and call me Max. It's shorter."

"Thank you, sir."

Max sighed as he opened a door with a key and preceded Con inside.

The room they entered was part office and part lab, with a couple of desks and two tall microscopes set up on the end of each. Papers and boxes of slides littered both surfaces. Only one of the desks was occupied.

A woman sat looking through the lens of one of the microscopes. Her hair was white-blonde and pulled back into a severe bun. She wore an army uniform with a lab coat over top. When she saw Max, she pushed away from the scope, stood and moved to meet them.

It was the blonde from last night. With her hair pulled back, she could have passed for even younger than twenty-four.

Fucking gorgeous. He took that thought, hog-tied it and shoved it into a dark corner. His personal mission left no room for anything beyond a professional relationship.

She also looked ready to rip someone's head off.

"Sophia," Max said. "This is your new partner, Weapons Sergeant Connor Button." He turned to Con. "Connor, this is Captain Sophia Perry."

Her mouth, pressed into a thin line, convinced him to pretend last night hadn't happened. He nodded at her respectfully. "Good to meet you, ma'am."

"Ma'am?" she asked, crossing her arms over her chest. "This is who you found to babysit me, Max? A fossil?"

Damn, she came out swinging. Maybe he'd let her win this bout. Con managed to keep a straight face and said in a hesitant voice, "I'm only twenty-nine."

"Would you rather I pair you up with someone who follows all the rules and regulations?" Max asked her, irritation showing in his rigid posture. "This guy—" he pointed a thumb at Con "—hates inside-the-box thinking as much as you do."

"Oh yeah?" she said, looking Con full in the face. A challenge. Why was she so pissed off? Because she didn't think she needed a babysitter?

He shrugged, then coughed to hide a chuckle. If he laughed now, she'd think he was laughing at her. "I don't like boxes. They're never big enough, and they're too... square."

She blinked at him, then narrowed her gaze. "What did you do to draw this duty? It had to have been bad."

Max opened his mouth, but Con didn't want to escalate things, so he spoke first, and went with the unvarnished truth. "I got blown up. I spent almost seven months in hospitals and physical therapy. The last three or four months I've been instructing and getting back into shape." He smiled at her. "When I found out what my first mission was going to be, bodyguarding some army doctor, I thought what the fuck? I sure as shit didn't want easy duty. But having talked with Max here, I've changed my mind." He shifted his gaze to Max's face. "This isn't easy duty, is it, sir?"

"No. It's not a matter of if there will be another biological weapon attack somewhere in this part of the world, it's when."

"My role isn't just to bodyguard Dr. Perry, is it?"

"No." Max began pacing back and forth between Con and Sophia. "We have intel that points to the Biological Response Team as a specific target. I don't want you to just protect Sophia, I need you two to be a team. All of us are being paired with Special Forces soldiers, even myself."

"Assassination?" Con asked. The idea of it made the back of his neck itch.

"Very possible. Sabotage is another danger."

"Have any attempts been made?"

"Yes. Dr. Samuels and her Green Beret were nearly killed in a trap I believe was set for them. We have an enemy who is intelligent, ruthless and fearless."

"Can I get everything you have on this guy?" Con asked.

"My assistant will have it ready for you in an hour or two." Max turned to him. "Have you been assigned quarters?"

"Yeah."

"I'm going to have you moved to the room next to Sophia's."

The woman in question opened her mouth to say

something unpleasant—he was sure from the way she'd screwed up her nose—which is why Con spoke first again. "Are you sure that's necessary?" He looked down, like he was thinking hard. "Do you want to advertise to the whole base that I'm her bodyguard, or would you like to keep it below the radar?"

Max gave him a dirty look. "Whose side are you on?"

"Hers, sir."

"Fine," Max said, with bit of an impatient edge to his voice. "I'll check to see where you're housed now. If it's not too far, you can stay where you are." Max pressed his lips together, glared at them both then stomped off.

Con looked at Sophia.

She looked back at him, snorted and went back to her microscope. "Nice attempt to come to my rescue. Again. But I don't need anyone to rescue me."

She needed to talk to someone about the moron. To prevent fear and anger from getting too deep a hold on her brain.

Despite how fast things had happened, the human mind had a way of warping events so the memory of them seemed to take a thousand times longer than the reality had.

Hell, he was a walking testament for how three seconds of hell could totally screw up the rest of a man's life.

Or take it.

Listen to him passing judgement on her mental state, when he'd done his level best to keep the shrinks out of his. Right now, he just had to convince her he was on her side. He wanted this assignment. "I know."

"Really?" Sarcasm turned the word into something

sharp and heavy. "You just met me. How would you know that?"

"I saw you in action last night."

She froze, and for a moment the expression on her face was a mixture of anger, fear and disgust. A second later, it was gone, smoothed away as if it had never been there.

Whoa. What was that?

Without looking at him, she said, "Babysitting me is going to be a complete bore for a soldier's soldier like you. I'll tell Max to find someone else."

Don't miss
LETHAL GAME by Julie Rowe
Available October 2015 wherever
Carina Press ebooks are sold.
www.CarinaPress.com